IN THE POLIT
TWENTY-FIRST
NEVE

A small-time drug dealer is murdered. The mayor's nephew is found dead. On the surface they are unrelated. But that surface has cracks, and Lieutenant Frank Carlucci is not a man to stop digging. He knows the murders are the tip of a long, corroded wire that twists deep into the San Francisco political machine. And it's a live one.

CARLUCCI'S EDGE

Praise for the award-winning work of
Richard Paul Russo . . .

"RUSSO'S VOICE IS MUCH NEEDED IN OUR DAY AND AGE." —*New Pathways*

"LEAN, MEAN, AND COMPELLING." —*Deseret News* (UT)

"[RUSSO] PAINTS [THE CITY BY THE BAY] like some kind of futuristic Inferno, graduated downward in levels ever more baroquely deadly . . . moves at a brisk, steady pace guaranteed to keep the pages turning." —*Minneapolis Star Tribune*

"RUSSO'S PEOPLE AND THEIR OBSESSIONS ARE DELIGHTFULLY REAL." —*Analog*

Ace Books by Richard Paul Russo

DESTROYING ANGEL
CARLUCCI'S EDGE

CARLUCCI'S EDGE

RICHARD PAUL RUSSO

ACE BOOKS, NEW YORK

This book is an Ace original edition,
and has never been previously published.

CARLUCCI'S EDGE

An Ace Book/published by arrangement with
the author

PRINTING HISTORY
Ace edition/June 1995

Cover art by Viktor Koén.

For information address: The Berkley Publishing Group,
200 Madison Avenue, New York, NY 10016.

ISBN: 0-441-00205-6

ACE®
Ace Books are published by The Berkley Publishing Group,
200 Madison Avenue, New York, NY 10016.
ACE and the "A" design are trademarks
belonging to Charter Communications, Inc.

PRINTED IN THE UNITED STATES OF AMERICA

10 9 8 7 6 5 4 3 2

This is for Dianne,
with love

And for my parents,
with thanks for all their support

PROLOGUE

SMOKE AND SWEAT and hot lights and the smell of beer filled the club, all cut through with the ripping wail and thunder of the slash-and-burn band on stage. Three women—drummer in tank top and blue jeans, bleached hair whipping up and down with the beat; guitarist in dark emerald-green shimmer pants and silver rag vest, black on black hair falling across her face; and Paula, in black jeans and boots and white T-shirt, tearing at the bass and shouting and howling out the vocals. Black Angels.

Paula sang and rocked in a kind of cocoon, earplugs protecting her from the worst of the sound. But she felt the bass pounding through her, driving into her bones, moving her. She was soaked with sweat, filled with fire. She was flying.

The Palms was jammed. It was a tiny club, more of a bar, really, but there must have been seventy or eighty people squeezed inside to see the Black Angels. Beer seemed to be the drink of choice, bottles and glasses everywhere; the smoke was a mix of cigarettes, pot, and fireweed. A few people up near the stage were trying to dance, jumping up and down in place. If she reached out, Paula could touch them.

She backed away from the mike and Bonita ripped into her solo, fingers clawing at the strings. Sheela lost a drumstick; it flew forward, bounced off the back of Bonita's head, but she didn't notice. This was their last song, they were too deep into it. Paula kicked the stick out of the way, pounding at her bass.

Too old for this? That's what Pietro had told her. Because she was pushing forty. Shit. The fucker didn't have a clue.

The screech of Bonita's solo cut through the earplugs, not painful, just enough to pump her up even more. The crowd was into it, too; Paula could see it in their faces—eyes clamped shut or wide open, necks, cheeks, and lips clenched tight. Bonita was burning tonight, and Paula hoped someone was getting it on-line. Damn, she wished Chick could have been here.

Bonita took it longer and further than usual, but eventually swung it back around and down, turning to Paula and Sheela, and then it was time for Paula to come back with the final rep of the chorus. She moved up to the mike, waited for it, then sang:

Yes, the night will drown us
And the stars will burn us
If we step out on the ledge.

Oh, the fear will take us
And it just might break us
When we live out on the edge.

Then back from the mike, Paula and Sheela and Bonita all facing each other, closing it down with the final strokes, all of them smiling. They knew they'd been burning tonight, they *knew.* A crash of drums and guitars, then another. Two beats of silence. One final crash. Lights out.

Paula felt good. Wrung out, but good. They were playing The Palms the next night as well, and they had all their equipment packed away and locked up in back. Bonita and Sheela were already gone. Time to go home, wind down, get some sleep. Or maybe go see Chick. It was only two-thirty, he was probably still up.

The Palms was nearly empty now. Recorded music played softly in the background. A few stragglers sat at tables and the bar, nursing their last-call drinks. Randy and Carmela and the new kid (what was her name, Laurel?) were cleaning up, trying to close. A guy at the bar tried to wheedle another drink out of Carmela, but she just ignored him.

Jacket over her shoulder, Paula headed for the front door, waving good night to Carmela and Randy.

"Hey, babe, need a lift?" It was a guy she didn't know, at the table closest to the door, so drunk he could hardly keep his head up. He wasn't going to be any trouble.

"No, thanks, Ace. You'd better get a ride of your own." The guy didn't look like he could drive five blocks without crashing.

The drunk gave her a sloppy grin, then pointed his finger at her like a gun, made a kind of shooting noise. Asshole.

Paula stepped through the front door and out onto Polk Street. The air was warm, muggy. San Francisco nights. She put on her jacket anyway, left it unzipped. There were still people out, wandering, or lost, and a few street soldiers were in sight. She smiled, shaking her head. The Polk was such a half-assed Corridor. The street soldiers always had their hands out, and a lot of them were as likely to try to nail you on your doorstep as give you safe conduct. Still, they kept the street itself relatively safe, and Paula could take care of herself.

So, home or Chick's place. Shit, she was too wound up to sleep. It had been a great set. Chick's place, then. It was closer, anyway.

She started up the street, headed uphill and west. There wasn't much traffic—a few cars, pedalcarts, and scooters. An electric bus heaved down the street, flashes of blue sparking off the overhead wires; it was almost half full. On the opposite sidewalk, a street medico was working on someone lying half in the gutter, two street soldiers standing over them. Paula watched, trying to figure if something shifty was going down, but she couldn't tell. She let it go.

She passed a stunner arcade that was still open, but it was mostly dark inside, and she could see only a single jerking figure within. A scooter cab swung to the curb alongside her, the old, long-haired driver lifting an eyebrow. Paula smiled and shook her head, and the cabby pulled away. Two men, hardly more than boys, staggered in tandem along the sidewalk, and Paula had to step into the street to avoid them. She could see it in their eyes, and their twitching—net zombies. Poor bastards.

Most places were closed, but a couple of eateries were still open, and Margo's Spice and Espresso Bar, a video parlor, Sherry's Shock Shop. Paula stopped in front of Tiny's, a twenty-four-hour donut house, seriously thought about going in. She had a real weakness for the damn things; all that fat and sugar, she knew they were bad for her, but she loved them. But the Mulavey twins were inside, the two women pouring coffee all over their donuts and the table, burning the cups with their cigarettes; coffee and ash and melted plastic dripped onto the floor. No, she didn't want to deal with that shit tonight.

She walked up two more blocks, still energized. She was starting to sweat under her jacket. Two street soldiers offered to escort her home, but she declined. Neither followed her.

She turned a corner and headed away from Polk. Chick's place was just two blocks down, but it was a creepy two blocks at night, not really a part of the Corridor. The street lights seemed to cast more shadows than light and the building windows were mostly dark. Paula didn't see anyone on either sidewalk, which was just as bad as seeing someone coming toward her. She put her hands in her jacket pockets and gripped the charged gravity knife with her right hand. She wasn't scared, but she wasn't completely comfortable either.

Nothing happened, no one jumped out from behind a parked car or out of a doorway. When she reached Chick's apartment building—a seven-story brick monstrosity called The Monarch—she unlocked the porch gate, went through, then climbed the half dozen steps and unlocked the building door. The lobby was well-lit for a change, but the elevator was still out of order.

She started up the stairs. Five flights. Good thing she was in shape. The building was quiet, though she did hear the faint sounds of a television as she passed the third floor, and saw the two Stortren kids sleeping in the hall on the fourth. Who knew what their parents were doing inside their apartment. Paula figured she probably didn't want to know.

The sixth floor was just as quiet. Only ragged strips of the carpet remained intact, huge sections worn through to the wooden floor. Her footsteps were a mixture of soft and hard sounds. Chick's apartment was at the far end of the hall, on the right. Nightclub notices for Pilate Error, the band Paula and Chick played in together, were tacked all over the door.

Paula knocked. No answer. She didn't hear any sounds, which meant he was asleep or had his headphones jacked in. Before she dug out her keys again, she tried the door. Unlocked, as usual. Dumbshit. The couple next door had been cleaned out just last week.

She pushed open the door and stepped into the tiny entryway. All three rooms led off from it, and lights were on in all of them. Jesus, the place smelled worse than usual. She pictured rotting food leaking out of his fridge.

"Chick?"

She stuck her head in the kitchen first. The usual piles of dishes and crap on the table and counters, but otherwise empty.

"Chick?"

She checked the front room, which, as always, was a mess,

books and discs and tapes scattered everywhere, half a dozen overflowing ashtrays. Chick was a chain-smoker and a slob: two of the reasons they didn't live together.

She said his name once more, then walked into the bedroom.

Oh, Jesus Christ, no.

Paula stood just inside the room, looking down at Chick. He was sprawled face-up on the floor, headphones plugged into his ears, and three holes in his head—one under each eye and one in the middle of his forehead. She couldn't move, just stared at him, at the blood and the bits of flesh and bone and hair sprayed out on the floor around his head.

No, Chick, no . . .

She closed her eyes, nearly lost her balance, opened them and reached back for the doorjamb to steady herself. Her heart was beating hard and fast, pounding up her neck, pulsing her vision.

"Jesus, Chick, I told you," she whispered. "I told you, one day . . ."

She took a couple of steps toward him, then stopped, shaking her head. She looked around the room, still dazed, not quite remembering it. The overstuffed chair, she could reach that without getting too close to him, without stepping in the blood.

She worked her way through the piles of clothes and books and scattered pieces of music, then dropped into the chair. Perfect spot, she could stare at Chick without moving her head. Jesus.

It occurred to her then that whoever had killed him might still be in the apartment. A shot of adrenaline arced through her and her heartbeat jumped up again. No, she told herself, she'd been in all the rooms; she couldn't believe someone was hiding in a closet or somewhere. Besides. Paula looked at the blood around Chick's head, the pieces of bone and flesh and, yes, Chick's brain, that were stuck in it. She wasn't an expert, but too much had dried; she could tell it must be hours old.

She tilted her head back and stared up at the ceiling so she wouldn't have to look at Chick. Flyers and posters covered the cracked plaster, yellowed and wrinkled notices for Pilate Error, Black Angels, his old band Tab Rasa, and even a couple for Sister's Machine, the first band they'd played in together, more than fifteen years ago.

She wasn't going to cry now, she knew that. She thought she should, and she knew she would later, but right now she just didn't have it in her. She was too damn numb, too wiped out.

She looked back at Chick, his skinny arms with all those fucking tracks, none of them fresh, but still . . . His blue eyes, cool and pale, now wide and staring. The tiny green snake tattooed on his neck. And those goddamn headphones socketed into his ears, cord trailing in the blood, along the floor, then up to the sound system, which was still on, the bright green peak meters spiking back and forth. Paula wondered what his destroyed dead brain was listening to.

"Oh, Chick," she whispered. She pushed herself off the chair, onto her knees, then moved across the floor and sat next to him, taking his cold hand in hers. "You stupid shit. What am I going to do now?"

Call the police, the practical side of her said. Yeah, yeah, in a minute. What's the hurry? No one's going anywhere.

Paula sat motionless on the floor, holding Chick's hand, and waited for the energy and will to move again.

PART ONE

ONE

CHRIST, DAYS LIKE this, Carlucci wanted to resign. And why not? He had more than his twenty-five years in, and at lieutenant he wasn't going any higher, he knew that—he'd pissed off too many of the wrong people over the years. Sometimes he was amazed he'd ever made lieutenant; the only reason he had was the capture of the Chain Killer three years earlier, and the fact that the higher-ups wanted him to keep his mouth shut.

He pushed his chair back from his desk, rolled it sideways until his face was directly in the wash of the fan. Sweat streamed down his sides, ran from his forehead and neck. Carlucci closed his eyes, letting the fan blow across his face and hair, and tried to imagine he was somewhere else, somewhere cool and breezy.

Carlucci was a stocky man, just over six feet, maybe fifteen pounds overweight, not much fat, really; he carried it well. His hair was short and black, heavily streaked with gray, and though he'd shaved this morning, he looked like he needed another. His shirt was soaked with sweat, and it itched, stuck to his skin. Carlucci opened his eyes, dismayed. No miracles. He was still here.

He pulled himself back to his desk and stared at the dead

computer screen. He picked up his coffee cup, looked down into it, saw a miniature oil-slick on top of the coffee, and drank it anyway. Cold and bitter, just the way he liked it.

The day had started off badly, and then had just gone to shit. First thing, five minutes after he'd arrived, Harker and Fuentes came in, demanding to be split up. Carlucci knew immediately that it was serious, not just the typical bitching that cropped up with regularity around here. Neither would say what the problem was, but both insisted they couldn't partner together anymore. Which probably meant that Harker had gone back hard and heavy to the booze, and Fuentes didn't want a drunk as a partner. Carlucci couldn't blame her; he'd feel the same way. He had told them he would work something out as soon as he could. It was going to be a pain in the ass trying to figure new partners, shift things around again. God damn.

Later in the morning the air conditioning had crapped out, the sixth or seventh time this summer. Summer, shit, it was late September, it was supposed to be fall. Once again they'd hauled out the fans, but the building's ventilation wasn't worth a damn, so the fans could only do so much—mostly they just stirred around the hot, sticky air, kept it from being completely intolerable.

Then the mayor's nephew was found dead in his penthouse apartment, throat cut, belly slit open. What a fuckin' mess. The mayor's nephew had been an asshole—a lot like the mayor, actually—and word was already on the street that he had tried to scam some black-market data sharks, and paid for it. But the mayor, ignorant bastard, was jumping all over the Chief, and the Chief was jumping all over Carlucci, and would keep on jumping until something broke. The mayor wanted justice. Sure thing, Your Honor. Carlucci was going to be wasting an awful lot of time on this bullshit, and it probably wouldn't go anywhere.

And finally this, Carlucci thought, still staring at the dead screen. The system had crashed. Again. He looked out the glass wall of his small office, watching the other men and women sitting around, sweating and swearing, talking on phones or to each other, everyone miserable. He glanced at the clock on his desk. Almost three-thirty. Fuck it, he wasn't going to get anything else done today. Go home. He nodded to himself, and prepared to leave.

Carlucci walked out of headquarters and stood in front of the building, trying to decide whether to take the bus or the streetcar. It didn't make much difference, he just liked to switch around a lot, try to keep the commute from being routine. The sky was a rust-brown haze hanging over the city. It hadn't rained at all for five or six days, and Carlucci wasn't sure whether that was good or bad. Probably bad. He thought he could feel the hot, filthy air turning his sweat into some putrid, oily substance.

He had just decided on the streetcar and started down the block, when a woman approached and stood directly in his path, forcing him to stop. She was wearing boots and jeans and a black T-shirt. There was a hard look to her, a sharp and dark edge.

"Frank Carlucci?" she said.

"Yes."

"Homicide, right?"

Carlucci nodded, wondering where this one was headed.

"My name's Paula Asgard. I need to talk to you."

"What about?"

"A murder."

Carlucci smiled. "Hey, there's a surprise. Look, I'm off-duty. Why don't you go inside the station"—he waved back at the building—"talk to someone who's on." He had a feeling she wasn't going to go for that, but he had to try. "I'm sure they can help you."

The woman shook her head. "I need to talk to *you.* And

privately, not in your office. Why do you think I waited out here for you?''

''Look,'' Carlucci tried again, laying it on thick. ''I'm a homicide detective, a lieutenant, we've got procedures. . . .''

''Mixer said you were the one I should talk to,'' Paula Asgard said.

''Mixer.''

''He's a friend of mine.''

Terrific, Carlucci thought. He started to shake his head, then turned it into a nod. ''All right, I'll let you buy me a cup of coffee, and we'll talk. I know a place nearby.''

''I appreciate it,'' the woman said.

Carlucci shrugged. ''Don't thank me yet.''

They sat at a small window table on the second floor of a place called The Bright Spot, a cafe just a few blocks from police headquarters. It was too late for afternoon coffee breaks, too early for dinner, so while the first floor was half full, the second-floor section was nearly empty—exactly what Carlucci had expected.

Neither said anything while they waited for their coffee. Carlucci's attention alternated between the street below and the woman across from him.

Paula Asgard. He liked the name. She was attractive, he thought, in a real earthy way. Somewhere in her thirties, about five-seven, five-eight, a few strands of gray in her dark hair. Almost but not quite slender. She looked strong, like she worked out.

Not much was happening on the street. A man with only one arm and one eye walked a string of three pit bulls leashed together with wire muzzles. Two thrashers on motorized boards ran the gutter directly below the cafe. A woman stood in front of an electronics store across the street, hawking her products and wearing a set of bone boomers; Carlucci got a headache just watching her. Then three teenage girls strolled past wearing rag vests, no bras, budding breasts appearing and disappearing among the strips. Christ, Carlucci thought. He watched until they were gone from sight, but nothing happened to them.

Margitta brought their coffees—iced for Paula Asgard, hot for Carlucci—and asked Carlucci how his wife was.

"Fine," Carlucci said, smiling. He knew what Margitta's game was: trying to guilt him just in case he was even *thinking* something funny about the woman across the table from him. Margitta and Andrea were good friends. "It's just business," he told Margitta. She shrugged and left.

Carlucci turned back to Paula Asgard. "So tell me."

"Mixer says you can be trusted." She turned her glass mug around and around, but didn't drink. "He said you're a cop who does what a cop is *supposed* to do."

"As opposed to all the cops who *don't* do what cops are supposed to do?"

A hint of a smile appeared on Paula's mouth. "You said it."

"Mixer." Carlucci shook his head and frowned. "That guy."

Paula's mouth moved into a full smile. "Yeah, that guy." She drank from her iced coffee, cubes rattling against glass. "He said you don't like spikeheads."

"I don't. I think they're fucking nuts. Self-mutilation doesn't do it for me." He shook his head again, picturing Mixer with the crusted, twisted spikes of skin all over his forehead. "But Mixer, well, we have an understanding of sorts. We get along all right."

"He told me you caught the Chain Killer."

"Not really," Carlucci said. "I was there, I was 'in charge,' but it was other people who were really responsible." He remembered sitting with Tanner at the Carousel Club three years earlier, telling him about the Chain Killer's faked death, "justice" taking it in the ass again—almost no one knew the Chain

Killer was still alive, locked away in some military compound. And he thought of a poor thirteen-year-old girl they had pulled out of a lagoon: Sookie. "One of them got killed," he said.

"A friend of *mine's* been killed," Paula said.

Carlucci looked at her, bringing himself back to the present, then slowly nodded. "Who was it?"

"A friend," she repeated, more quietly.

Carlucci watched her, wanting to look away, not wanting to see what he saw in her eyes. She might be a hardass on the outside, but he could see hints of what was happening inside her, the way she was fighting to *keep* it inside. Someone she loved had died, been killed. He knew that look, because he had seen it too many times.

And then he thought of his older daughter, Caroline, and he wondered if he would have that look in *his* eyes when she died. One day he would be grieving over her death, a day that would be way too soon in coming.

"His name was Chick Roberts," Paula finally managed. She looked out the window, swirling the ice cubes and coffee.

"A friend," Carlucci prompted. The name wasn't familiar. Should he have come across it? Maybe not. He wanted to get straight to it—when was he killed, how, why, whatever—but he knew he'd have to take it slow, at her pace, ease into it.

"Yeah, a friend. More than a friend. I don't know, boyfriend?" Paula turned back to him and shook her head. "Doesn't seem the right word." She drank from her coffee. "Lover?" Then she tried to smile. "Never liked that word, either, but I guess that's as close as I'm going to come. We'd known each other a long time. Sixteen, seventeen years."

"Did you live together?"

"No," she said, almost laughing. "Tried once. Didn't last a year." She didn't offer any explanation, and Carlucci wasn't going to ask her for one.

"When was he killed?"

"A week and a half ago. I stopped by his place after a gig,

found him dead. Shot three times in the head."

She didn't go on, and Carlucci let the silence hang between them for a bit. He was tempted to ask her for more details, but this wasn't his investigation, probably never would be. But there was one question he had to ask if she wasn't going to get to it herself.

"Why me?" Carlucci asked. "Why are we here?"

Something in her expression changed, hardened. The grief was gone, replaced by anger.

"I want to know what the hell is going on."

Yeah, Carlucci thought, we all do.

"What do you mean?" he asked.

"I've been trying to keep on top of it, the investigation, the case, whatever it's called." Paula finished off her iced coffee, set the mug down, shook the ice cubes. "I want to know who killed him, and why. I want to see whoever did it pay." She pushed her mug to the side, and Carlucci could see the anger burning inside her. "His parents don't give a damn, but *I* do."

"So what's the problem?"

"I call the cop who's supposed to be in charge, see what's going on, and he gives me the biggest crock of shit I've ever heard. First, he tells me the investigation has been a dead end, no leads, nothing. Fine, I can sort of accept that, though I don't really buy it." Paula grabbed her mug again, tried to drink coffee that wasn't there, then put it back down. She looked hard at Carlucci. "But then the guy tells me the case is closed. Now, you tell me how the case can be closed if the cops have no idea who killed him?"

"Well," Carlucci said, "there's closed and there's closed."

"What the fuck is *that* supposed to mean?"

"*Technically* the case won't be closed. What he meant is that they think they've gotten as far as they can, which apparently is nowhere. They don't think they'll be able to solve it, and they probably won't be putting much more time into it."

"They haven't put jack into it yet."

"You don't know that," Carlucci started. "I'm sure . . ."

"Bullshit!" Paula was getting angrier; her neck muscles had tightened and her fists were clenched. "As far as I can tell, they haven't talked to any of Chick's friends about it, they haven't asked anyone anything. That's why I can't buy this dead-end crap." She leaned forward. "They haven't even asked *me* a damn thing, and I found him."

Carlucci was starting to get a bad feeling about this. He was beginning to wish he had never agreed to talk to her. "What do you mean by that?" he asked. "One of the investigating officers interviewed you, right?"

"Wrong." Paula shook her head. "They asked me about five questions when they first showed up that night, sent me home, and told me they'd get back to me. No one did."

"No one?"

"That's what I said. I found out who was in charge of the case, talked to him, but all I got was the runaround. Said he didn't need to talk to me, that they had all the information they needed. I even volunteered to come in and talk to him, but he said no. That's when I started checking with people Chick knew. Cops didn't interview *any* of them. Now, you tell me what that's all about."

He had no answer for her. He signaled to Margitta for more coffee. She came over, refilled his cup, then poured some over what remained of the ice cubes in Paula's mug. Carlucci could see the ice cubes melting from the hot coffee. "Want some more ice, hon?" Margitta asked. Paula shook her head, not looking at the waitress, holding her stare on Carlucci. Margitta took the hint and left without another word.

"Who was the investigating officer?" He had to ask. He didn't want to hear her answer, but he had to ask.

"Ruben Santos."

Not a name Carlucci expected to hear. Two or three other names, sure, he wouldn't have been surprised. But Ruben?

"Ruben Santos," he said. "Are you sure?"

"Yes, I'm sure. How do you think I came up with the name? Picked one at random?"

Christ, the whole thing was turning on him. He had been prepared to take Paula Asgard pretty much at her word—he'd seen this kind of thing often enough—but now he began to doubt her. Ruben was about as straight a player as cops came. Carlucci really didn't know what to think.

"It gets better," Paula said.

"How?"

"Last time I talked to this guy Santos, he said they were looking into the possibility that it was suicide."

Sure, Carlucci thought, a kind of backdoor way out, even if it was bullshit. "Could it have been?"

Paula let out a chopped laugh. "Right. Three bullet holes in the face, half the back of his head blown off, and no gun in the apartment. The most amazing goddamn suicide in history."

Yeah, but Carlucci could see how they'd play it. The girlfriend, wanting to avoid the stigma of suicide, pops him a couple extra shots in the face to make it look like murder, then dumps the gun. All bullshit, but the cops just might make that case to close it up, and the coroner could be depended on not to shut the door completely on it.

"Why would the cops want to let this case go?" Carlucci asked. "Laziness? Maybe they just think it's unimportant?"

Her eyes got real hard again. "Unimportant to who?"

Great. That hadn't been the most sensitive thing he'd ever said. "Point taken," Carlucci said.

"Besides," Paula went on, "they're not just letting it go, they're trying to bury it."

"Maybe so." *Probably* so, he thought. But Ruben? He couldn't shake his doubts. "But why? Do you have any idea why they'd want to cover it up, or not find out who killed him? There must be some reason; they wouldn't do something like this just to be assholes."

"You tell *me*. That's why I'm here." Paula sighed, looked away from him. She picked up her coffee mug, drank absently from it. There was no ice left. She turned back to him.

"Chick—" she began. She gave him a half smile. "Chick made a living his own way, and most of the time his own way wasn't exactly legal. Low-end stuff, really. Deal a little bit, run a scam on a jack lawyer, middle-man something hot, things like that. Nothing too big, nothing that would catch the attention of the sharks. You know what I mean?"

"Sure," Carlucci said. A bottom feeder, picking up the crumbs and the crap.

"That was the biggest reason we didn't live together. I couldn't tell him how to run his life, but I didn't want to be a part of that shit, not even on the edges."

"I understand."

Paula looked away, out the window. "Theory is one thing, the real world is another. Trying to stay small-time, out of the way of the sharks, well, impossible to do all the time." She turned back to Carlucci. "Every so often he'd get himself in over his head, riding on the edge, but he always managed to slip out of it. My guess is he got in over his head again, and this time he couldn't get out. In with the sharks, chewed up and spit out." She paused. "And the cops don't want to touch it. I don't know, you tell me why."

Carlucci looked down at his coffee cup, didn't drink, then looked back at Paula. "What do you expect me to do? I can't go in and take over the case. I can't interfere in the investigation without damn good cause."

"What investigation?"

"You know what I mean."

Paula nodded. The anger was gone from her expression, replaced by exhaustion and a return of the grief. "I don't know. *Something* should be done. Mixer said you could help.

Do *you* like it when your fellow cops try to bury something? Don't you want to know why?" She shook her head slowly. "Somebody should be trying to find out who killed him." She paused, and Carlucci thought he saw tears welling in her eyes, but she managed to keep them back. "Chick deserves better than this. Anybody does. He wasn't a saint, but he never hurt anyone if he could help it. This may sound weird, but for all his fuckups, Chick was a good person. Do you have any idea what I mean?"

"I think so."

"And he deserves better. He deserves *something.*"

Carlucci didn't say anything for a while. Not everyone gets what they deserve, he wanted to tell her, good or bad. But he realized she already knew that. Still.

"All right," he finally said. "I'll look into it. No promises, though. Understand? I'll have to be careful, and I don't know how much I can push it."

Paula nodded. Her expression didn't hold out much hope. She wasn't naive.

"I may not be able to do much at all," he said.

Paula nodded again, but didn't say anything.

"Where can I reach you tomorrow? Afternoon or evening?"

She blinked, as if she'd been thinking of something else. "Um, at Chick's place, actually. His parents don't want any of his things, so I'm going to go through his stuff, clean out his apartment." She smiled sadly. "He was such a fucking slob." She shook her head. "You have something to write with?"

Carlucci took two of his cards and handed them to her along with a pen. "Keep one for yourself. Write Chick's number and your number on the other."

She wrote the numbers on the card and handed it back to him.

"I'll call you tomorrow, or the next day. And when you go

through Chick's things tomorrow?"

"Yes?"

"Make a note of anything you think is missing."

"And if there is, who will have taken it?" Paula asked. "His killer, or the cops?"

Carlucci didn't answer. "No promises, remember?" he said again.

Paula nodded. "I understand."

Carlucci got up from the table. "You coming?"

"No. I think I'll stay here a while."

Carlucci wanted to say something to her, something that would be comforting, or reassuring. But there wasn't anything. He stood for a few moments, watching her, then turned away and left.

TWO

LONG AFTER DARK, Paula and Sheela were still out on the fire escape outside Sheela's apartment, drinking beer. A hot, muggy night, no rain in the air. Sheela was smoking the longest, skinniest cigarettes Paula had ever seen—Silver Needles. Paula was sitting on a crate, her back against the building; Sheela sat on the metal grating, legs and arms and head dangling through the railing and over the edge. A block and a half away, a vacant lot served as the neighborhood dump, and a methane fire burned on the street-side slope of the huge mound of garbage.

"Pilate Error was supposed to play at The Black Hole tonight," Paula said. She'd gone through seven or eight beers, and she was fairly drunk, but it didn't seem to do much to blunt the pain inside her.

"Chick was a pretty good guitar player," Sheela said. "Not as good as Bonita, but pretty good." Sheela had dropped three melters about fifteen minutes ago, but they hadn't kicked in yet, so she was still coherent. Still, Paula knew she would lose her soon.

"Bonita never liked Chick much," Paula said.

Sheela giggled. "She hated his guts."

Paula smiled, brought her beer up to her mouth, and drank.

Cold and bitter and smooth, biting her throat. "Yeah, I guess she did."

"*I* liked him okay," Sheela said. "Even if he did try to prong me that one time." She turned and looked at Paula, her blonde hair covering one eye. "He didn't know I don't go for guys."

Oh, God, Paula thought, let's not go through this again, not tonight. When Sheela got drunk . . .

"You want to stay here tonight?" Sheela asked.

"No. I want to be in my own place, sleep in my own bed." She also had to meet Mixer at midnight, but she wasn't going to tell Sheela that. Sheela would misunderstand. "But thanks."

"I could always . . ." Sheela started. Then she turned away and stuck her head back between the railing bars, looking down at the street. "Sorry."

"It's all right," Paula said. And it was. They'd been close friends for too many years.

A corporate recruiter van appeared on the street a few blocks away and headed toward them. The van, lights flashing and rolling, moved slowly, at little more than a crawl. White text and images flowed along the side of the van, but it was too far away and the angle was wrong, so Paula couldn't make out the words or the pictures.

"I wonder what they're trolling for tonight," Sheela said. She drank from her bottle, shook it, then set it down. She coughed violently, whacking her head against the metal railing. She'd had a terrible, hacking cough for years, and never seemed able to shake it. When the coughing let up, she said, "Have you ever thought about going for one of those deals?"

"No," Paula said. "You?"

Sheela nodded. "Once, a few years ago. I was broke, I was living in the cab of an old truck, and I was sicker than shit. Thought I had brain fever, even though I didn't have the rash. Turned out to be some bad flu, but I didn't know it then."

She held her beer bottle up to the light from the street lamp across the way. "I need another." She set the bottle on the grate beside her. "A recruiter for the New Hong Kong orbital rolled down the street one night while I was out trying to scrounge up some food cash. I watched it roll past, all those pictures of outer space, gleaming apartments, clean air and healthy plants, glittering lights and fancy restaurants, tables filled with food." She shook her head. "I almost went for it. I knew what it would really be like for someone like me—scut work, a tiny hole to live in, institutional food. But I almost went for it. Actually got the van to pull over for me. But as soon as it stopped, and the side doors opened, I freaked. Ran like hell. I thought they were going to come after me and force me to go." She paused, gripped the railing bars tightly and pressed her head against them. "I told a friend of mine about it the next day, and that night she went out looking for the van herself."

Paula thought she knew how this story ended. She drank the rest of her beer, then said, "And she found it?"

Sheela nodded. "She found it. Signed up and went off to New Hong Kong."

"What happened to her?"

"I don't know. Never heard from her again. Never tried to find out for myself." She turned to Paula. "You know, I hear the medicos up in New Hong Kong are working on immortality."

Paula shook her head. "Not immortality. Life extension."

"Same thing."

"Not really." Paula shrugged. "Those stories have been drifting around for years. *Everyone's* searching for longer life."

"Yeah," Sheela said, "but I hear they're getting close."

"I've been hearing *that* for years, too. I doubt it. Doesn't really matter if they are. You think *we'd* get a shot at it? They sure as hell won't want people like us living forever with them."

"Yeah, I guess." Sheela looked down at the beer bottle once more. "Want another?" she asked.

"Sure."

Sheela grabbed her empty bottle, pulled herself to her feet, then reached out for Paula's empty. Paula handed it to her, and Sheela said, "I'll be . . ." then stopped. She dropped the bottles, her head jerked twice, a kind of smile forming, and she slowly, slowly crumpled to the metal grating. The melters had kicked in.

Paula sighed, looking down at Sheela, some of the lyrics for "Again," a Black Angels song, going through her head:

I'm never . . .
I'm never . . .
I'm never gonna get
Fucked up
Like this
Again!

In fact, Sheela had written those lyrics. Sheela, who now lay in a crumpled heap on the fire escape, eyelids fluttering, fingers twitching occasionally. Live forever? Right. Why in hell would you want to be doing this any longer than you had to?

Paula moved the bottles out of the way, then knelt beside Sheela and grabbed hold of her under her arms. She pushed herself slowly to her feet, leaned back, and pulled Sheela to the open bedroom window.

After that it was a struggle—propping Sheela against the building, going in through the window, reaching back out to take hold of Sheela again, heaving her up and onto the windowsill, dragging her over the sill and into the apartment. Once she had her inside, it was a little easier. She dragged

Sheela across the floor, then pulled and pushed her onto the bed. It was plenty warm, so there was no need for a blanket. Besides, the melters would be heating her just fine.

Paula sat on the edge of the bed for a few minutes, recovering her breath, and watched her friend. Sheela didn't move much, other than the fluttering eyelids and the mild twitching of her hands and feet. One day, Paula thought, Sheela's nervous system was going to do a hard crash if she didn't stop this. She was one hell of a drummer, but she put way too much shit into her body.

Paula looked at the glowing digital clock in the wall next to the bed. Eleven fifteen. She should be leaving soon to meet Mixer. She got up from the bed and crawled back out onto the fire escape to get the empties. The recruiting van was almost directly below her now, and she could read it.

ATLANTIS II, the huge, lighted letters spelled out as they flowed across the panels attached to the van roof. So it *wasn't* for New Hong Kong. On the side of the van itself, three video panels showed a running series of images—color shots of the first undersea dome being built on the floor of the Caribbean, along with computer-generated conceptions of how it would look when completed. The images were probably even more appealing than the ones Sheela had seen of New Hong Kong. Crystalline blue water, lush aquatic plants; a dome filled with spectacular buildings and gardens; incredible views of the water through the dome itself, with schools of brilliant tropical fish.

Then more text scrolled across the roof panels: WORKERS NEEDED ** SKILLED OR UNSKILLED ** EXPERIMENTAL SUBJECTS ** GOOD PAY, FINE HOUSING, EXCELLENT BENEFITS. The pictures and images and text repeated as the van rolled slowly past and continued down the street.

Atlantis II, the undersea dome. It all sounded so peaceful and inviting, Paula thought. Paradise on Earth. And New Hong Kong was Paradise in Orbit. It might almost be tempting if she didn't know what was really being offered. Still, this recruiter might do all right. It was probably a better contract than most, and there were always people desperate enough to go for it, even if they knew the reality.

Paula picked up the empties and crawled back inside. It was time to go meet Mixer.

Paula stood on the roof of her apartment building, waiting for Mixer. Midnight meetings on rooftops. Mixer was a romantic at heart—mystery, melodrama, suspense, atmosphere. From here she could see the upper reaches of a corner of the Tenderloin: elliptical strings of blinking lights marking the rooftop mini-satellite dishes; spinning reflections of seeded catch traps; irregular outlines of razor wire; a couple of small fires, shadowed figures moving among the flames. The Tenderloin. Mixer's home.

Gravel crunched, and Paula turned to see Mixer walking toward her. He was wearing jeans and a long-sleeved shirt, and as he approached, she could see lines of metal—narrow tubing, wire, complex joints—surrounding his right hand and fingers and extending up his arm beneath his shirt. Exoskeleton. She wondered how far it went, and why he had it.

"Hey, Paula," Mixer said, grinning and saluting her with his right hand, metal brushing the twisted spikes of crusted skin on his forehead. She could just barely hear the soft whir of the exoskeleton's motors. She could also see now that it extended all the way along each finger, past the last knuckle, with special finger pad attachments so he could grip normally, hold onto things. "What do you think?" he asked. "It's an exoskeleton."

"I know what it is," Paula said. "You do something to your arm?"

Mixer shook his head. "No, it's just an augmentation." He stripped off his shirt, revealing the entire thing. The exo ran up his arm to the shoulder, where it connected to a metal, plastic, and leather harness that fit across his upper back and chest. "Rabid, isn't it?"

"How did you manage it?" A true exoskeleton was incredibly expensive, and had to be custom-designed, built, and calibrated.

"I did someone a favor." He put his shirt back on. "It took six months and a dozen fittings before it was finished." He stretched out his right arm and looked at it with admiration, though only the hand section of the exo was now visible. "Final fitting just an hour ago." He flexed the fingers, then wiggled them at a fantastic speed, metal flickering like a strobe.

"Must have been some favor."

Mixer shrugged. Paula knew he wouldn't tell her about it, which was fine. She didn't want to know.

"So you saw Carlucci today?" Mixer said.

"Yes."

"What did you think?"

"What's to think? I talked to him for maybe half an hour." She put her hands in her jacket pockets. "You're probably right about the man. I got a good hit off him."

Mixer nodded. "He's a good cop. An honest cop."

"Maybe so. But I don't know if he'll be able to do anything," Paula said. "He kept telling me, 'No promises.' "

"He's got to be careful," Mixer said, nodding slowly. "If the cops are trying to sink this thing, he'll have to go real easy." He shrugged.

"Sounds to me like he might not be able to go after it at all."

"He'll go after it," Mixer said. "I know him. And if he doesn't go on his own, I'll give him a nudge."

Paula looked at him. "You know something about Chick's death?"

"Maybe." He shrugged again.

"Jesus, Mix, how much *do* you know?"

"Nothing, really," Mixer said, "and that's the truth, babe.

I've heard some things, been hearing some things for weeks. I tried to warn Chick, told him he might be getting in up to his neck again. Looks like he got in a hell of a lot deeper than that." Mixer shook his head. "I don't know who killed him, Paula. I don't really know *why* he got himself killed, but I have an idea or two."

"Like *what*?"

Mixer shook his head; he wasn't going to say any more.

"Jesus, Mixer, I hope you're not in this enough to get yourself killed, too."

"Not me, babe."

"Mixer." Paula sighed heavily. "Don't call me 'babe.' We-'ve been through that before."

"Yeah, yeah, you're right. Sorry."

They stood together at the edge of the roof, looking out at the night. Paula hadn't heard a siren in a long time, which gave the night an eerie, quiet feel, though of course it wasn't all *that* quiet. On the street below, an all female thrasher pack cruised past, motorized boards growling at low idle. A trio of rollers wandered in and out of the street, chanting, their head-wheels spinning. And from somewhere nearby came the distorted racket of metal-bang rock.

"I miss the skinny bastard," Mixer said.

"Yeah."

Mixer turned to look at Paula. "How are you doing?"

The ache jammed up against her chest again. When was it going to stop? "Got a hole in my heart," she said.

Mixer nodded and put his arm around her shoulder, pulling her close to him. The ridges of the exoskeleton felt strange to Paula, yet comforting.

"Need anything?" Mixer asked.

Paula shook her head.

Mixer leaned into her, kissed her on the cheek. "Let me know." Paula nodded. "And let me know what you hear from Carlucci." Paula nodded again, and he let her go. "I'll talk to you.'' He turned and walked toward the roof ladder, gravel crunching under his shoes.

Paula gazed down at the street below and listened to Mixer's footsteps until he'd crossed the roof, descended the ladder, and was gone. Gone. Just like Chick, except she'd never see Chick again. ''Aw, shit,'' she whispered to herself. ''Chick . . .'' But she didn't know what else to say except his name. ''Chick . . .'' she said again, then nothing more.

Paula remained on the roof a long time, fighting the tears until she just didn't have the energy to hold them back any longer. She sat on the roof ledge, legs dangling, arms pressed into her sides, and cried.

THREE

MIXER WAS BACK on home turf, surrounded by light and sound, crowds and moving vehicles, color and the crash of city music. Walking the streets of the Tenderloin at night. One in the morning, the Tenderloin was still peaking, humming all around him. Message streamers shimmered above the street, swimming in and out of existence, hawking goods, announcing special events, calling for job applicants, crying for help or love.

Mixer didn't pay much attention to the activity around him. He was feeling out of sorts. It was his talk with Paula about Chick, about Carlucci. He liked Carlucci all right, but thinking about the homicide cop always made him think about Sookie, which brought up the old aches inside him. No, he didn't just feel out of sorts, he felt damn shitty.

Sookie. Thirteen years old, the final victim of the Chain Killer. Tanner and Carlucci had caught the bastard, and the guy had ended up dead, but not before he had killed Sookie, tattooed angel wings onto her eyelids, and grafted metal bands and chains to her wrists and ankles. Mixer had been at the lagoon with Tanner and Carlucci when she'd been pulled out of the water. Shit, he wished he hadn't seen that. Three years later it still made him sick when he thought about it, still gave him nightmares once or twice a month. He had seen a few dead people in his life, and some things a lot worse, but nothing had ever bothered him like that. Sookie had been special to him, and he figured it must be like losing a sister or daughter, though he'd never had either.

Mixer stopped in front of a crasher shop and lit a cigarette. He had a little trouble flicking the lighter with the exoskeleton, but he managed it. He still hadn't decided whether to keep the exo on around the clock, or just put it on for special occasions. For now he'd leave it on, see how awkward it was. Might be worth any hassles, it was pretty fucking rabid.

Mixer checked his watch. Ten minutes to his meet with Chandler. Better move it. He started down the street, thinking how Chandler would be impressed with the exo. But, impressed enough to tell him something about Chick?

Two blocks, walking fast, he tossed the cigarette, then shot across the street, darting through traffic. He bumped into a patchwork beggar who was stumbling along the sidewalk with eyeblinds and a fingerless stub for a hand. The beggar cried out, swung his good fist blindly toward Mixer, but Mixer blocked it with his right arm, and the beggar's fist banged into the exoskeleton. The beggar yowled and staggered away. The exo *was* good for something, Mixer thought.

He pulled open the lobby door of the Caterwaul Building, twelve stories of ugly, and stepped inside. Gunther, the beefy security guard with a hole in his face where his nose should have been, looked up from his chess game, recognized Mixer, and waved him through to the elevator. The chessboard spat a bishop at Gunther's face, but he caught it inches away from his forehead, grinned at Mixer, and put the bishop back on the board.

The elevator doors were already open and waiting, and Mixer entered. He hesitated, breathed deeply, and pushed the twelfth-floor button. As the doors closed, his chest tightened.

There was a click, then the elevator lurched upward. Mixer started to sweat.

Mixer hated elevators. Something like claustrophobia, he guessed. He had an irrational fear that the elevator would get stuck between floors and he would be hopelessly trapped for hours. But to meet Chandler he didn't have a choice; Chandler had blocked off the stairs at the tenth floor, making the elevator the only access.

Mixer stood in the middle of the elevator as it slowly rose, listening to the double *ca-click ca-click* at each floor, counting silently . . . five . . . six . . . He realized he had stopped breathing, and forced himself to start again, slowly in and out . . . ten . . . eleven . . . The elevator ground to a halt with a terrible groan. The doors slid open. Mixer stepped out.

Chandler had gutted the entire twelfth floor several years back, turning it into a single, enormous room. Chandler traded in almost anything, and usually there were crates and cartons and foam-pack bundles stacked against the walls, several tables and chairs scattered throughout the room with computers, printers, and various kinds of analyzers and measurement devices, a dozen or more people, half of them security, and the whole place lit with lamps strung from the ceiling. Now, though, the room was nearly empty, silent, and dimly lit by a single overhead light. A few boxes against the right wall, under a window. A single folding chair in the middle of the room. Two wadded pieces of paper on the floor. Dust rolls.

No Chandler. Nobody at all.

Something was very wrong.

The elevator doors started to close behind him. Mixer turned, watching them close and seal. He could have reached them in time, kept them open, but his gut said to let them go. Might not be a good idea to be in the elevator when it reached the ground floor. A groan sounded, and the elevator began its descent.

On the other hand, if someone—Chandler?—wanted him,

why hadn't they been waiting when he stepped out of the elevator? Mixer scanned the shadows of the vast, empty room, half expecting someone to appear, lights to go on, or some explosion to go off. Nothing happened.

Mixer felt calm and unafraid. There was no way to know what was going on here, no way to know if it even had anything to do with him. Chandler was into all kinds of shit, with all kinds of people, even New Hong Kong. The body-bags were only a sideline for him. This could be anything.

Mixer walked around a little, listening to his own echoing footsteps. He could search the place, maybe find something. A clue. Right. What he should do is get out. Now. Stupid to take chances.

But how? He still didn't like the elevator. And the fire escape was out. Chandler had ripped it off the side of the building years ago. Elevator shaft, maybe. Force open the door, climb down the shaft to the tenth floor, force that door open, and he'd be able to reach the stairs, maybe find a way out on one of the other floors.

He went back to the elevator, tried to force open the outer door. There was nothing to grip; the edge of the door went too far into the wall, and the door didn't budge. The exo would give him extra strength, but it wasn't any help if he couldn't get a grip on anything.

He gave up on the elevator shaft, and stood gazing around the huge, empty room, thinking. He still wasn't much worried, but he didn't want to stay here any longer than he had to. Shadows, pillars, barred windows. Ventilation shafts way too small.

Stairs. The stairwell was in the corner, now deep in shadow. They were blocked at the tenth floor, but there might be a window in the stairwell, or . . . something. Mixer walked to the corner, slowing as the darkness increased, letting his eyes adjust. He hesitated at the top of the stairs, looking down, unable to clearly see more than a few steps in front of him.

No sign of a window. Hell, just go. What else was there? He started down.

Halfway to the next floor the stairs cornered and switched back, actually got a little bit brighter, light coming in from the door opening onto the eleventh floor. He stopped on the landing and stuck his head into the hallway. There was a window at the far end of the corridor, and open doors on both sides, light emerging in angled bands from most of them. He didn't see or hear anything, but there was a mild stench coming from somewhere. He'd never been allowed on this floor, never known what Chandler used it for.

Mixer looked down the stairwell. It got darker again. No window, and access to the tenth floor was blocked by brick and concrete; he'd seen the barrier the one time he'd tried using the stairs in defiance of Chandler's instructions. No choice, then. He had to see if there was a way out on this floor.

The window at the end of the hall was probably his best shot. He took a few steps into the hall, then stopped, listening for voices or other sounds. Nothing. He continued slowly along the hall, trying to keep his footsteps silent.

The door to the first room on his left was open, and light emerged through it. No sounds. Mixer stopped, then leaned forward and looked inside. Empty. The stench was worse; he could almost feel it wafting out of the room, but he couldn't see anything that would cause it. What the fuck had Chandler been doing in here? Bare walls, bare floor, boarded windows, an overhead fluorescent light. Nothing else.

Mixer moved on. The next room was on his right; it, too, was open. When he looked inside, he again saw bare walls, bare floor, a fluorescent light. Once more he felt and smelled the stench, heavy and warm and cloying.

Bad, bad, bad. He hadn't been afraid on the floor above, standing in that vast, empty room. But here? Something was wrong, seriously wrong, and Mixer was damn sure he didn't want to be here.

He moved quickly now, not quite jogging, a fast walk, still trying to stay quiet. No more looking into the rooms as he passed them; he hoped there wasn't anyone or anything inside. Just get to the window, he told himself, and get out.

Mixer reached the end of the hall and looked out the window. Good and bad luck. The next building was no more than eight feet away, but the roof was at least a full floor below, maybe more. The gap would be easy, the drop a bitch. At the far end of the roof was a rat-pack hut with a few soldiers moving in and out of the lights. Mixer knew the building, knew the head rat. He wouldn't get free passage, but he'd be able to buy his way down.

The window was old, counterweight and pulley. Mixer grabbed the bottom handle and pulled up. The window rose smoothly, surprising the hell out of him. He opened it all the way, put his head through and looked down. A cement ledge ran along the wall about two feet below the window. Narrow, but wide enough to use as a launch pad.

Mixer pulled his head back in and was just about to put his leg through the open window when he sensed something approaching from behind. He spun and crouched, preparing himself, but the hall was empty. The sensation remained, however, the feel of some presence there in the hall with him. There were no sounds, no signs of movement, just the steadily increasing stench and the eerie, prickly feeling that flowed over him. *Fuck me*, Mixer thought. *I've got to get the hell out of here.*

He worked his way backward through the window, feeling his way with his shoes to the ledge below, never taking his eyes off the hallway. When his footing was secure, he eased his chest and head through, keeping hold of the sill, watching the hall. Still nothing.

He didn't want to turn his back to the hall, not for more

than a few seconds, anyway, so he geared himself up to turn and jump at the same time. He ran through it in his head, glancing back and forth from the hall to the roof below. He'd jump, land feet first, buckling his legs and doing a tuck and roll to absorb the impact. Okay. One last look down the hall, and go.

Mixer turned, let go of the windowsill, and pushed off the ledge, leaping across the gap and down. Almost immediately he hit the roof hard, pain flaring in his ankles as he pitched forward and sprawled across the rough surface, scraping his arms and hands and face. Shit, so much for the tuck and roll theory.

He pushed himself up to hands and knees, then slowly to his feet. Both ankles hurt, the left worse than the right, but he'd be able to walk. The exo had protected his right hand and arm, but the other was badly scraped and bleeding in several places.

Mixer turned around and looked up at the eleventh-floor window. Nothing. He was about to turn away, when he thought he saw something, a shadow, a shimmer of movement. He stared hard, but didn't see anything else. A minute passed. Nothing. Then the window slowly, steadily, slid down and closed.

Fuck me, Mixer said to himself again.

He kept watching the window, listening to the rat-pack soldiers coming toward him, but he saw nothing more. One hard, long shiver rolled through his body. Mixer turned away and limped across the roof to the rat-pack soldiers waiting for him.

FOUR

CARLUCCI WAS ALREADY exhausted by the time he got to his office and dropped into his chair. His morning coffee-hash at Spade's had gone almost three hours, most of that time spent trying to organize the murder investigation of the mayor's nephew with LaPlace and Hong, who were in charge of the case. They were getting almost as much heat as he was, and so far they were getting nowhere. They'd arranged to meet later that afternoon at the nephew's penthouse for another look-through. Then, after dropping him off at the station, LaPlace and Hong had gone off to talk to people they knew weren't going to tell them a damn thing.

The air conditioning was still out, but the fans had been left on all night, and it was early, so the air wasn't too bad yet. Carlucci cleared a spot on his desk, piling files and notepads on top of other piles, then turned on his computer terminal. To his surprise, the system was back up and running. He logged on, then called up his file on the nephew—William Kashen. There wasn't much in it, and there wasn't much to add—the official report would be done by LaPlace and Hong, since it was their case—but with all the political pressure on this thing he had to keep a kind of management file to show he was staying on top of it.

Carlucci spent a half hour working on the file, most of that time staring at the screen and doing nothing, not even thinking about the case. When he thought he'd done enough, he printed out a hard copy, grabbed the sheets from the printer on the side of his desk, and stuffed them in the blue case folder. Then he sat staring at the monitor for a while longer, thinking about Paula Asgard and Chick Roberts.

Gotta start sometime, he thought. Carlucci called up the case file for Chick Roberts. The cover sheet came up on the screen, which gave the most basic information: case number, date, first officers on the scene, investigating officers (Santos and Weathers, Santos senior-in-charge), and status (open, pending). When Carlucci tried to call up the rest of the case file, he got "the message."

FILE ACCESS RESTRICTED
CAPTAIN MCCULLER/CHIEF VAUGHN FOR AUTHORIZATION

Pretty much what he had expected. A temporary dead end. There was no way he could go to McCuller or Vaughn for authorization. At this point he didn't want either of them to know he was at all interested in the case.

Carlucci exited the case file and logged off, then picked up the phone and punched in Ruben Santos's number. There was no answer, and after three rings Carlucci heard the click as he was transferred through to the front desk.

"I'm looking for Ruben Santos," he told the clerk.

"Ah, let's see . . . he's out with Weathers, interviews, probably back this afternoon. Page or message?"

"No." Carlucci hung up.

One step at a time, no hurry, Carlucci told himself. Chick Roberts wasn't going anywhere, and he had to be careful. But it nagged at him, and he had a crappy feeling about the whole thing. He wanted to move on it, or forget about it completely. Forgetting about it, though, wasn't something he could do.

So . . . patience. There was nothing more he could do until he talked to Santos. For now, just muck around at the desk, grab a bite to eat, then go out to the nephew's. Chick Roberts would have to wait.

The nephew's apartment was still a mess. The only thing missing was the body. Even the stink of death remained, if only a trace. Blood was spattered everywhere in the front room, dark and dry now. Deep, solid patches on the white carpet radiated from the vague outline of a body, interspersed with wide, fanning streaks. Everything in the room was white—carpet, walls, furniture, lampshades, even the entertainment system and picture phone—and in the bright lights the blood stood out like phosphor. There were even a few splatters on the white textured ceiling.

"We should rip up the carpet," LaPlace said. "Frame it, and put it up in a gallery. Post-neo-industrial-modern-slasher art, or something like that."

Peter LaPlace, a heavy, balding man, removed his glasses, rubbed the bridge of his nose, then replaced them. Joseph Hong, who was taller and much thinner than LaPlace, also wore glasses, and a lot of the homicide cops called them the Spec Twins.

LaPlace turned slowly, gazing around the room and through the doorways into the rest of the apartment. "Fuckin' weird place to live," he said.

"Weird guy," Hong said, shrugging.

Carlucci just nodded. They'd been through the apartment pretty thoroughly the day before while the coroner's men worked on the body. Most of the rooms were monochrome, like this one, furnishings matching the wall paint and carpeting. The two enormous bedrooms were all black, an office room was blue, the bathrooms bright red, the kitchen white. The dining room was the exception, a combination of white and black and chrome.

None of them were quite sure what they were looking for. The crime scene techs had already gone through it with all their sophisticated detection equipment, slicking up prints, hairs, fibers, skin flakes, and various other particles which they were now analyzing with a fortune in lab machinery. With the mayor on their asses, no expense would be spared. And plenty would be wasted. Additionally, the three detectives had already tagged and bagged several boxes of articles from the apartment, which were now back at the station and which they would go through again and again later on, along with the dozens of photographs that had been taken. They were here now hoping to see something they'd missed, or think of something, or get kicked off into a line of thought that none of them had come up with before. They were searching for intangibles and gut feelings. Anything.

And Carlucci wanted to talk to Hong and LaPlace alone, where they wouldn't be overheard by department squeakers, the way they might have been at Spade's this morning. Carlucci hadn't seen anybody suspicious, but he hardly trusted anyone these days.

"Pete, Joseph," Carlucci said. The two men looked at him. "I've got something I want to say. Didn't want to talk about it at Spade's."

"Squeakers?" LaPlace said.

"Yeah, Pete, you just never know."

Hong slid a cigarette from his shirt pocket, stuck it in his mouth, dug out a lighter from his pants, and lit the cigarette, all his motions slow and deliberate. Hong thought they were about to get ragged on, Carlucci realized.

"Look, this is your case," Carlucci said. "You two are in charge, you make all the decisions, handle it the way you think best. The only reason I'm here is because of all the heat from the mayor and the chief. I'm not trying to butt in on the case, I've just got to do this for appearances. It's all bullshit, but I've got no choice. As much as possible, we do this like we would any other case—it's yours, and you report to me. I'll be around more, I'll be on the streets with you once in a while, but I'll try to stay out of your way." Carlucci shrugged. "I don't like this arrangement any more than you do."

Hong and LaPlace looked at each other, Hong nodded, then LaPlace turned back to Carlucci. "Joseph and I have already talked about it," LaPlace said. He half smiled. "We can see what's going on. We just didn't know how you were going to be about it. Hell, Frank, you might have decided to jump all over our asses. We didn't think you would, but who the fuck knows? We figured if you did, we were going to be assholes about it. But hell, since you're not, we'd just as soon you actually worked with us as much as you can. This is going to be a bitch investigation, for a lot of reasons."

"Yeah, it is." Carlucci sighed and nodded. "All right, then. Everything's clear between us?" Hong and LaPlace both nodded. "Good. Then let's get to work, see if we can find *anything* in this freaking place."

They split up. Each man would go through the entire apartment separately, hoping somebody would spot something the others missed. Wasn't much of a hope, Carlucci thought, but it was worth a shot.

As he worked his way through the apartment, Carlucci had to struggle to keep from being distracted by all the extravagance and luxury, the fortune in high-tech gadgets and the incredible views, even though he'd seen it all the day before. Picture phones and internal video systems were built into the walls of every room, including the bathroom, along with control panels for the Bang and Olufsen entertainment system, which also had speakers and monitors in each room. The larger of the black bedrooms had a set of neural head-nets, and hanging in the closet was an assortment of exotic sexual electronics, some of which Carlucci didn't even recognize. The other bedroom, aside from the friction bed, had a set of bunked bubble tubes, one of which was still half filled with a pink, gelatinous fluid.

The blue room was filled with computers, data-scanners, and more electronic equipment that was only vaguely familiar to Carlucci. Most of the equipment had been damaged or destroyed, presumably by the nephew's killer. The department's electronic salvage crews had been in and removed what few disks and chips and bubbles were left behind, and were working to recover any data that remained. Carlucci didn't hold out much hope for that line of investigation, either.

Saunas and whirlpools and automated massagers in the bathrooms, auto-chef and espresso machine and ionizers in the kitchen. A heat scanner in the dining room, digitizing paintings on the hallway walls. And the entire penthouse wired with the most sophisticated alarm and shield system Carlucci had ever seen, which hadn't prevented the mayor's nephew from being gutted in his own living room.

The nephew. He had a name, Carlucci reminded himself. William Kashen. Except no one referred to him by name. He was the mayor's nephew, which was his most significant feature as far as the investigation was concerned.

Carlucci didn't spot anything in any of the rooms that seemed worthwhile, and an hour after they had begun, they met back in the living room, where they stood looking down at the largest of the bloodstains on the carpet. Hong was on his fourth or fifth cigarette, which actually helped cut the leftover stink in the apartment. Nobody had found a thing.

"Bet we get the autopsy report pretty damn quick," LaPlace said.

Carlucci nodded. "Prelim's due on my desk this afternoon. Maybe we can go over it later today, or first thing tomorrow."

"Tomorrow," Hong said. "My grandmother-in-law is one hundred today. We're having a dinner celebration in our flat tonight. Twenty people, and I'm the cook."

Carlucci smiled. "Tomorrow, then."

"Bet the report says he was still alive through most of the gutting," LaPlace said.

"I wouldn't be surprised." Carlucci ran his gaze over the wide scattering of blood once again.

"I suppose they're going to put the slugs on it, aren't they?" Hong asked.

"Yeah," Carlucci said. "They've got one on it now, and they'll put all of them on it once the autopsy report comes in and a good chunk of the lab work is done. Everything's got a goddamn rush on it. Info-Services is already putting together the Prime Level Feed for them, and a few people are working on the sublevel feeds. They might start the rest of the slugs tomorrow or the next day." Carlucci didn't look forward to it. It had been years since he'd had a session with the slugs, and the thought of doing another made him queasy. The slugs were repulsive—bodies, limbs, and faces twisted and distended by the frequent injections of reason enhancers and metabolic boosters. He had a hard time even thinking of them as human.

Hong put out his cigarette in an immaculate white porcelain ashtray atop a quartz table; then, as if reading Carlucci's thoughts, he frowned and said, "The slugs aren't people, not anymore. We don't need them."

No one was going to argue with him. Most cops hated the slugs and felt they got a lot more credit than they deserved, felt they got in the way more than they helped. Carlucci knew they *had* been responsible for real breakthroughs in several major cases that had dead-ended before the slugs were put on them, but if he had a choice he would as soon do without.

"Anything else?" he asked.

Hong and LaPlace both shook their heads, then LaPlace said, "I'd like to keep the apartment sealed off another couple days or so. I'd like to be able to come back and look around."

"Sure." Carlucci understood. They were all afraid they had missed something important, and probably all three of them would come by here at least one more time, alone, most likely in the middle of the night. "We done here for now?" Both men nodded. "All right, then, let's get out of here."

Back in his office, there was no preliminary autopsy report, which was just fine with Carlucci; it would shift some of the heat from him to the coroner, at least for today. He punched up Santos's number on the phone, and a woman answered.

"Weathers."

"Toni, this is Frank. Ruben around?"

"Yeah, somewhere. I'll go see if I can find him."

"Thanks."

"By the way," Weathers said, "how's progress on that paragon of virtue, the mayor's nephew?"

Carlucci snorted. "We're pursuing several potentially fruitful lines of inquiry," he said, imitating the PR hack who'd been on television the night before.

Toni Weathers laughed. "You haven't got jack shit."

"That's about right."

"I'll go see if I can find Ruben."

He heard the clunk of the receiver being dropped to the table, then a scattering of background noises as he waited, including what sounded like an incredibly long and loud belch.

Toni Weathers, like Ruben, was a good homicide cop, and as straight as Ruben. They'd been partners for more than ten years. Carlucci wondered what *she* thought of the Chick Roberts case.

More clunking sounds, then, "Frank?" Santos's voice.

"Yeah, Ruben."

"What's up?"

"Got a half hour? Buy you a cup of coffee."

Santos didn't answer at first. Carlucci could hear his deep, raspy breath over the phone.

"There something you need to talk to me about?" Santos asked.

"Oh, just this and that, get your thoughts on the mayor's nephew."

Another hesitation, then, "You want to come by here and talk to me while I write up these interviews?"

"I thought we'd take a walk. Get out of this damn hot box. Get some fresh air."

This time the pause was even longer. Santos probably had a good idea what Carlucci really wanted to talk about, and didn't want to touch it. But he would also know he couldn't avoid it for long.

"Sure, Frank," Santos finally answered. "I'm suffocating in here anyway. Meet you downstairs in, say, fifteen minutes."

"Fine," Carlucci said. He hung up.

They met in the station lobby, and immediately left the building. Santos was thin and wiry, with curly hair the color of rust, and was growing a beard again. Carlucci figured it was about two weeks along, and there was more gray in it than there was the last time around.

It was late afternoon, and hot. It looked like it might finally rain for the first time in days, orange-brown clouds moving across the hazy sun, the air heavy and charged and damp. Carlucci stopped at the Cuban bakery on the corner and bought two large cups of coffee, then he and Santos continued down the street, sipping at it through openings torn in the lids. The coffee was strong, and so hot it burned Carlucci's tongue and lips.

"Chick Roberts," Carlucci said when they were several blocks from the station.

"Fuck the Virgin Mary," Santos said. "I *knew* you were going to ask me about that goddamn case. Mayor's nephew, my ass. God damn!" He turned to glare at Carlucci. "I'm not saying a fucking word about it."

"Come on, Ruben. This isn't like you. What the hell's going on?"

"Frank, I'm not screwing around. I've got nothing to say."

"Ruben, shit, it's *me* you're talking to. Why are you burying this thing?"

Santos didn't answer. He led the way across the street and down half a block to a vacant lot that had only recently started filling up with garbage. Five kids around nine or ten years old sat in a shallow cave dug out of the side of the garbage mound, playing some kind of game with a batch of dead green neurotubes.

"Hey!" Santos called to the kids. "Why aren't you in school?" They looked up at him but didn't respond. Santos repeated his question in Spanish. Still no response. Santos shrugged. "Hell, they probably don't even know what school is."

"Why, Ruben?" Carlucci asked again.

Santos drank some more of his coffee, then suddenly threw the cup at the mound of trash. The lid flipped off and coffee sprayed in twisting arcs through the air. Santos turned to Carlucci, eyes glaring.

"How the hell do *I* know why I'm burying it? Jesus Christ, Frank, you think they tell me why? You know better than that. 'Bury it, Ruben.' That's all they said. So I'm fucking burying it."

"Ruben . . . Christ, Ruben, why not demand reassignment?" Automatic reassignment was an option that had always been available, to allow any cop to stay as straight as he wanted. The vast majority of investigations proceeded on regular tracks, but there were always a few that the top hogs, for whatever political or financial reasons, wanted buried, or fouled up, or just ghosted, and anyone involved in one of those cases had the option of being reassigned so they wouldn't have to be a part of it. It was an informal arrangement that had worked well over the years. Any cop could get off a dirty case, and in return they agreed not to raise a stink—they let it go. A clean cop could *stay* a clean cop.

Santos seemed to sag, and he slowly shook his head. "You think I didn't ask, Frank?"

"They turned you down?" Carlucci could hardly believe it. The reassignment option was one of the few things cops counted on.

"They fucked me, Frank. That shit McCuller, he'd bend over for anyone above him who said 'asshole' in his hearing. Called me before I even got to the scene, asked me if I wanted my job and my pension and my health benefits. I asked for reassignment right then, before he had a chance to tell me what he wanted done. I didn't even want to know." He stopped, gazing at the mound of garbage and the kids playing in their cave. "McCuller said there would be no reassignment on this case, unless I wanted to resign and forfeit all my pension and benefits." Santos turned to Carlucci. "I've got twenty-three years in, Frank. I'd never get another job as a cop, you know that. What the hell am I supposed to do, start all over again someplace? Doing what? At my age? With Consuela and the kids?" He paused, breathing deeply, shaking his head. "Jesus Christ, Frank, they're not supposed to be able to do this to us." He stopped again, ran his hand through his hair, then rubbed at his neck. "I had about thirty seconds to make my decision. I thought about fighting it, bringing it to the Association, threaten to go public, whatever, but I didn't think about it long." He looked at Carlucci. "I couldn't afford to lose that one, Frank. So I made the decision, and I'm stuck with it."

They started walking again, slowly, neither speaking. When they came to a liquor store, Santos went in, then came back out with a pack of cigarettes. He opened it, shook one out and lit it.

"I've been trying to quit," he said. "I'd been doing all right until you called. God damn you, Frank." He dragged in deep on the cigarette, and they continued along the street.

"How's Toni feel about it?" Carlucci asked.

"The same. She hasn't said anything, but I think she's going along with it mostly for me. She's younger, she's got no kids. I think she'd have been willing to fight it, try to blow these fuckers out of the water, if it wasn't for me. Which only makes me feel worse about the whole fucking mess."

"But why wouldn't they let you and Toni off the case?"

Santos shook his head. "I've been thinking about that. Two possibilities. One, they want clean cops on the file so it looks like nothing funny's going on. Or two, they just don't want more people to know about the case." He shook his head again. "I don't know, Frank. I think someone panicked on this thing."

"Why?"

"You know anything about this Chick Roberts? A part-time rocker, part-time two-bit petty thief, ex-junkie who probably still popped too much shit. If nobody says anything to us, how much time and effort were we going to put into the case? Not a hell of a lot. We'd have written it off to a drug deal gone to shit, something like that. Probably would have just faded away all on its own. Now? Who knows, it might stay buried. But it just might blow up in somebody's goddamn face."

A shimmering flash of light appeared in the clouds, followed a few moments later by a roll of thunder. The first drops fell on the two men. They hurried around the corner and under the shelter of an abandoned bus stop just as the rain poured full force from above. Santos dropped his cigarette to the ground, crushed it with his shoe, then turned to Carlucci.

"This isn't some kind of official inquiry, is it, Frank?"

"Ruben. You know me better than that."

Santos shrugged. "I had to ask." He lit another cigarette, dragged on it. "How the hell did you find out about this thing? The files and reports were supposed to bypass you completely."

"They did," Carlucci replied, but he didn't say any more.

"Then . . . ?" Santos cocked his head, then nodded to himself. "The girlfriend, right?" Carlucci didn't answer. "Yeah, has to be; she'd been dogging me about it. I thought she'd finally gotten the message and dropped it." He shook his head. "You talk to anyone else about this, Frank?"

"Of course not. I came to you first, Ruben."

"Then leave it that way, for Christ's sake. And tell the girlfriend the same thing. I don't know why they want this thing buried, and I don't want to know. You don't either, Frank. Go find out who killed the mayor's nephew, get a citation, and leave this case the fuck alone."

"You really don't know why it's being buried, Ruben? Not even a hint?"

"Shit, Frank, if I did I wouldn't tell you. Forget this goddamn case. *I'm* trying to. And forget we even talked about it."

They stood under the shelter, the rain pouring down all around them. Another flash, then rolling thunder. It pissed Carlucci off, what McCuller and Vaughn had done to Santos. It just wasn't fair. Well, shit, he told himself, not much *was* fair. Santos knew that, and Paula Asgard probably knew that as well. He was going to have to talk to her soon, and what the hell was he going to say?

Carlucci turned to Santos and nodded. "You're right, Ruben. We haven't talked about this."

Santos nodded back, but didn't say anything. They remained in the shelter, silent, waiting for the rain to stop.

FIVE

WHAT A FUCKED day. Paula lay back on Chick's bed and closed her eyes, incredibly tired. Her arms and legs felt heavy, and the heat seemed to drain all the energy from her; the air was so still and quiet, and she didn't want to move. So don't move, she told herself. Why bother?

First there had been the horrible stench of the place after being closed up for almost two weeks. Then, seeing the bloodstains all over the rug. She'd almost walked away and left everything, but in the end she just couldn't do that. So she'd stayed, and spent the day going through all Chick's stuff, trying to decide what to keep, what to get rid of.

There were surprises. Like tens and twenties stashed all over the apartment, in books, wedged onto shelves; she must have found over three hundred dollars so far. A collection of twentieth-century Hungarian postage stamps. A complete set of Torelli's fifteen vortex novels. And finally, she'd found a box of all the letters she'd ever written to Chick over the years. She'd had no idea he'd saved them, no idea that they would be important to him, and that had made her even more tired and depressed.

Paula was nodding off, almost asleep, when someone pounded on the front door. Before she could get up and out of the bedroom, the pounding was repeated, louder this time.

"I'm coming!" she called as she came into the entryway. At the door, she looked through the peephole. It was Graumann, the building manager. Paula unlocked the door and opened it.

Graumann was huge; not much taller than she, but at least three hundred and fifty pounds, large arms and legs and an enormous gut. His puffy face glistened with sweat and he was breathing heavily.

"You've got to get out of here," he said. "I gotta rent this place."

Good afternoon to you, too, asshole, Paula thought. "I'm going through Chick's things now," she said. "I need some time to sort through it all, pack it up, and move it."

"You haven't got time," Graumann said. "You want me to call the cops? The owner's on my butt. You've gotta get out, unless you wanna make up all the back rent. Chick was behind again."

Of course he was. Chick was always getting behind on his rent, and then he'd pop something, catch up, maybe even pay a little ahead, and slip Graumann three or four hundred dollars for letting it go so long. It had worked out fine for both of them.

"Give me a fucking break," Paula said. "I've got a lot of shit to go through."

"No one's paying rent," Graumann said.

"Chick's dead, for Christ's sake!"

Graumann looked down at the floor for a moment, but then returned his gaze to her. A bead of sweat hung from his chin. He shrugged, knocking the bead free, but didn't say anything.

The telephone rang. Oh, terrific. Graumann looked over her shoulder. What did he expect to see, Chick appearing to answer the phone? It rang again. Okay, okay. Paula dug her hand into her pocket and pulled out the wad of bills she'd collected. She shoved it all into Graumann's hand and said, "I need three or four days.'' A third ring. Fuck.

Graumann shrugged again. ''Okay,'' he said and Paula slammed the door in his face. The phone rang once more and Chick's answering machine clicked on. Shit, she'd forgotten about that. Chick's voice spoke from the machine, and she felt like crying again. Or laughing.

''This is Chick, and you can suck my dick. Or leave a message. Your choice.'' A high beep sounded, followed by another click.

''Ah . . . this is Lieutenant Frank Carlucci, calling for Paula Asgard. I'll try to . . .''

Paula hurried into the bedroom and looked around for the phone.

''. . . this message you can . . .''

She spotted it under the edge of the overstuffed chair, crossed the room, dropped to the floor and picked it up, interrupting Carlucci's message.

''Hi, this is Paula.''

''What? Oh, yes, this is Lieutenant Carlucci. I just wanted to let you know that I've checked into the case.''

Jesus, he sounded so damn formal. ''And?''

''And, well, I'm afraid there's nothing I can tell you. Everything possible has been done, but unfortunately without much success. Despite a thorough investigation, there have been no leads. Although the case is not technically closed, for all practical purposes it is pretty much over.''

Paula was speechless. It was Carlucci's voice, she was sure she recognized it, but it hardly sounded like him, spouting all this crap.

''I'm sorry, Ms. Asgard,'' Carlucci went on, ''that I couldn't have been more help.''

God damn, the bastard was caving with the rest of them. ''That's all you've got to say?'' she asked him.

''No, there is one more thing, Ms. Asgard. I know this has been difficult for you, and that it's especially frustrating when the person or persons responsible for the death of your friend have not been apprehended, or even identified. But I think it would be best if you put this whole thing behind you.'' He paused. ''Let this go, Ms. Asgard.''

''Just like that, huh?''

''I know it won't be easy, but yes. Forget about it, Ms. Asgard. Believe me, it will be better if you do.''

All right, I've got the message. ''Fine,'' she said to Carlucci. ''I get the picture. Thanks a lot for nothing.''

''I'm sorry, Ms. Asgard.'' There was another long pause, and when Paula didn't reply, Carlucci said, ''Goodbye, Ms. Asgard,'' then hung up.

''Yeah, goodbye, asshole.'' Paula sat on the floor for a minute, holding the receiver, listening to the dial tone. Terrific. Carlucci, the wonder cop. Mixer didn't know his ass from a gravity well. She hung up the phone, then pulled herself up off the floor and into the overstuffed chair.

She'd been right here that night, sitting in this chair and staring at Chick's body on the floor, what was left of his head surrounded by thick, dark blood. All that remained now were the stains in the rug. She shouldn't have bothered going to Carlucci in the first place. What did it matter in the end? Chick was dead, and he was going to stay dead no matter what happened.

But she had thought it was important, important that somebody at least *try* to find out who had killed him and why. It still was important, she decided, but it obviously wasn't going to happen. And since it wasn't, Carlucci was right. She should just forget about it. Mixer said he could ''nudge'' Carlucci into it, but she would tell him not to bother. If Carlucci wouldn't do it on his own, then fuck him. Just fuck 'em all.

Half an hour later, Paula decided to pack it in for the day. She was hungry and tired and depressed. She'd had enough. She would take the box of letters and a few other things with her, and leave the rest for later; tomorrow or the next day she would call Nikky and see if she could borrow her van.

Before she could pull everything together, she heard knocking at the door. Oh, God, not Graumann again. What the hell would he want this time? Paula went to the front door, looked through the peephole, and was surprised to see Carlucci.

She didn't know whether to be pissed, or just more depressed; whether to open the door, or scream at him to leave. When Carlucci knocked again, Paula threw back the bolts and pulled the door open.

"Hello, Ms. Asgard." He looked uncomfortable, which was fine with her.

"Why are you here, Lieutenant Carlucci?"

"I want to apologize for what I said on the phone."

"Yeah?"

"Yes. Look, I need to talk to you. You can forget everything I said on the phone, all that . . . well, that was just to cover my ass, and yours." He scratched behind his ear. "This case is making me paranoid, and I'm trying not to take any chances."

Paula's anger and depression lifted a little, but she remained wary. "Are you saying you *are* going to look into Chick's death?"

Carlucci scratched again, frowning, then nodded. "I think so. That's why I want to talk to you."

"But the phone call. You think your own phone is bugged?"

Carlucci shrugged. "I'd be surprised if it wasn't. Look, have you had dinner yet?" When Paula shook her head, Carlucci said, "Why don't we go get something to eat, then, and talk about this?"

Did she really want to? Did she really want to get worked up again, maybe get shot down one more time? Or should she just let it go? Paula finally nodded. "Sure. I was just getting ready to lock up here. I've had it for today. Let me get my jacket."

Carlucci waited in the hall while she walked back to the bedroom, got her jacket, checked to make sure her wallet was secured inside, then rejoined him. She closed the door, locked the dead-bolts.

"You know a good place around here?" Carlucci said. "I'll buy."

Paula nodded, throwing her jacket over her shoulder. She should give him a choice. "Thai, or Mex?" Hoping he would say Mex; she had a real yen for chile rellenos and black beans.

"Mexican," Carlucci said.

Paula smiled. Maybe things were picking up. "Great," she said. "I know just the place."

Christiano's was small and colorful, noisy and crowded, with brightly painted dolls and masks and pictures hanging on the walls and from the ceiling. Traditional cantina played through tinny speakers mounted in the corners. Isabel met them as they came in, and Paula spoke with her in Spanish. They exchanged hellos, and Isabel hugged her, offered condolences for Chick. Carlucci surprised her when he introduced himself to Isabel, also in Spanish. Isabel said they would have a table cleared in a few minutes, and left.

Christiano's was one of Paula's favorite places, with good food and good people, a real neighborhood place. As they waited just inside the front door, she looked around for familiar faces. In the back, at a small table next to the kitchen door, was Pascal, the neighborhood scrounger, sitting alone and drinking coffee with his see-through arm. Three years ago Pascal had replaced his perfectly healthy right arm with an artificial limb sheathed in some kind of clear material so that all the inner workings were visible. Word on the street was that he'd done the same thing with his cock, but Paula wasn't about to check it out for herself.

Jeff and Robert were at a table by the front window, holding hands, Robert batting neon lashes at any man who walked by. Paula liked them both a lot, and waved when she caught Jeff's eye. Jeff and Robert waved back, smiling. Deena sat with three men Paula had never seen before, which worried her a little, but Deena seemed all right; Deena could usually take care of herself.

Isabel returned with menus and led them to a booth against the left wall. Carlucci sat facing the front of the restaurant, which left Paula with a terrific view of Pascal and the kitchen door. Carlucci glanced through the menu, then looked at her. "Any recommendations?"

"Everything's good," Paula said. "I go for the chile rellenos myself. But whatever you get, have an order of their black beans. They're great."

When Isabel came by again, Paula ordered three chile rellenos and black beans; Carlucci ordered *pollo con arroz*, a side of the beans, and a bottle of Diablo Negro beer.

Paula made a face at him after Isabel left. "God, you can drink that stuff?"

Carlucci smiled. "Sure. Why not?"

Paula just shivered. It was foul-tasting beer, very high alcohol. She had gotten tanked on Diablo Negro once, and she'd been sick for days. She'd never touched it since. Isabel came by with the beer, poured half the bottle into a glass, and left. Carlucci picked up the glass and raised an eyebrow at Paula. She gave him a sick smile, and said, "Go right ahead." Carlucci drank deeply; he seemed to actually enjoy it. Paula shook her head.

She picked up a tortilla chip and nibbled at it. "You wanted to talk," she said. "So let's talk."

Carlucci scanned the restaurant, checking the people around them, and Paula wondered if he thought coming here was a mistake. But there was so much noise between the music, conversations, and the shouting and cooking sounds from the kitchen, she didn't think he had to worry. She couldn't make out the conversations of *anyone* nearby; it was all just babble. Carlucci apparently came to the same conclusion, because he shrugged and looked back at her.

''I told you,'' he said, his voice just loud enough for her to make out. ''This case is making me paranoid. We both have to be careful of what we say, and where. I just don't like any of this.'' He paused, turning his beer glass around and around on the table. ''Look, I want you to think damn hard about whether or not you really want me looking into this. If I go ahead, I'll be sticking my neck out, but it's going to put you at risk as well. I'm sure of it. Believe me, I'll be damn careful, but I can't guarantee anything, for either of us. I've got no idea how dangerous it could be, but we should assume the worst.'' He picked up his glass, stared at it, put it down without drinking, and looked back at Paula. ''If you want me to just forget about the whole thing, I'll drop it right now. Let the case close, let them bury it.''

''So they *are* trying to bury it,'' Paula said. She hated it, but it felt good to hear Carlucci say it, to know she'd been right.

''Yes,'' Carlucci said, nodding. ''And that might be the smartest thing to do, let them.'' Then he shook his head. ''No, it *would* be the smartest thing. Certainly the safest.''

Paula scooped salsa onto a chip, put it into her mouth, and chewed on it as she watched Carlucci. She was trying to figure what his real feelings were on all this. Was he simply trying to warn her of real dangers and risks, or was he trying to scare her off?

''What about you?'' she asked. ''Do *you* want to look into it? Forget about me for a minute. If you were on your own, would you be trying to find out what happened?''

''How am I supposed to forget about you?'' Carlucci said, smiling. ''If it wasn't for you, I wouldn't even know about the damn thing. There'd be no decision to make.''

"You know what I mean," Paula said.

Carlucci nodded. "Yeah, I do." He drank more of his beer, then poured the rest of the bottle into the glass. "Probably," he said. "I'd be digging into it, yes. Friends of mine are being screwed over by this case. I'm not going to go into details, or tell you any names. You don't need to know any of that, and we're both better off if you *don't* know."

"I think I can guess one name," Paula said. "Besides, you don't really know how much you can trust me, right?"

"There is that," Carlucci said. "It's not personal."

"I understand," Paula replied. "You don't know anything about me."

"I don't. I have your phone number, but I don't know where you live. I don't even know what you do for a living. You at least know that about me."

Paula smiled. "Most of the time *I* don't even know what I do for a living." She shrugged. "Mostly, I manage the Lumiere Theater, which gives me very irregular paychecks. And I play bass in slash-and-burn bands, which makes me pretty much no money at all."

"Slash-and-burn?" Carlucci raised an eyebrow. "Like Chick."

"Yeah, like Chick. We played in the same band, Pilate Error. As in Pontius Pilate. We played together off and on for a lot of years. And I play in an all-woman band called Black Angels."

"How old are you?" Carlucci asked.

"Thirty-nine." She watched him, waiting for the question, but Carlucci didn't say anything. He made a grumbling sound and drank from his glass. "You aren't going to ask me if I don't think I'm too old for slash-and-burn, rock and roll?" Paula asked.

Carlucci smiled and shook his head. "Not me. I'm not touching that one."

Paula smiled back at him. She was beginning to like Carlucci, no doubt about that. Maybe Mixer wasn't so crazy after all. She let the smile fade.

"So, are you going to look into it?" she asked him.

"Do you want me to? I was serious about the risks. Someone with heat wants this thing buried, and we both could get scorched but good."

She'd thought a lot about it before she'd even gone to Carlucci; she'd known from the beginning that it wouldn't be easy. "I'm willing to risk it if you are," Paula said. "I trust your judgment. I think."

Carlucci frowned. "Yeah, you think. Well, like I said before, no promises. I'm willing to dig around a bit, stick my neck out a little, but I'm going to be damn careful, and if it looks like I'll get my head chopped off, I'll pull the plug. I'm not willing to sacrifice everything I've got for this. Understood?"

"Understood." She nodded. "I wouldn't expect anything else."

"Good enough."

"So," Paula said. "What's next?"

"I want to get together with you for a couple of hours so we can talk about Chick, the people he knew, anything you know about what he was doing, that kind of thing."

"All right. When?"

"I've got another case I'm working on, but I'm off this weekend. Either Saturday or Sunday, any time."

As Paula was thinking about it, their food arrived. Isabel warned them about the hot plates, asked Carlucci if he wanted another beer. He said no, and she left them alone.

"Sunday would be best," Paula said. "If we can do it early, say eight or nine in the morning. We've got a Final Films Festival this weekend at the Lumiere, and I've got to be there and make sure the thing doesn't completely fall apart."

"Final films?"

"Yeah. Final films of the great directors. The last films of

Malle, Maxwell, Scorsese, Godard, Herzog, Blanchot, Fassbinder.''

Carlucci nodded. ''I know Malle. *Elevator to the Gallows.*''

''Sure, one of his early films. You've seen it?''

''No. I just know the soundtrack. Miles Davis. Great music.'' He smiled. ''I'm a jazz and blues man myself.''

''Really? Do you play?''

''A little. Trumpet.''

Yes, Paula thought, she was going to like Carlucci just fine. ''So is Sunday morning all right?'' she asked.

''Yeah, probably. I'll call you in a couple of days, confirm it, and we can decide where.'' He looked down at his plate, then back at her. ''Right now, how about we eat while it's still hot?''

''Absolutely.'' Paula dug her fork into one of the chile rellenos, brought it to her mouth. The egg coating was light and fluffy, the chile had a sharp bite, and the cheese inside was hot and smooth. Wonderful. She looked up at Carlucci, who seemed to be enjoying his own food. She thought about the letters Chick had kept, and Carlucci showing up at the apartment, saying he would look into Chick's murder, and now delicious food in a place like this. The day had turned out all right after all.

SIX

CARLUCCI SAT IN the dark basement of his home in the Inner Sunset, trumpet in hand, one of his old Big Eddie Washington discs playing on the sound system. Eddie Washington—a great blues guitarist with a harsh, haunting voice. Washington finished singing a verse of "Devil Woman Blues," and Carlucci brought the trumpet to his lips. As Washington began his solo, Carlucci broke in, counterpointing Washington's guitar with his own solo trumpet.

After his family, this was Carlucci's love—jazz, yes, but most of all the blues. Listening to it, and playing it. It took him away, not in escape, but into a world that seemed to mesh with his gut and with his heart; it brought up sadness and pain, but in ways that were somehow beautiful, and affirming.

He had been in the basement for over an hour, listening and playing. Christina, their younger daughter (not so young anymore, seventeen), had been the only one home when he came in after taking Paula to her apartment. Christina said that Andrea had called from the office and wouldn't be home until nine or ten; then she had taken off to meet Marx, her boyfriend, for a night of bone-slotting down in the Marina. Which had left Carlucci the house to himself.

The song ended and Carlucci sat back in the old sofa, rest-ing the trumpet on his thigh, thinking about Caroline, his other daughter. Caroline, who had just turned twenty and wouldn't live to see thirty. Right after the Gould's Syndrome had been diagnosed, Caroline had moved out of the house, and they hardly saw her anymore. Carlucci thought he understood, and he didn't hold it against her, but knowing she didn't have that many years left, he wanted to see her as much as possible. Instead, they only saw her once or twice a month, and didn't even talk to her much more than that.

The next song's solo began, and Carlucci played a few notes, then stopped, returning the trumpet to his thigh, thoughts moving for some reason from Caroline to his old blues band. Death on his mind, he guessed. When he was younger, a lot younger, he had been part of a quartet with three other cops. Right after Caroline had been born. They'd called themselves the Po-Leece Blues Band, and they'd been good enough to play in some of the clubs around the city; not regularly, but often enough to stay fresh and tight. Then Baker, the bass player, and Johnson, the drummer, had both been killed in a race riot in front of City Hall, and that had been the end of the band. Carlucci had never tried to put together another, and he had contented himself over the years with playing alone in his basement, playing along with the old greats and the new.

There were three more songs on the disc, but Carlucci just listened to them, eyes closed, silently pumping the valves with his fingers. Then the disc ended, and Carlucci remained motionless in the dark, listening to the near silence.

Sometime later he heard the muted sounds of the front door, then footsteps overhead. Andrea was home.

By the time he got upstairs, she was already in the shower. Carlucci knocked on the door, stepped into the bathroom. "It's me," he said. He watched her moving behind the shower door, her image distorted by the wedge-cut glass.

"I hope it's you," Andrea said. "Were you in the basement? I didn't hear any music.''

''Yes.'' Carlucci closed the toilet lid and sat on it, leaning back against the tank. ''I was listening to music earlier. Then I was just thinking.''

''Sitting alone in the dark again,'' she said. ''Brooding, I'd bet.''

Carlucci didn't reply. He listened to the way the water sounds changed as she moved beneath the shower head. ''How was your day?'' he asked. She was an attorney at a firm that specialized in environmental law. She only worked three days a week, but they tended to be long days.

''Terrible and way too long.''

''Why?''

''I don't want to talk about it,'' she said. It was her standard answer. Andrea never wanted to talk about work when she got home. The next morning would be different, and she would tell him all about it over breakfast. But he always asked.

Andrea turned off the shower. ''You want to hand me a towel?'' she said. ''Please?''

Carlucci stood, got a dry towel from the rack, then brought it to the shower. Andrea opened the door, stuck her head and arm out and took the towel from him. ''Thank you.'' Before she had a chance to retreat, Carlucci leaned forward and kissed her, getting his mouth, cheek, and nose wet. Andrea dried his face with the towel. ''How was *your* day?'' she asked as she pulled the door shut and began drying herself.

''About like yours, I imagine. Terrible.''

''The mayor's nephew, or that other matter?'' The ''other matter'' was Paula Asgard and Chick Roberts. Carlucci had told her the night before about his talk with Paula at The Bright Spot.

''Both,'' he said. ''And they're both getting worse, in their own ways.'' He stood in front of the sink, watching the water drip from the faucet. He still hadn't gotten around to replacing the damn washer.

Andrea stepped out of the shower with the towel wrapped around her head, and Carlucci gazed affectionately at her nude body. She was about five foot six, and no longer as slender as she once had been. In recent years she had put a little weight on her hips, a small pot had formed on her belly, and her breasts had begun to sag a bit. She was absolutely beautiful.

"You're beautiful," he said.

Andrea smiled, then waved at him to leave. "Go on, let me do my things."

Carlucci walked out of the bathroom, leaving the door partway open, and lay on the bed, listening to the sounds Andrea made at the sink.

"How bad is it?" she asked.

"Which one?"

"The one the woman came to you about."

"Worse than I'd thought it would be." He turned onto his side, facing the bathroom door, and watched her shadow move across its surface. "Ruben's being forced by McCuller and Vaughn to stay on the case and bury it."

"Frank, I thought they couldn't do that."

"So did I," he said. "This is the first time I've heard of it." He sighed heavily. "He probably could have fought it and won, but he's afraid. He's got too much to lose."

Andrea's face appeared in the doorway. "Does this mean they could do it to you, Frank?"

"I don't know." It was the only answer he had for her. That was another reason he was willing to take risks and dig into this thing. If the honchos got away with it this time, they would be more likely to try it again, maybe even with him.

Andrea slowly shook her head, then returned to the sink. "What are you going to do?"

"A little digging. I hate what they're doing to Ruben. And

to Toni Weathers. But also for self-preservation. I don't want them even *trying* something like this with me."

She didn't ask any more, and Carlucci lay on the bed in silence, listening to her, watching the shadows, and thinking. After a while he closed his eyes, not trying to sleep, just to stop the burning.

"Frank?"

He opened his eyes, and she stood in the doorway, the towel now draped over her shoulder, her wet hair falling free. "Yes?"

"Why don't you get undressed and get into bed?"

"It's too early."

"No it's not," she said.

He knew that tone in her voice. "Ah," he said, smiling. "Aren't you tired?"

"Not even close." She smiled back at him. "I'll be out in a couple minutes."

Carlucci sat up on the bed and began to undress. He could hear the hair dryer going now. When he was completely undressed he pulled back the covers and lay naked on the bed. It was too warm to cover himself with even a single sheet.

The dryer stopped, and Andrea came out of the bathroom without the towel. She got onto the bed down near his feet, and he lay there motionless, waiting for her. She kissed her way up his legs until she came to his cock, which she gently took into her warm, wet mouth. He was hard within seconds.

A minute or two later Andrea resumed her movement upward, along his belly and chest, then lay fully across him, her face just inches from his.

"Hi, there," she said, smiling.

Carlucci wrapped both arms around her and squeezed. "Hi." They kissed deeply, then Carlucci moved his hands up across her shoulders, her neck, then to the sides of her face, holding her head gently in his fingers. "I love you," he said.

"I love *you,* Frank."

Carlucci wrapped his arms around her once more and pulled her tight against him, wanting to never, ever let go.

Near midnight Paula sat on the recliner in her bedroom and watched one of Chick's homemade music videos on her TV. The track was a Pilate Error song Paula had written, "Love at Ground Zero," a rare slow piece, slow and melancholy, a kind of slash-and-burn blues song. She wondered if Carlucci would like it.

Intercut with a distorted, digitized image of Chick singing the lyrics was footage of two naked people making love in slow motion on a sagging mattress. The faces were hidden by shadow, but Paula knew who the people were: herself and Chick. Sweat glistened on skin, on breasts and arms and thighs, reflecting orange and yellow light. She hadn't known he was filming them at the time. He hadn't asked, because he knew she would have refused. But once it was done, and mixed into the video, what could she say? No one would know who it was, and the footage was effective. Damn effective.

She was crying again. Soft and quiet now. God damn, she missed him.

The song ended, and then there was a close-up of Chick's face, looking directly at her. Paula knew what was coming, and so the ache drove into her chest again. Chick silently mouthed the words, "I love you," and then his digitized image began to slowly, slowly come apart.

"I'll find out who killed you," she said to his disintegrating image. "I will, Chick."

And then what? No idea. Paula was sure that justice was not going to be easy to come by. It might even be impossible. *No promises,* Carlucci had said to her. Was she trying to make promises to a dead man?

The last bits of Chick's face disappeared, leaving behind a

random scattering of light and shadow. Paula stopped the player, turned off the TV.

"All right," she said to the blank screen. "No promises."

Paula lay back in the chair, closed her eyes, and tried to ease away the pain.

PART TWO

SEVEN

CARLUCCI WAS DREAMING. He was on a train to Seattle, and had just realized something was terribly wrong, when a phone started ringing somewhere on the train. He couldn't see the phone, but it seemed to be getting closer, louder with each ring, and then he realized he was dreaming and the phone was his own, pulling and dragging him out of the dream.

The train shook and broke apart and Carlucci opened his eyes. The phone beside the bed rang again. The clock said 3:25 A.M. Fuck. He was still half back in the dream, only barely awake. When he was younger he came awake almost instantly. Another ring and he grabbed for the phone, picked it up, put it against his head. ''Yeah?''

''Frank, this is Pete. Sorry to wake you up.''

Oh, shit. ''What is it, Pete?''

''You're going to want to see this one, Frank.''

''Who's the victim?''

''I'd rather not say. Let me give you the address.''

''All right, hold on a sec.'' Carlucci swung his legs over the side of the bed and sat up, turned on the tiny nightstand lamp, picked up the pen and pad beside it. ''Fire away.''

It was an address in Pacific Heights, but it wasn't familiar.

Carlucci repeated the address back to LaPlace, then took down the phone number.

"Is Joseph there with you?"

"Yeah," LaPlace said. "He's going through the place right now with Porkpie."

"Good. Okay, I'll be right out. See you in a few minutes."

Carlucci hung up the phone and remained seated on the edge of the bed, still trying to wake up. He felt old.

"Who was that?" Andrea asked, her voice little more than a mumble.

"Pete." He looked over at her, but she was on her side, facing away from him. Usually she slept through his middle-of-the-night phone calls.

"Somebody dead?" she asked.

Carlucci almost laughed. "Yeah, of course." He expected her to ask who, but she didn't say anything. "I was dreaming," he said. Andrea mumbled something. "I was on a train to Seattle. I'd thought I could take the train to Seattle, do some business, then take the train back in time for dinner the same day. Once I was on the train, I realized I'd badly miscalculated, that it took twenty hours to get to Seattle. Then the phone rang and I woke up."

"You can't take a train from here to Seattle," Andrea said. "You have to go over to Oakland."

"I know that," Carlucci said. "It was a dream." He realized then that Andrea was still half asleep. "I've got to go," he said. He got up from the bed. "I'll be back when I can."

"Is somebody dead?" Andrea asked again.

"Yes," Carlucci said. "Somebody's dead."

Carlucci had to show his police ID to get through the security checkpoint and drive into the Rio Grande section of Pacific Heights, which turned his foul mood even blacker. Rio Grande, what a crock. The only running water in Pacific Heights was in the water mains and sewers. Carlucci hated the whole setup—the residents had put together a self-appointed council and talked and bribed the city into selling them the public roads in the Rio Grande section so they could put up their own checkpoints, hire their own security forces, and keep out the "undesirables." Two other parts of the city had done the same thing since, and several more were working on it.

Carlucci parked several houses down from the address LaPlace had given him and remained in the car a minute, looking over the street. It was still dark, without even a hint of the coming dawn. Two unmarked police cars, a black-and-white, the coroner's van, and a Rio Grande Security car were all congregated in front of a beautiful three-story Victorian house, its windows lit up. All the other homes on the street were dark, but Carlucci thought he could make out movement in some of the windows—morbid curiosity tugged at the wealthy, too.

He got out of the car and walked up to the brightly lit Victorian. A Rio Grande Security guard stopped him on the porch, then let him through after he again showed his ID. Carlucci was ready to chew someone's nose off.

Just inside the front door, bare feet swinging about eye level with the three cops standing around it, the blood-streaked body of a naked man hung from the stair railing above the entryway, neck impaled on a huge, sharp metal hook; a long, thin spike ran through his belly and emerged from his spine. Carlucci stared up at the dead man's face for a minute, but couldn't place it. It didn't even look familiar. It also didn't look happy—undamaged, but in agony, eyes and mouth both open wide.

Hong was one of the cops. Mason, the coroner's assistant, was another. Both men were smoking. Carlucci didn't recognize the third, a woman uniform.

"Jesus," Carlucci said. He looked at Hong. "Who is he, Joseph?"

"Robert Butler."

Robert Butler? Then it hit him, and he realized why LaPlace had called him. Robert Butler was one of the names on the Prime Level Feed given to the slugs on the mayor's nephew's case. Business partner or something like that.

Carlucci stepped around Butler's body, toward the uniform, and put out his hand, gaze flicking back and forth between her and the body. Butler had been in good shape, maybe even handsome. Hard to tell with that look on his face. "Lieutenant Carlucci," he said.

The uniform shook his hand. "Officer Martha Tretorn," she said. "My partner and I were first-on-scene."

"Tretorn," Carlucci said, looking at her. "I've heard good things about your work."

She gave him just a touch of a smile, said, "Thank you, sir."

"Where's Pete?" he asked, looking at Hong.

"In the first-floor flat," he said, gesturing down the hall at a closed door. "Talking to the woman who found the body. Butler owned the building, lived on the upper two floors, and rented out the first. The woman found him. On her way out, or in—there seems to be some 'confusion' over that."

"She doesn't know whether she was coming home or going out when she found the body?" Carlucci said.

Hong nodded. "Let's just say the story is in a state of flux. I couldn't get much from her; she didn't seem to want to talk to me." Hong gave Carlucci a hard smile. "Wrong kind of eyes, I think. That's why Pete's with her now."

"Hey," Mason broke in. "Can we take him down now? Porkpie's got all the pictures. They wanted me to wait until you got here so you could see him." Mason grinned. "They probably wanted you to see the schlong this guy has. Pretty fucking amazing, isn't it?"

"Yeah," Carlucci said, not smiling. "Amazing." He shook his head, then nodded. "Sure, Mason, take him down. Where's Porkpie?"

''Upstairs, on another run-through of Butler's place.''

''All right, Joseph, let's go up. You've been through it once?'' Hong nodded, and Carlucci said, ''You can give me a rundown, then.'' He turned to Tretorn. ''Go ahead and help Mason get the body down,'' he said. ''You'll love working with him. He's a lot of laughs.''

Again, that touch of a smile from Tretorn. ''I've noticed, sir. I'll be glad to help.''

Carlucci and Hong climbed the wooden steps, followed by Mason and Tretorn, who would have to work on getting the body down from the top of the stairs. As Carlucci and Hong reached the open door, Tretorn said, ''Lieutenant?''

''Yes?''

''My partner's inside with the crime-scene techs. Sinclair. Could you send her out to give us a hand?''

''Sure.'' Sinclair. He knew that name. What had he heard about her? But then, entering the hall and looking toward the kitchen, where Sinclair stood in the doorway, he remembered. Sinclair was a stunning woman about six foot four, with long blonde hair tied at the base of her neck and hanging halfway down her back.

''Sinclair?'' Carlucci said. The tall blonde turned to him. ''Tretorn needs a hand out there.'' Sinclair nodded and walked past them and out of the apartment.

Carlucci stuck his head into the kitchen. One of the crime-scene techs was on her hands and knees, picking up something with tweezers. Porkpie was sitting on a stool at the counter, smoking a cigarette. He shook his head at Carlucci, which meant he was working, thinking about something, and shouldn't be disturbed. Which was fine with Carlucci. Porkpie was the department's top crime-scene tech. Carlucci backed out of the kitchen and gestured for Hong to join him in a room off the hall, which turned out to be a library. All the walls were covered by bookcases; there was a large work desk and chair, and two reading chairs.

"Joseph, how did you and Pete get called in on this? Not just coincidence, is it?"

Hong smiled. "No. Pete and I got McCuller to let us put a tracer into the system, keyed to all the names, addresses, and phone numbers on the Prime Level Feed. Anything that would come up on any of those people, even a parking ticket, would trigger a call. When Butler's address came up on the 911 call, Minsky called us in. We weren't far behind Tretorn and Sinclair. We held off until we had a pretty firm ID on Butler, then Pete called you."

Carlucci nodded, said, "Good work, Joseph. Look, I haven't had a chance to go through all the Feed text yet; all I did Friday was take a run at the names. What's Butler's connection to the nephew? Something about business dealings, right?"

"Yes. They owned several companies together. An investment firm, another that does bio-implant research, a pharmaceutical distributor, and the largest recruiting company in the city."

"Recruiters? The vans?"

Hong nodded. "Yes, that kind of recruiting. Scumbuckets. The companies have been indicted several times."

"Ah," Carlucci said, interest rising. "What for?"

"Securities fraud. Attempted bribery. Data theft. Twice for false imprisonment."

"False imprisonment because of what the recruiters were doing?"

"Yep."

"Let me guess," Carlucci said. "No convictions."

"You got it."

Carlucci nodded. "Big fucking surprise." He glanced around the library, but didn't see anything that immediately caught his eye. "All right, let's go look around the place, show me what you and Porkpie found."

As they moved from room to room, and from the second

floor to the third, Carlucci tried comparing this residence to the penthouse apartment of the mayor's nephew, and he was surprised at how different they were. Butler and the nephew may have been in business together, but as people they didn't seem to be anything alike.

All the expensive high-tech equipment and gadgetry was here, just as it was in the nephew's, from picture phones and A.V. environments to computer links and reality-sims to slotters and ion poles in every room. There was even a similar security system, which had apparently been just as ineffective, now completely dead. But here everything was made or covered with natural colors and fabrics and expertly integrated with real wood and cloth and leather furniture, plaster walls, wood trim, nature-tone carpeting, and hundreds of books; various other objects, such as glasses, pens and notepads, vases and planters and candles, made the place look lived in. The nephew's penthouse was cold, sterile, a metal-and-glass showcase. Robert Butler's house was warm and comfortable—a home.

They were on the third floor, and had just entered a room set up for entertainment. There was a small sofa, two large foam chairs, and a huge video-and-sound system built into one wall.

"See what Porkpie found in here," Hong said. He went to the video control panel, powered up the system, read from a piece of paper he'd taken out of his pocket, and punched a series of buttons. He tuned the monitor to a channel of static and video snow, then punched more buttons. The wall adjacent to the monitor gradually became transparent, revealing a huge wall safe surrounded by computer-driven access panels.

"Jesus Christ," Carlucci said. "How in hell did Porkpie find this?"

Hong smiled. "You know Porkpie. He said he's seen a few of these setups, and downstairs he found this taped to the bottom of the coffee maker." Hong held up the piece of paper.

"Something just clicked in his head, he claims, and he started looking around for it. Fiddled with this until he figured what the numbers on the paper meant, and here we are."

"That guy." Carlucci shook his head, staring at the safe through the transparent section of wall. "I'd sure like to see what's inside that thing."

"Porkpie says getting into the safe is going to be a lot harder than finding it."

"Yeah, no shit. Who's that guy the department calls in, Collins?"

"Collier."

"Right, Collier. Wonder how he'll do with this."

Hong shrugged, but didn't say anything. They stood staring at the wall safe for a minute until LaPlace walked into the room and joined them.

"Brings tears, doesn't it?" LaPlace said, gesturing at the safe.

"Only if we don't get in," Carlucci said. He turned to LaPlace. "So what's with the woman?"

LaPlace shook his head. "Changing stories, that's what. First she told Joseph she found the body on her way *out*. Then she said no, she didn't mean that—she was shaken up, all that—she had been *coming home* when she found Butler. Where had she been? Real vague on that, who she was with, said it was her personal business, cha cha cha. I let it go for a while, but a little later on, she lets it slip again, that she was going *out* when she found him. I didn't say a thing, and she didn't realize she'd said it again. If I had to bet on it, I'd say she was on her way out when she found Butler."

"What's she worried about, if that's the way it happened?" Carlucci wondered aloud.

"Maybe she doesn't want to tell us where the fuck she was going at two o'clock in the morning," LaPlace said. "Or how, if she was up and awake, getting ready to go out, she didn't hear a thing while old Robert Butler was being gored and having a hook rammed through his neck. Couldn't have been all that quiet. Anyway, we finally reached a point where she wasn't going to say any more without her fucking lawyer. I told her she wasn't a suspect, but she jammed up anyway." He shook his head. "She'll be in Monday with her attorney to make an official statement." He shook his head again. "I didn't see any point in pushing it, she wasn't going to open up."

"Anything else?"

LaPlace sighed. "No. She rented the first floor from Butler, but didn't know anything about him. She paid her rent, he left her alone, he seemed like a nice guy, but she really didn't know him, cha cha cha. I don't believe any of it, but that's all she'd say. End of interview."

"All right," Carlucci said. "Christ, this is getting swampy on us. Think we can keep the connection between Butler and the mayor's nephew quiet? Out of the news?"

"I don't see why not," Hong said. "The three of us are the only ones who know about it."

"Good. Let's try and keep it that way." He shook his head. "All right, let's wrap things up here. Do a quick chop on the reports, then go home. We'll get together first thing Monday morning at Spades, see where we are."

The sun was up by the time Carlucci pulled into the driveway. He shut off the engine, but remained in the car for a minute, looking at their house. It was a good home, well over a hundred years old, a little ragged in spots, but in fine shape. A good neighborhood, too, a small, tightly knit community for the most part, several blocks of families that watched out for each other. An island of security in the city. It had been a good place to raise their two daughters, and he hoped it would remain a good place to retire. Hard to know.

Carlucci got out of the car and walked up the steps to the

front porch. No Sunday paper yet; too early. He unlocked the front door and went inside.

The house was quiet, almost silent. He stopped by Christina's bedroom and looked in through the open door. The bed was a twisted, misshapen bundle of sheets, blanket, pillows, and his daughter. He could make out a shock of wavy hair up in one corner, and a bare ankle sticking out from the sheets at the foot of the bed. Another year or two and she would probably be moving out, just as her older sister had done. He didn't want Christina to leave. Knowing Caroline didn't have many years left, he wanted to hang onto Christina as long as he could, as though he might lose her too. Afraid to wake her, he mentally kissed her on the forehead and moved on down the hall.

Andrea was still asleep, lying on her side. Carlucci bent over, kissed her lightly on the lips, then her cheek. Andrea smiled, murmured, and dug her face deeper into the pillow, but her eyes didn't open. Carlucci quietly left and walked to the other end of the house and the kitchen.

He looked at the clock. Ten after six. Lots of time before he was due to meet Paula Asgard. He made himself a cup of coffee and took it out to the small backyard deck, where he sat in one of the plastic chairs. The air was warm and quiet, a little muggy, but not too bad, and the sky was orange and pink and blue, the colors not yet looking sick as they almost certainly would later in the day.

Things were getting more complicated with the mayor's nephew, and he would start getting deeper into another mess when he talked with Paula Asgard, but for now Carlucci put all those thoughts aside. He wanted to enjoy the two free hours he would have this morning.

A thumping sounded on the fence, and a furry gray face appeared over the top, golden eyes wide, followed by the rest of the stocky cat's body. It was Tuff, the next-door neighbor's manx. Tuff crouched atop the fence for a moment, then dropped into Carlucci's yard, padded through the flower beds, and hopped up onto the deck. As Tuff approached the chair, Carlucci reached down and scratched the old gray cat's ears and cheeks and chin. Tuff purred loudly and deeply, and closed his eyes.

The cat was missing most of one ear, and had a nasty scar across his nose, just missing his left eye. He'd been a hell of a scrapper, fighting all comers, until Harry and Frances next door finally decided it was time for Tuff's balls to go. Tuff still defended his turf when he had to, but now he was fat, and incredibly gentle with people.

Tuff ducked away from Carlucci's hand and came around to the front of the chair. Carlucci held his coffee out of the way in anticipation, and the cat jumped up onto his lap, claws digging through his pants to his skin. Tuff turned one complete circle, then settled down across Carlucci's thighs, the deep purr kicking in again.

I could do worse than this, Carlucci thought to himself as he laid his free hand on the old gray cat. A lot worse. He brought the cup to his mouth and drank, scratching Tuff's head with his other hand. Things were going to get swampy, the rot was going to go deeper, but for now Carlucci felt as he imagined the old cat felt: warm, relaxed, and content.

EIGHT

PAULA SPOOKED. SHE spotted Boniface across the street and up a few blocks, heading her way. She ducked into Mama Buruma's spice shop and stopped just inside the door, blinded by the shift from bright morning light to heavy shadows and dim orange flames. Paula didn't move for a minute, listening to the East Asian techno-folk, letting her eyes adjust to the darkness.

Mama Buruma's—a long, narrow store lit only by small flickering candles—was empty except for Mama Buruma herself, who sat on a massive cushion behind the counter. Mama Buruma was fat, maybe even heavier than Graumann. The shop smelled of burning tiki spice, fireweed, and sweat. Tins and baskets and gel bubbles filled the display cases running the length of the shop. Vines and lush plants hung from the ceiling, insects flying among them.

''Ms. Asgard,'' Mama said, shifting position on her cushion. She wore a huge, loose dress of bright floral patterns, and her flesh shook with every movement. ''Can I help you with something?''

As Paula stepped farther into the shop, she could make out the ten or twelve multicolored dermal patches on Mama Buruma's neck. She imagined them pulsing as they fed the big woman a steady stream of head juice. "No thanks, Mama. Well, maybe yes. Some mondo perv was tracking me out on the street."

Mama Buruma grinned and the flesh tightened around her eyes. "You want something to spike him with?"

"No," Paula said. "I was thinking of a way out. Through your stockroom."

Mama Buruma sighed and the smile melted back into her face. "You're too nice, Paula." She sighed again and waved her arm, flesh and sleeve flapping. "Go ahead."

"Thanks, Mama." Paula squeezed around the display case, pushed through the hanging tapestry, then worked her way around the crates and tubes and foam-packs in the stockroom. She pushed open the heavy metal door, stepped out into the alley, and let the door slam shut.

Paula leaned against the brick wall and waited, trying to decide what to do. It was probably coincidence, seeing Boniface just now. She had no reason to think he was looking for her. She couldn't stand the guy, because he'd hit on her repeatedly over the years, refusing to get the message, but he'd never come around looking for her. Still, she had just given Carlucci his name half an hour ago.

Paula thought he was a fuckhead, but there wasn't anything all that special about Boniface. He was one of a dozen or so names she'd given Carlucci: the people Chick hung with or brought in on his scams, people Chick had seen in recent weeks. Boniface hired out part time as a games courier, and it was hard to imagine that he had anything to do with Chick's death. But how could she know?

You're getting paranoid, she told herself. It came from spending two hours with Carlucci, talking about what Chick did, and who he did it with, running all those names at one time, seeing their faces one after another in her mind. People on the edges, like Chick, any one of which was all right alone. But talking about *all* of them had made Paula skittish.

Paranoia, she told herself again. Yeah, but that doesn't mean they're not after you. Ha, ha. So what was she supposed to do? She looked at her watch. Already late getting to the theater. Besides, Boniface knew she worked at the Lumiere; if he was trying to find her he could just go there. Or her apartment. He knew where she lived. Yeah, terrific, they *all* knew where she lived.

She shook her head, pushed away from the wall. *Relax, girl.* Boniface wasn't looking for her. No one was. Chick had been dead two weeks now, and nobody had shown up in her face. *Relax.*

She walked down the alley, emerged onto the sidewalk. Her throat closed up and her heart slammed against her ribs, *bam bam bam*. Boniface was twenty feet away, walking toward her.

Paula couldn't move. Boniface came up to her and stopped. Up close, she could see that under his street clothes he was in full courier rig, armored from neck to toes—someone would have to blow or chop his head off to stop him, and they still wouldn't be able to get what he was carrying.

"Hey, Paula," Boniface said, laying a gloved hand gently on her shoulder. "Heard about Chick. I'm real sorry. He was all right with me, you know that."

He pulled his hand back just before Paula would have knocked it away. Adrenaline was making her twitchy. Relax, she told herself once more.

"Thanks, Bonny," she said; he hated being called that.

Boniface frowned, then glanced over her shoulder. "I can't stay and talk now," he said, looking back at her. "I'm on a run. But if you need anything, a few bucks . . ." The frown slid into that nasty smile he'd used every time he'd hit on her. "Or maybe just some comfort. You know where I am."

Yeah, I know where you are, asshole. But she managed some kind of smile, said, "Thanks, Bonny," again, and stepped aside, waving him down the street.

Boniface's smile turned into a frown again, but he nodded

and walked away. Paula watched him walk down the block, cross the street, then go into Ah Minh's. He *was* on a run. It *had* been a coincidence. But he was just as scummy as ever.

Paula breathed deeply several times, tried to shake out the excess adrenaline. Then she jammed her hands into her jacket pockets and headed for the theater.

By mid-afternoon most of the jitters were gone, and by the six o'clock intermission after the showing of *Xerxes Agonistes*, Paula was feeling almost normal. They had close to a full house, so the lobby was crowded now, people lined up for food and drinks, lined up at the bathrooms, the smokers huddled together in the corner next to the ventilators. Paula wandered through the lobby, checking on things, but everything seemed under control; for a change, everyone had shown up for work today so she wasn't understaffed.

She was headed for the stairs up to the projectionist's booth when a man moved in front of her. He looked familiar, though she didn't think she'd ever met him before. An inch or two taller than she was, slender, with short hair and wire-rim glasses. Kind of good-looking, in an odd way. She couldn't really tell how old he was—he could be in his late thirties, or he might be a youngish forty, forty-five.

"Excuse me," he said when she stopped. "Paula Asgard?"

"Yeah. Do I know you?"

"My name's Tremaine. I don't think we've ever met."

So, that's why he was familiar. The guy tried to keep low-profile, but he couldn't keep his own face completely out of the media. A bit of irony there.

"I'm a freelance journalist," he said when she didn't respond.

"I know who you are," Paula said. "I've read your stuff."

Tremaine smiled. "Is that good or bad?"

"Good." The guy did real investigative reporting, not sensationalist cheap-shotting, and if he couldn't get the papers or magazines or television to run his stories, which was often, he sent them out over the nets. He'd made a lot of enemies, but probably not very much money. He found stories where there shouldn't have been any, stories no one else could find, stories no one else knew existed. The anti-cancer implant scam at the UCSF medical school. The firefly distribution ring run by two senior partners of Maxie and Fowler, the largest and most prestigious law firm in the city. Like that.

"I want to talk to you," he said.

"What about?" Paula asked, instantly wary.

"Chick Roberts."

Paula didn't say anything at first. The sounds and images of the people in the lobby became a smeared blur, highlighting Tremaine's face. His voice had been neutral, as if what he was asking had little real importance, and his expression was just as unconcerned. But hearing Chick's name made her feel sick, and the morning's jitters came back.

"What about Chick?" she managed to say.

"I'm trying to find out why he was killed."

"Why?"

Tremaine shrugged, but didn't answer, and it was obvious to Paula that he wasn't going to say any more about it right now. "I'd like to get together with you," he said. "An hour, maybe longer, somewhere private. Any time, any place you like."

Paula didn't know what to say to him. Carlucci had warned her against talking to anyone, and she didn't feel good about the idea, anyway, talking to a stranger about Chick. But why did Tremaine want to know what happened?

"I can't," she finally said. When he didn't respond, didn't ask her why, she repeated herself. "I can't. I don't know anything about it."

"I'd still like to talk to you about him." He handed her a small black plastic card with light gray printing—his name, and several com numbers. Paula put it in her back pocket.

"Just let me know." He started to turn away, then looked back at her. "Let me buy you dinner."

"I don't want to talk about him," Paula said, shaking her head.

"Just dinner," Tremaine said. He gave her a disarming smile. "You get to know me a little better, I get to know you, maybe you'll change your mind."

Paula shook her head again, unable to keep from smiling back. There was something damn charming about the guy. "I can't take the time. In fact, I'm on my way upstairs to fight with the projectionist over the sandwiches we're sharing for dinner."

"I understand," Tremaine said, still smiling. "I'll be back for the ten o'clock show. If you feel any different . . ."

"You're coming back to see *City Dogs*?"

"Wouldn't miss it."

"I guess that might be your kind of film."

Tremaine nodded, then said, "Enjoy your sandwich."

"I will."

Termaine turned, then worked his way through the crowded lobby to the front doors.

Why did he want to know about Chick? What story was he working on? Christ, she had a feeling she was going to end up talking to the bastard. Paula turned and climbed the stairs.

Mixer was waiting in the lobby when she came down from the projectionist's booth as the last film was ending. Leah was opening the front doors, and the coffee bar was closed up, but Mixer had managed to get a cup for himself anyway; he was holding it with the exoskeleton.

"Hey," Paula said. "What are *you* doing here?"

"You saw Carlucci this morning, yeah?" When Paula nodded, he said, "I want to talk. I'm hitting a wham-wham tonight, and I want to hear about your Carlucci talk before I go."

People began to filter out of the theater as the closing credits ran, and Paula and Mixer moved out of the way, behind the coffee bar. ''Leah can lock up for me,'' Paula said, ''but let's hold off until we empty out here.''

The crowd coming out into the lobby grew, moved past them before narrowing as it squeezed through the front doors and out onto the street, loud and noisy. People who knew Paula waved or nodded to her as they passed, and Paula nodded back. The crowd eventually thinned, and then there were only a few stragglers as the credits finished and the theater went silent.

Tremaine was one of the last people out, and he stopped in front of the coffee bar. He smiled, glanced at Mixer, nodded, and said, ''Good night, Paula Asgard.''

''Good night.''

Tremaine strolled out the doors, moved into the street traffic, and was immediately gone from sight.

''Who was that?''

Mixer's voice had a testy edge to it and Paula looked at him, but his face was almost expressionless. ''What?''

''I'm just asking who that guy was.''

''Tremaine. Why?''

''The reporter?''

''Yeah.''

''You know him?''

''No. He wanted to talk to me about Chick.''

''Chick?''

''Yeah, Chick. He said he's trying to find out why Chick was killed.''

''Tremaine? Why the fuck is *he* digging into this?''

''I don't know, Mixer. He wouldn't tell me.''

''You're not going to talk to him, are you?''

''Why shouldn't I?''

''Hell, I don't know. He worries me, that guy.''

Paula sighed and nodded. ''Yeah, well, he worries me,

too.'' She smiled at Mixer. ''No, I'm not going to talk to him.''

Mixer shook his head, but didn't say any more. Paula checked the theater to make sure it was empty, then asked Leah to lock up after Pietro, the projectionist, left. She got her jacket from the locked cabinet under the coffee bar and left the theater with Mixer.

They walked down to the corner, then swung right and headed up Polk. Sunday night, the street was full but low-key, people thinking about actually getting some sleep or heading off into dreamland of one kind or another. Mixer stopped at the street window of Sasha's Bad Eats.

''Let's get some coffee,'' he said.

''You want to go inside?''

''Not a chance. I'm going to be cooped up for hours with the wham-wham, I'd better stock up on fresh air.'' He turned to the purple-eyed kid at the window. ''Large coffee and''—he glanced back at Paula—''large decaf, right?''

Paula nodded at the kid, who was bobbing to music Paula couldn't hear. The kid drew the coffee, then handed the cups out through the window after taking Mixer's money. Mixer and Paula sat on one of the concrete benches built along the front of Sasha's.

''So what did you and Carlucci talk about?'' Mixer asked.

''Not much, really.'' She sipped at the coffee, which was almost as good as it was hot—she burned her tongue and nearly enjoyed it. ''I told him what I know about what Chick had been up to lately, which is damn little. You know Chick, he didn't tell me shit, which was always fine with me. I gave him some names of people Chick ran with, his 'business' contacts.''

Mixer cocked his head at her. ''You think that's wise?''

''Jesus, Mix, you're the one who told me to go to Carlucci, what a great guy and honest cop he was. What's the point if I don't tell him what I know?'' She shook her head, blowing on her coffee, sipping it. "Carlucci's already told me the whole thing could be risky, I'm willing to chance it for now. It's either that or drop it."

"What did you tell him about me?"

Paula turned to look hard at him. "Oh, I see. That's what you're worried about. Well, he does want to talk to you, Mixer, that's clear. If you don't go to him soon, he'll come looking for you, count on it." She sighed. "What was I going to tell him, Mix? He knows you knew Chick."

"Does he know Chick and I . . . did business?"

"Yes. But I didn't tell him what kind of business. And I didn't tell him about you talking to me the other night like you might have some idea why Chick got himself killed."

"I didn't say that."

"Not right out, you didn't."

Mixer didn't respond to that. He drank from his coffee, looking away from her. Paula put her hand on his knee, and he tensed for a moment, staring down at it.

"What is it?" Paula asked.

"Nothing," he said, shaking his head. He laid his free hand across hers, wrapping his fingers around it.

Paula felt cold sweat from his hand, and she could have sworn she felt his heart pounding hard now through his leg and wrist. What was going on? *God, don't tell me Mixer's got it for me, too.* Jesus, what was it today, was she secreting some kind of pumped-up pheromones? First Boniface, and what, now Mixer?

Mixer sighed heavily, then let her hand go and drank more of his coffee. "So Carlucci wants to see me," he finally said.

"Of course, Mixer." Paula took her hand off his knee and stuck it in her jacket pocket. Maybe she was just imagining things. "You going to tell him what kind of business you and Chick did?"

Mixer shrugged. "I don't know. Probably. What's he going to do, arrest me? Arrest Chick?" He shrugged again. He finished off his coffee, crushed his cup, then looked at his watch. "Gotta go. Checking out my own lines tonight on Chick."

"In a wham-wham?"

Mixer nodded.

"Careful," Paula said.

Mixer looked at her, smiled. "Always." He leaned forward, kissed her warmly on the cheek, then stood. "I'll be in touch. And don't talk to Tremaine." Before she could say a word, he was off and walking away, his right hand still working at the crushed coffee cup.

Paula watched him stride up the street, slipping in and out of the crowds until he turned a corner and was gone. She looked down at her own coffee cup, which was still half full and steaming. Some days, she thought, life is just one fucking mess after another. She set the coffee on the ground beside her, got up, and headed for home.

NINE

WHAM-WHAM, ALL right. Mixer hadn't been stupid, he'd pumped himself full of neutralizers before coming in, but the air in here was so gassed he felt like he was swimming through it, and the neutralizers were barely holding their own. He kept getting these sharp, intense flashes of desire, but the desire never locked onto anything specific; the neutralizers were doing their job. Mixer wondered what the gases were targeted for: booze, fireweed, gambling, booth time, smoke, heavy tipping. Probably *all* of the above. Without the neutralizers he'd be broke, fucked up, and out on the street in less than an hour. Which was, of course, just what some of the people in here wanted.

The wham-wham was underground in a Tenderloin subbasement warren. Mixer worked his way through the crowd in a maze of ion poles, cubicles and booths, tables and minibars, music pounding through dim colored phosphor lights. Close to capacity. There was just enough room to move from one spot to another without having to touch someone if you didn't want to.

Mixer was looking for Chandler, or if not him, then his proxies, Karl and Skeez, the freakoid twins. One or more of them were supposed to be here tonight, but Mixer almost hoped that if Chandler himself wasn't around, he *wouldn't* find the freaks. Bad news, those two.

The music was a loud, heavy machine dub, maxed out on the bass, and Mixer felt like he had bone boomers strapped all over his body. He should have taken aspirin along with the neutralizers; he was going to have a hell of a headache before too long.

Mixer moved over to one of the minibars, bought a bottle of Beck's, then wandered through the crowd, watching faces, latching onto snatches of conversation.

". . . something burning inside his head . . ."

"Style, man, kicks and style . . ."

" . . . and he was taking his clothes off, enough to make you lose your breakfast."

". . . blood rushing up his neck . . ."

"Yeah, give me your slots, I'll bang your head . . ."

". . . *rush* . . ."

". . . slide, baby, into that body-bag . . ."

". . . *rush* . . ."

"Give. Give me those kicks, you . . ."

". . . RUSH . . ."

Rush, all right. Mixer stopped listening, letting the words wash through him with the pounding of the dub. A slow, high guitar was cutting through the heavy bass now, fine, fine stuff; he could just grab a seat somewhere, drink his beer, and listen. But he needed to find Chandler.

Chick got himself offed, and Chandler disappeared at the same time. Could be coincidence, but Mixer didn't believe it. Not when Chick had been trying to set up a deal of some kind with Chandler—wouldn't say what, just that it was big. Mixer didn't think Chandler had killed Chick, but there had to be a connection.

He passed a booth with its door still open. Inside was a naked man wrapped in a body-bag—a full body neural net—twitching and shaking on a cot, mouth open and drooling as the net sparked and sputtered. Fuck me, Mixer thought, no one should have to see that. He pulled the curtain shut and moved on.

Next to the booth was a gambling alcove, all the spots occupied. One woman was winning big, but she looked sick—apparently she was here to lose, maybe even go broke; she sure wasn't happy winning. The others were a mix, some of them pleased, some as sick as the woman. All of them appeared to be losing. That was one of the things that made a wham-wham interesting to Mixer—you never knew who would want what, and watching them was always a discovery.

"Hey, spikehead!"

The voice came at him from out of the noise and crowd and lights, and Mixer wasn't sure he wanted to find the source. The voice was vaguely familiar.

"Spiiiiiiikehead!"

From his left. Mixer stepped around an ion pole, static raising his hair for a moment, and saw the two freaks in an open booth, drinking from tall, fluted glasses. Karl, who leaned back against the booth wall, was six and a half feet tall; when he'd lost his right arm, he'd replaced it with a batch of three-foot-long metal chains that hung from his shoulder. Like Hook's croc, you always knew when Karl was getting close—*clink, clink, clink.* Skeez was shorter and stockier, with one eye that was a bright green glow-globe. Lots of stories about how *that* happened. He was sitting forward, saluting Mixer with his glass.

"Hey, spikehead, have a seat," Skeez said.

Mixer tossed his half-full beer into a trash barrel and moved forward to within a few feet of them, but remained standing. "I'm looking for Chandler," he said.

Skeez laughed, and Mixer swore the green globe in his eye got brighter.

"Chandler doesn't want to be found," Karl said. He shrugged his right shoulder and rattled his chains. "He's gone to ground, says you should have gotten the message."

"When?"

"At the Caterwaul. A ghost message."

Mixer shivered inside, remembering that freaky, invisible presence on the eleventh floor, the window being pulled shut after he jumped. Ghost messages. He wouldn't be surprised.

"Yeah," he said. "I got the message."

"But here you are looking for Chandler," Skeez said.

"I *got* the message. I just didn't know what it was. Now I do."

Skeez slowly shook his head. "Not good enough."

Mixer started to back away, but Karl was too fast, on his feet and rushing forward, dipping and swinging the chains up and around, across Mixer's shoulders, wrapping around his right arm. Which was the exo. The chains clanked on the exoskeleton and Mixer grabbed them in his augmented fingers, twisting out and away from Karl, unwinding himself, but hanging onto the chains. Then he jerked the chains with everything he had, which sent streaks of pain down his back, but also pulled Karl off his feet and sent him sprawling across the floor.

Mixer still had hold of the ends of Karl's chains, was getting ready to drag the guy into a wall, when he glanced at Skeez. Skeez had a cattle prod out, pointed at Mixer.

"Drop the chains," he said. Mixer did. "We're going to have to make *sure* you've got the message," Skeez said. "Chandler insists."

"I told you," Mixer said. "I've got the message."

Skeez shook his head again, smiling. "Chandler's given us free rein." Karl struggled to his feet, hand on the table, and rattled his chains a few times. "We can have all the fun we want," Skeez went on. "As long as there's no permanent damage, nothing that can't be surgically corrected."

Karl started toward Mixer again, grinning, then abruptly

stopped. The grin vanished, along with Skeez's smile, and they were both looking past Mixer.

"He's mine," a voice said.

Mixer turned to see a tall, stunningly beautiful woman standing just a foot behind him. Her hair was a glistening auburn, and her clothes were a dark, deep blood-red. "You'll come with me," she said, looking at Mixer.

Mixer looked back at Karl and Skeez. Both looked pissed as hell, but they didn't object, they didn't say a word. Skeez even sheathed the cattle prod and laid it across his lap. Mixer turned back to the woman.

"I can go with you?" he said.

"You *will* go with me."

Mixer didn't like the sound of that, and he had no idea who this woman was, but going with her *had* to be better than having the shit pounded out of him by the two freaks.

"All right," he said. "Let's go."

The woman hooked her arm through his and led him away from the freaks. They worked their way through the wham-wham, and people moved to make way for them. Uh-oh, Mixer thought, what didn't he know about this woman?

"Who are you?" he asked.

"Saint Katherine," she replied.

"Oh, shit."

"Exactly," St. Katherine said, smiling.

Before Mixer could move, he felt the collar whip around his neck and lock up. A jolt went up into his head, white lights exploding behind his eyes. Oh, fuck me, Mixer thought. Then there was another jolt, harder, his vision blacked out . . . and then there was nothing.

TEN

LATE TUESDAY MORNING, the air conditioning kicked back on. Carlucci looked up from his desk and stared at the wall vent; he watched the bits of whirling dust, listened to the clicks and whirs and squeals of obsolete machinery trying desperately to come back to life. He sat without moving, waiting for a cool wash of air, some relief from the heat and stagnation, but all he really noticed was the stench of burning oil, a smell the air conditioning always seemed to have in this building. The relief would come eventually, he knew that, but for now all he got was the stink. Everything back to normal. He left the fan running.

Carlucci looked down at the crumpled sheet of yellow paper on the desk—the list of names Paula Asgard had given to him. He should be working on the other two murders, Butler and the mayor's nephew, the two "real" cases at the top of his list. But he couldn't get the Chick Roberts case out of his mind. Fuck it, he thought. He picked up the phone and punched up Diane's number.

"Info-Services, Diane Wanamaker." That wonderful, throaty voice.

"Diane, this is Frank."

"Frank. The man of my dreams."

"Right," Carlucci said. "There's never *been* a man in your dreams."

Diane laughed. "True enough. What can I do for you?"

"Let me buy you lunch."

"That I can do, man o' mine. I'm scheduled for twelve-thirty. That all right with you?"

"Sure," Carlucci said. "Want me to come by?"

"No, I won't put you through all that. I'll meet you out front. And Frank?"

"Yeah?"

"Take me somewhere nice."

"Of course."

"Ah, yes." She sighed. He could almost see her shaking her head. "I don't think you even *know* any nice places."

"Twelve-thirty, in front of the building."

"Okay. See you then."

Carlucci put the phone down and picked up the sheet of yellow paper. He read over the names again, waiting for one of them to emerge from the others, carrying with it some special meaning, setting off a flash of memory or insight. Nothing happened. He took a pen and added Chick Roberts and Paula Asgard to the top of the list, then folded the sheet and put it in his wallet.

Carlucci sat on the concrete steps in front of the station, waiting for Diane. The sidewalks were swarming with the midday crowds, every bench and available seat occupied by men and women eating their lunches. The air was heavy with the heat and damp, the sun glaring through thin, mustard-colored clouds overhead. The city was still waiting for the first cool-down that was supposed to come with autumn; sometimes Carlucci wondered if one year the fall and winter wouldn't even arrive, and the stifling heat and humidity of summer would just continue on without relief, relentlessly baking them all until everyone in the city went mad.

Carlucci closed his eyes, and for a few, brief moments imagined himself at Pine Crest, on the shore of the lake high in the Sierras. He could feel the cool, clean air washing over him, could even smell the pungent aroma of pine needles and wood smoke. It had been years since he'd been there, far too many years since he and Andrea and the kids had stayed at Tony and Imogene's cabin. Too many years since he and Tony had gone out on the lake before sunrise, the boat purring through the deep, cold water, surrounded by the dark green of trees as they headed for one of their secret spots for a few hours of fishing.

A hand on his shoulder abruptly brought him back, and he opened his eyes to see Diane standing over him.

"You looked like you were in heaven, Frank."

Carlucci smiled and nodded. "I was." He got to his feet and tugged at his pants. "And you brought me back to earth. Thanks a lot."

"Sorry."

Diane was a beautiful woman in her forties with light brown curly hair; her large, round glasses were attractive on her, and her smile always cheered Carlucci. She was, probably, the happiest person he knew.

"You look terrific," he said.

"I always look terrific." Diane took his arm in hers and they walked down the steps to the sidewalk. "Where to?"

Carlucci led the way through the crowd and into a stream of people flowing north. "Not far," he said. "A few blocks."

"Have I been there before?"

"Yes."

"Oh, God. Then it's one of your holes." But she smiled at him and squeezed his arm.

Pine Crest. With the heat and humidity and the people and noise pressing in on him from all directions, he could almost believe that Pine Crest was nothing more than a fantasy, that it didn't really exist. How long had it been? He hadn't talked to Tony or Imogene in years, didn't know if they even owned the cabin anymore. Was the lake still there, as cold and blue and deep as it had always been, or had the interior drought killed it off as well? He had no idea.

Carlucci cut off the street and into a crowded, shop-lined alley. Two doors up they entered Pattaya Thai Cafe, one of his regular places. Inside was swirling air from half a dozen fans and a babble of voices even louder than the noise outside. One of the waiters looked at Carlucci, pointed at the ceiling, then held up three fingers. Carlucci nodded, then led Diane through the jammed maze of tables and toward the back.

They had to go through the kitchen to get to the back stairs. "I remember this place," Diane said, shouting over the hissing, sizzling, clanging noises of the cooks. "They must have a dozen health code violations in here."

Carlucci just shrugged and smiled and motioned her up the wooden steps. They climbed four cramped half-flights, and by the time they reached the top, Carlucci was breathing heavily and sweating.

"You're out of shape, old man," Diane said.

"Thanks a lot. It's this damn heat."

The third floor was much quieter than the first, but it was nearly full as well, and they couldn't get a table anywhere near the open windows. The circulation was better, though, and the air was almost comfortable. They sat at a table under a pair of carved shadow puppets mounted on the wall; Carlucci could not decide whether the puppets were preparing to fight or embrace.

They ordered pork satay, hot and sour soup, lard nar rice noodles with shrimp, and Thai iced tea. Diane would eat at least as much as he would, but it wouldn't go to her gut like it did to his. She was right, he was out of shape; he needed to exercise. Christ, there were times he felt like an old man.

"How's Lissa?" Carlucci asked.

Diane smiled. "Still making me happy. We're going to

Alaska in a couple of weeks, ten days of camping in what's left of the Refuge.'' She shook her head. ''Even after nearly four years together she worries about the age difference. But that'll be fine. Our relationship may go into the toilet someday, but it won't be because of the age difference.''

The waiter came by with their iced tea. Diane picked up her glass, said, ''Cheers,'' then drank deeply. She set down the glass and looked at him.

''So tell me, Frank. What do you need from me?''

''Information,'' Carlucci replied.

''Frank.'' There was irritation in her voice. ''Just tell me.''

''What I need, I need off-line, Diane. I can't have Vaughn or McCuller or *anyone* know what I'm looking into.''

''No record of a download, no trace of the search itself, that's what you want? Serious stuff, Frank.''

Carlucci nodded. ''Have you got a demon who could do it?''

Diane smiled, shaking her head. ''What you mean, is, someone who can do it, who would be willing to do it, and who can be trusted.''

''Yeah. That's it.''

''How important is it, Frank?''

''Pretty damn important, I think, or I wouldn't be asking.''

''You *think*?''

Carlucci didn't respond. He took out his wallet and pulled the yellow sheet of paper from it. For a moment he hesitated; then he unfolded it and handed it to her.

''I need whatever you can get me on these people,'' he said. ''Especially any connections to each other.'' He almost asked her to concentrate on Chick Roberts, but decided it was better if he didn't steer her one way or another.

Diane studied the list, a frown working into her expression. She glanced up at him, back down at the list, then looked up at him again.

''Frank, even doing an off-line demon run isn't going to

get you any more than what you've already got on these people."

"I haven't got *anything*," Carlucci said.

She looked at the list, shaking her head. "Chick Roberts . . . Tory Mango . . . Boniface . . . Jenny Woo . . . I don't know, maybe not *all* the names, but a lot of them. You've got what's in the feeds. I can't get you any more than that, Frank, even with a demon."

"What are you talking about?"

"That's where you got these names, isn't it?"

"From *where*, for Christ's sake?" Carlucci was getting that bad feeling in his gut again, burning through him along with his confusion.

"The slug sublevel feeds," Diane said. "For the mayor's nephew's case."

Oh, shit. Carlucci leaned back in his chair, looking at her. He didn't want to hear this. He picked up his glass and drank deeply from the thick, sweet, creamy iced tea. The cold liquid felt like molten ice in his belly, solidifying. He set down the glass and shook his head.

"I didn't get the names from the feeds. I haven't had a chance to look at any of them except the Prime and first sub."

"Then where . . . ?"

"A different case," Carlucci said. "Something completely unconnected to the mayor's nephew. At least that's what I thought." He leaned forward. "Which names—?" he started, but the waiter came by with the satay, cutting him off. When the waiter was gone, Carlucci started again. "Which names on that list are in the sublevel feeds?"

"Hell, I can't tell you for sure, Frank. My memory's good, but not *that* good." She looked down at the list. "Not all of them, probably, but at least half. The ones I mentioned, plus, oh, Poppy Chandler, I think . . . Ahmed Mrabet . . . maybe Rossom." She looked back at him. "I can take these back and check for you, Frank, but you can do it yourself. You've got all the feeds, right?"

Carlucci just nodded, staring at the sheet of yellow paper. He reached across the table and picked it up, stared at the names for a minute, then folded the sheet and put it back in his wallet.

"If you want," Diane said, "after you've checked those against the feeds, I can arrange a demon run for the names that *aren't* in the feeds."

Carlucci shook his head. "Thanks, but . . . I've got a feeling the ones I want *are* in the feeds."

"What's this mean, Frank? About what you're doing?"

"Shit, I don't know. Nothing good." He shook his head again, then gave her a half smile. "Let's eat."

Carlucci picked up one of the skewers, dipped the meat in hot mustard sauce, and bit into it. The satay was good, but he was no longer hungry, and eating was nothing more than something to keep his hands occupied. He chewed, swallowed, then dipped the meat again.

What *did* this mean? Carlucci tried to organize his thoughts and work it all through logically. It was possible, barely, that the overlap of names was just coincidence—strange coincidences were more common in this job than most people thought. But Carlucci didn't believe it. Not this time, not with so many names overlapping the two cases. There had to be a connection.

Pressure was coming down through Vaughn and McCuller on both cases. But the pressure was to solve the one case, and bury the other. That didn't make sense, did it? If there *was* a connection, solving the one was liable to blow open whatever was involved in the other. So what was going on?

A couple of possibilities, it seemed to him. One: the pressure was coming from two different sources, down through the same conduit of Vaughn and McCuller, unknown to each other and, presumably, for different reasons. Or: the pressure was coming from the same source, but whoever it was didn't realize the two cases were connected; they wanted the one case solved, for one reason, and the other buried, for a completely different reason, unaware that the one could screw up the other.

The soup and noodles arrived. Carlucci continued to eat mechanically, hardly noticing the food, hardly noticing Diane. She knew him; she would let him alone as he ate and thought, and she wouldn't take offense.

So, two possibilities, and Carlucci didn't like either one. And of course there might be a third, or even a fourth possibility that hadn't yet occurred to him. And there was always the fallback position, which he liked even less: that *nothing* was what it seemed.

Fuck. This whole thing was far messier than he'd ever imagined. Until he had a better idea of who was applying the pressure on the cases, and why, he'd be stumbling blind, and there were too many ways to sink into deep shit.

"The food's not that bad," Diane said.

Carlucci looked up at her. "Oh, you still here?" he said, smiling. Her plate was empty, the serving plates were empty, but his own plate was still half full. Only the soup was gone. Carlucci put down his chopsticks. "I'm not hungry anymore."

"How bad is it?" Diane asked.

"Bad," Carlucci said. "Bad enough I'd really like to walk away from it all."

"But you can't."

Carlucci shook his head. "I can't."

"There's something else, Frank. Might be unimportant, but it probably won't make you feel any better."

"Great. What is it?"

"Tremaine's been digging around in the nephew's case. He's requested interviews with you, which we've turned down, of course. And he's been asking about the Butler case, wanted to know who was in charge of *that* one."

Terrific. What the hell was Tremaine after?

"Is there anything I can do to help?" Diane asked.

"No. Well, yeah. Forget you saw that sheet of paper. Forget we talked about anything except Lissa and the damn weather."

The waiter came by, raised an eyebrow at Carlucci, and, when Carlucci nodded, picked up the plates and took them away. Carlucci finished off his tea and chewed on what little ice remained.

"You'll crack your teeth," Diane said.

"Nag." He crunched twice more on the ice, then swallowed the tiny pieces.

"Frank?"

"Yeah?"

"If there's anything I can do . . ."

There won't be, Carlucci thought. He wouldn't allow it, he wasn't going to get her mixed up in all this. He would get *himself* out of it if he could.

"Thanks," he said. "I'll let you know."

He looked up at the shadow puppets on the wall. Fighting or embracing? Making love or war? He could see it now. He knew: they were preparing to do both.

ELEVEN

THE ONLY REASON Paula saw him come in was because the place was half empty. It was Dead Wednesday at The Final Transit and the Black Angels were playing the ten o'clock slot, filler until the hip-lit crowd arrived and the Deconstruction Poets took over the stage for another of their shouting fests—poetry reading as primal scream therapy. Or was it the other way around?

The Black Angels were halfway through "The Dead Drive Better Than You," Paula backfilling with her bass for Bonita's solo, when Tremaine came into the club. Paula nearly missed a beat when she saw him standing in the doorway, staring at her and smiling, but she kept it together and moved farther back from the spots on Bonita, wishing for a moment that she could disappear from the stage altogether. What was it about Tremaine that made her feel so weird? She watched him work his way to a table against the side wall, maybe thirty feet back from the stage.

Then it was her time, and she moved up to the microphone, hot red light glaring down on her, and began to sing:

"There you go again,
Driving the wrong side of the road,

Forgetting all your Zen,
  Flashing along in hit-and-run mode.

There you go again,
  Swerving and skidding and sliding,
Scattering women and men,
  You at the wheel, but no longer driving.

So never make fun of that Haitian Voodoo,
  'Cuz the walking dead drive better than you do.''

As always when she sang those last two lines, Paula had to work hard to keep from laughing. Stupid lyrics. Worst of all, she'd written them herself.

She glanced over at Tremaine, who was shaking his head and smiling; he held up his glass and tipped it toward her, then drank. Christ, Paula thought, she'd hardly met the guy, and she had to admit she was attracted to him, somehow, despite the fact that he wanted to talk to her about Chick. It was all too weird. She looked away from him, backed off from the mike, and dug into her guitar as if she were trying to rip the strings from her heart.

When the set was over, Paula put her guitar in its case, set it by the drum kit, then asked Sheela and Bonita if they could get by without her, loading up all their equipment.

''Sure,'' Bonita said, shrugging. ''Fergus and Dolph are here tonight.''

Fergus and Dolph were Bonita's two inseparable, six-and-a-half-foot-tall boyfriends. Huge men. Paula got the shivers whenever she thought about the three of them in bed together. Fergus and Dolph could handle all the loading by themselves, and would enjoy it.

''What's up?'' Sheela asked.

''A friend dropped by during the set.''

''Oh, yeah? Who?'' Sheela stood on her toes to look past

Paula and Bonita, searching the tables.

"Just a friend." Paula turned to Bonita. "Take my bass home with you?"

Bonita nodded. Fergus and Dolph came out of the club's back door, stepped onto the stage, and started unplugging the sound equipment. Bonita turned away and joined them.

"Who is it?" Sheela asked again. "That guy by the wall?"

Paula turned to see who Sheela was looking at, sure that somehow Sheela had picked out the right guy. Yeah, she had. She was looking right at Tremaine, who was calmly returning her gaze.

"Yes," Paula said. "That's him."

"Jesus, Paula, Chick's hardly been dead a couple of weeks."

Paula grabbed Sheela's arm, jerked at it until Sheela turned to face her. "Hey, back off, Sheela. You don't know what the fuck you're talking about. He's just a friend. Besides, anything like that, I don't answer to anyone but myself and Chick. And, as you so delicately pointed out, Chick's dead. Got it?"

Sheela pulled her arm out of Paula's grasp and looked down at the floor. She nodded slowly and walked back to her drum kit. Dolph was breaking it down, but Sheela pushed him away and set to work on it herself.

Christ, Paula thought, what's going on around here? She grabbed her jacket, stepped down from the stage and made her way to Tremaine's table. She leaned on the back of the empty chair across from him, but didn't sit down.

"Hello, Paula Asgard."

"Hello, Tremaine. You're not going to tell me this is a coincidence, are you?"

Tremaine smiled. "Of course not. I came here looking for you." He gestured at the chair. "Please, have a seat. Let me buy you a drink."

Paula looked at her watch. "A short one," she said. She pulled out the chair, hung her jacket over it, and sat. "The poets are set to go on in twenty minutes, and I want to be out of here when they start.''

''The poets?''

Paula shook her head. ''Don't even ask. Take my word for it, you don't want to be here either, unless you can get into two hours of incoherent screaming.''

''Sounds lovely,'' Tremaine said.

''Yeah.'' Paula flagged down a waiter and ordered a Beck's; Tremaine ordered another warm ale.

The club was filling up. The Black Angels audience was almost gone, but the hip-lit crowd was pouring in; *flowing* in, Paula thought, with their capes and longcoats, several men and women draped in window-silk, the shiny fabric projecting television shows in shimmering color.

The waiter came by with their drinks. ''Maybe we can go somewhere else,'' Tremaine suggested. ''Where it's quieter.''

''Maybe,'' Paula said. ''I'll think about it.'' She still wasn't sure what to do about Tremaine. She drank deeply from her beer. Damn, it was good; she hadn't realized how thirsty she was. ''You caught about half our set,'' she said. ''How'd you like it?''

Tremaine shrugged. ''It was all right. Good energy. But I guess I like my music slower and quieter.''

Paula laughed. ''Most people do. Fast and loud is the whole point of slash-and-burn. Like a shot of speed to your heart and head.''

''You like it, don't you?'' Tremaine said.

''I *love* it. It keeps me alive.'' Paula turned the bottle around and around in the ring of moisture that had formed beneath it. ''So tell me,'' she said, cocking her head at him. ''What keeps *you* alive?''

Tremaine didn't say anything for a minute. ''The stories I do,'' he finally said.

''I can't talk about Chick,'' she told him.

''Why not?''

"Look, I don't know why he was killed, and I don't *want* to know why."

"Yes you do," Tremaine said.

Paula drank from her beer. "All right, sure. I want to know who killed him. But the whole thing scares me a little."

"It should."

"Thanks. That's reassuring."

He gazed steadily at her without speaking for a minute, then said, "Okay, we won't talk about Chick. Let's go someplace quiet and just talk, have a drink. No business, just personal, the two of us."

Paula smiled. "Bullshit. I got a feeling that with you, *everything's* business."

Tremaine smiled back. "That's probably true. But that doesn't mean it can't be personal at the same time. I'd like to know you better."

Paula drank again from her beer. She still didn't know what to think about him. She wanted to get to know Tremaine better, too, but she didn't know how much he could be trusted. Still, she thought it might be worth finding out, and she was about to suggest they go to a nearby pub, when Amy Trinh walked up to the table.

Amy Trinh was half-Vietnamese, half-Cambodian, and beautiful. Tonight she was wearing black jeans tucked into knee-high black leather boots, and an open, worn leather jacket over an incredibly bright white T-shirt. On her face was heavy eye shadow and liner, dark red lipstick, and an expression Paula didn't like one bit.

"Aw shit, Amy, you don't look like you've got good news."

Amy Trinh shook her head. "I don't, my good friend." She glanced at Tremaine, then looked back at Paula. "It's Mixer. Word on the nets is he got picked up by Saint Katherine a few days ago."

Paula stared at her, unable to speak for a minute. Her

breathing had stopped, and she wondered if her heart had, too. Then, "Jesus Christ. How the *hell* did that happen?"

"Don't know. Something about a wham-wham. No details. But . . . He's due to go through the trial tonight. At least that's the hard-core guess. Midnight, probably. But definitely tonight."

Paula felt something heavy and cold drop in her stomach, a dull vibration rippling out from it and through her body. Oh, Mixer.

"We'll never find him before the trial, will we?" Paula said.

Amy shook her head.

Word always went out about the trials, flexing along the nets, but unless you were a part of the Saints inner circle you'd never learn the actual location. "You free tonight?" Paula asked. "Got your scoot?"

"Yes, and yes," Amy said, nodding twice.

"We can try anyway, can't we?" The dull, sick vibration was still thrumming through Paula.

"Sure."

"If nothing else, maybe we find him after, when they let him go." An ache was sinking into Paula's bones. "Pull him off the streets before the scavengers rip out whatever's left of him."

"Sure," Amy said again. She almost smiled.

A slow, steady grinding worked through Paula, cut through now with a demanding surge of adrenaline. She turned to Tremaine. "Gotta go. Another time, maybe."

"Who is—?" Tremaine started, but he cut himself off with a shake of the head. "Like you said, another time." As Paula was getting up from the chair, he said, "You still have my card?" When she nodded, Tremaine smiled. "Do what you have to do. I hope things work out." He paused. "And I'd like to see you again."

"Could be." Paula picked up her jacket and punched her arms through the sleeves. A strange thought flashed through her mind: Sheela would be glad to see her bailing on Tremaine. She turned to Amy. "Let's go." With one final glance at Tremaine, she said, "Bye and thanks for the beer," then she and Amy headed for the street.

Amy's scoot was half a block up from the club, plugged into a charger, and a teenage boy was squatting beside it, yowling. He'd tried to take the scoot, or rip something off it, and got juiced. Amy chuckled, then yelled "Asshole!" at the kid. "Leave my bike the fuck alone!"

The kid scrambled away, still howling, while people around them laughed. Amy de-commed the defense system, unlocked the two helmets and handed one to Paula. Amy climbed on first, then Paula got on behind her. The scoot was small, just big enough for the two of them, but it was jazz. Amy put everything she had into it—time and money and sweat—and it had all the power and cool she could ever want. She punched the scoot to life, the engine humming so quietly Paula wasn't sure she even heard it; then Amy flicked it into gear and they shot out into traffic.

The scoot was smooth and quick, and Amy maneuvered it gracefully in and out of traffic, shooting narrow gaps between moving and parked vehicles, leapfrogging around cars and vans, even riding the curb once to get past a city bus. Paula hung on tight as they headed for the Tenderloin.

The Saints. God damn, Mixer, what the hell happened? Crazy women living in the Tenderloin who had taken on the names and characteristics of historical saints—St. Lucy, St. Apollonia, St. Christina the Astonishing. The worst of them was a woman who sounded completely insane to Paula, the "head" Saint: St. Katherine. The Saints held periodic "trials" of other men and women, the trials based on what their namesakes had been put through, and St. Katherine's trials were the worst. Paula didn't know exactly what was done to the victims, but they emerged from St. Katherine's trials as complete neurological wrecks, with their language capacities pretty much shot to hell. Those that lived. The survivors of St. Katherine's trials made the net zombies look functional. *Jesus Christ, Mixer, how the hell did you let yourself get taken by her*?

The Tenderloin rose before them, growing as Amy weaved through traffic, headed straight for it. Then, as they reached the edge of the district, Amy swung the scoot around and they moved along the perimeter, slower now. A nearly solid wall of buildings loomed ten and twelve stories above them, marking the border of the Tenderloin; the wall of buildings, broken only by hidden, narrow alleys, enclosed something like sixty square blocks of a city within the city. A city that ran full speed through the night, slowing only when the sun rose. Paula had lived here once.

Amy braked, jumped the curb, Paula grabbing her harder; then they crossed the sidewalk and plunged down a flight of concrete steps, the scoot bouncing and jerking its way to basement level. At the bottom of the steps was an opening into a weirdly lit, covered alley. Amy headed the scoot into the dim alley, even slower now, her boots out and brushing the concrete for balance. The alley walls and ceiling were covered with what appeared to be patternless stretches of phosphorescent molds, which gave the alley a shimmering look.

Ahead, a metal gate barred their way, and Amy rolled to a stop. A short, thin man, hardly more than a boy, emerged from a doorway in the alley wall and barked something at them in what Paula thought was Chinese. He held something that might have been a weapon under his arm, though it looked more like a console of some sort.

Amy shook her head. "Don't speak that shit to me, you little fucker!" Then she shifted into Vietnamese.

The boy answered, still in Chinese, anger in his face. Amy snapped back at him, and finally the boy answered in Vietnamese. The two spoke back and forth for several minutes, the only words intelligible to Paula being "Amy Trinh" and

"Paula Asgard." Finally the boy did something with the console and the gate crackled, a pulsing glow flowing over the metal. Then the boy disappeared back into the doorway.

"Fucking young punks," Amy said to Paula. "No pride. The Chinks still have the most power inside, and a lot of the young kids coming up want to be just like them. No pride, and no sense of history." She shook her head.

"Where did he go?"

Amy turned to her, grin visible under her visor. "Kid thinks he's bad shit, but he's afraid of making a mistake, let the wrong person through. He doesn't know me, so he juiced the gate and went to get authorization."

The kid reappeared, followed by a tall, handsome man with a thin moustache. "Amy," the tall man said, nodding.

"Hello, General," Amy replied.

The tall man smiled and shook his head. "Are you in a hurry?"

"Yes."

"Then this is not the time to talk. Perhaps some other night."

"Sure, General."

Still smiling, the tall man switched to Vietnamese and spoke to Amy for a minute. She responded, after which the man turned to the boy and said a few words. The boy, stiff and silent, fiddled with the console; there was more crackling from the gate, the metal dulled, a click sounded, and the gate swung open. Amy gave the tall man a mock salute, flicked the scoot into gear, and they shot forward.

The alley beyond the gate was more of the same: enclosed, and lit by the pulsing swatches of green and blue. Near the end, as pale gray light began to appear ahead of them, another gate was already open, and they drove through, Paula glimpsing a shadowed form standing back in a wall opening. Then the alley ramped upward, a rectangle of light appeared, and moments later Paula and Amy shot up and into the Tenderloin night.

They emerged in the Asian Quarter. The sky was filled with lights: message streamers swimming through the air in flashing red, three and four stories up; above that a shimmering green, red, and gold dragon undulated, sparks shooting from its eyes, smoke pouring from its nostrils, and advertisements flowing along its body; and high above the dragon, a network of bright white lights and tensor wires webbed across the street, connecting one building to another, pulsing rapidly against the night sky.

The streets and walks of the Asian Quarter were as full of people, vehicles, and movement as the sky was of lights. Amy maneuvered the scoot into the thronging street traffic, a mass of bikes and scoots and carts and riks and vans. They were in the heart of the Asian Quarter, and they had to get out. The Saints were definitely a Western thing; no trace of them would even be allowed here. Paula and Amy would have to make their way to the Euro Quarter.

Paula had lived in the Tenderloin for six years, right where the Asian and Euro Quarters merged together. She had loved the energy, the unrestrained *life* that flowed through the streets and the air. She had lived here and breathed all of it into her, giving just as much back in her own way—with her music. The days had been for sleeping, the nights for living. An endless cycle of energy. But as she'd grown older, it had become too much for her. When you lived in the Tenderloin, you couldn't ever get away from it. Paula had come to need times of peace and quiet, relaxation, things she could never get while she lived here. She still loved the Tenderloin, but now only as a visitor.

Their pace was agonizingly slow. Paula craned around Amy's neck, but didn't see anything that unusual, just a typical street jam. Then, as they crept forward, she saw it: a pedestrian spillover from the sidewalk, flooding the street. Paula finally spotted the source, Hong Kong Cinema disgorging a huge audience through three doors while a crowd waited to get in for the next showing. The marquee floated in the air directly above the street, rolling the titles in Chinese, English, Vietnamese, and French. Paula hooked onto the only one she could read: *Ghost Lover of Station 13*. Shit, Paula thought, no wonder.

They slowed even further as they got closer to the theater, now at a lurching crawl. Paula breathed slowly, deeply, trying not to think of what might be happening to Mixer. She let her gaze drift slowly from side to side and behind them. Familiar places, old haunts. Hong Kong Gardens, the cafe next to the theater. Shorty's Grill across the street, sandwiched between Tommy Wong's Tattoos and Ngan Dinh Body Electronics. Back half a block, a favorite hangout of Paula's—Misha's Donuts and Espresso.

And then, amid the familiar places, Paula spied a familiar face, a woman legging a pedalcart three vehicles behind them. Jenny Woo. Like Boniface, a name Paula had given to Carlucci just a few days earlier. Like Boniface, someone she couldn't stand.

Paula swung around to face forward again. Another coincidence, like seeing Boniface? After all, Jenny Woo *did* live here in the Asian Quarter. But still . . . Boniface was harmless. Jenny Woo wasn't. Jesus.

They were finally past the Hong Kong Cinema, traffic eased, and their speed picked up a bit. Amy found a break at the next intersection and turned hard left, giving the scoot a blast to shoot through and down the street. Now they were headed straight for the Euro Quarter, only three blocks away.

Paula turned around again, but didn't see Jenny Woo. There were riks and bikes and a pedalcart behind them, but no one familiar in any of them. Maybe it *was* another coincidence. Maybe it wasn't even Jenny she'd seen.

For the next three blocks, Paula kept looking behind them, but never saw Jenny Woo again. Then they were crossing into the Euro Quarter, and Paula turned her attention back to the street in front of her and the shops and sidewalks around them. She couldn't worry about Jenny Woo. Mixer was more than enough to worry about. And it was Mixer's face, more than any other, that she wanted to see again.

Amy and Paula gave up just after dawn. As they'd expected, they'd had no luck ferreting out the site of St. Katherine's trial, they just got further confirmation that it was to take place, or already had, and that Mixer was definitely the "defendant." So they had spent the last hours of darkness cruising the streets of the Euro Quarter, occasionally venturing a block or two into the other Quarters, searching for a staggering, catatonic wreck. They'd come across an astounding number of candidates, but none of them had been Mixer.

Amy dropped Paula off at her apartment building as the sun was rising, with a promise to return later that afternoon to pick her up for another run through the Tenderloin. They both needed sleep and food, and rest for their burning eyes. Unspoken was what they both knew—the fact that they hadn't found Mixer within an hour or two of the trial, whenever it had been held, was bad. Real bad. The two most likely possibilities? Scavengers had picked him clean before Paula and Amy could find him. Or he hadn't even survived the trial. Paula didn't try to decide which was better.

She climbed the stairs to the third floor, walked down to her apartment, and unlocked the door. She stood in the doorway for a minute, listening. The building was so quiet. This early, most people were either still in bed or just waking up. She stepped inside and closed the door behind her.

The apartment seemed terribly empty. Paula wandered through it, making several circuits of the two rooms until she finally sat on the edge of her bed and stopped. Yes, it was the same place, nothing had changed. Except . . .

Two weeks ago she'd lost Chick. Now it looked like she'd lost Mixer as well. It was just too much. Paula lay back on the bed, staring up at the ceiling. She was tired, so tired. She closed her eyes, and wondered if she would ever get up again.

TWELVE

THIS TIME WHEN Mixer came to, he was naked from the waist up and strapped to a large, flat, horizontal wheel, his arms and legs spread-eagled, bound at the elbows and wrists, thighs and ankles. He was on his back, sweating in the stifling heat, his blurred gaze trying to bring the ceiling overhead into focus.

The ceiling seemed very far away, and after several moments Mixer realized it *was*—twenty, twenty-five feet above him. He found he could move his head, and he raised it, turned it from side to side. The wheel was about three feet off the floor, supported by . . . what? He couldn't tell. Though the ceiling was high, the room was smaller than he'd expected, maybe twenty by thirty. At the moment it was empty. There was a door at the other end of the room, but no windows. The walls were covered with prints and paintings and photographs depicting saints and martyrs, some dispensing good works, others being tortured and killed.

How the *fuck* did I get into this? Mixer wondered. And why St. Katherine? Why not one of the others, like the one who pulled all your teeth out of your head without any anesthetic? Right now he'd take that over having his brain gouged and jittered by St. Katherine's Wheel.

He let his head fall back on the wheel. He flexed his hands and feet, his arms and legs. Not much give. But his right arm. . . . They'd left the exoskeleton in place. He wondered if there was enough power in the exo to tear out the straps.

Mixer turned his head to the right. His vision was sharp now, and he could see the straps over his right arm and wrist, wrapped tightly over the exo. He didn't much like what he saw. The straps were made of woven metal strands. What were the chances of ripping through that, even with the exo? Not good, not fucking good at all.

Mixer rolled his head back, facing the ceiling once again, then closed his eyes. His stomach was fluttering, knotting up on him. Man, oh, man, he was scared. Dying was one thing. This was another. He'd seen a survivor of St. Katherine's Wheel. The guy had been a mess, like he had perpetual epilepsy—a walking seizure, with two "pilgrims" caring and begging for him like he was a holy man. And that's where I'm headed, Mixer thought. His one hope was that he'd be so far gone when it was over that he'd have no idea how fucked up he was, and how much he'd lost.

What he could use right now were a few of the neutralizers he'd taken for the wham-wham. Or *some* kind of drug. Something to freeze him down. Of course, that was part of what got him into trouble at the wham-wham, the neutralizers fucking up his judgment.

Goddamn wham-wham. How long had it been? Hours, or days? Days, he thought. The Saints had kept him doped, he knew that much. Good stuff, though, since he felt pretty clearheaded. He'd come to several times, and he thought he remembered being given food and water, being taken to the can, but it was all pretty vague. He remembered different faces. St. Katherine's, hers he knew best—long and sharp and, he had to admit, beautiful; if she wasn't so crazy, and if she wasn't going to scorch his brain, he could fall in love with a woman who looked like that. There was another woman, older, dressed all in black, with a hard, worn face. And then a third, a woman with the most incredibly beautiful eyes he'd ever seen. Electric blue. Couldn't have been real, those eyes. St. Lucy.

Mixer opened his own eyes again. How long was he going to be here? The "trial" was going to start soon, he was sure of that. Why else strap him to the wheel?

The straps. Why not try? Nothing, absolutely nothing to lose. Mixer breathed deeply twice, closed his right hand into a fist, then pulled, trying to rip his right arm free. There was no give, and he pulled harder, trying to use his elbow for leverage. He could hear the whine of the exo motors straining, getting nowhere. Sweat dripped down his face, his neck, slid off his arm.

Nothing.

He kept on, but pain started in his wrist and moved up along his arm to his shoulder, then around his neck and back. The pain jacked up; he felt like something in his bones was going to pop, and he finally quit. The straps hadn't loosened a bit. His arm throbbed, and he felt a sharp pain in his shoulder. Damn exo. What good *was* it?

Fuck me, he thought. He was stuck here, and he was going to die. No, worse than die.

The door opened. Mixer wanted to close his eyes, pretend to still be out, but instead he turned his head and watched St. Katherine walk toward him. She was alone, dressed as she had been at the wham-wham—deep, blood-red cloak over more layers of red.

When she reached the wheel she stopped and looked down on him, smiling. He was at waist level to her, and she reached out, placed her warm fingers on his cheek, lightly brushing his skin. God, she was beautiful.

What the fuck am I thinking? Mixer asked himself. She might be beautiful, but she's insane and she's going to scorch my brain.

"It's all right," St. Katherine said, moving her fingers to his forehead. No, it's *not* all right, Mixer thought. But there was something quite calming about her touch, and he almost believed her.

"How are you feeling?" she asked.

Even her voice was beautiful, deep and smooth, washing over him. For a moment he wondered if the air in the room was gassed, but decided it wasn't. St. Katherine's impact on him, he was sure, was all her own.

"Cat got your tongue?" she said, smiling.

What the hell did that expression *mean*? he wondered. "I'm feeling just terrific," he finally said. "What do you think?"

"Your trial will begin soon," she said. "I'm here to prepare you."

"Prepare me?" Mixer almost laughed, but it came out as a choking sound. Why was he even talking to this woman?

"Don't you want to know why you're here? What the trial is for?" She ran her fingers lightly across his face, down his neck, like soft warm feathers, then down his chest, tingling his skin. "Why I've chosen *you*?"

She was gazing into his eyes, and he could not turn away from her as her fingers moved downward, over his belly, and finally across his pants and to his crotch, where they circled and brushed and pressed lightly at him until, astoundingly, he began to get hard. This is fucking insane, he told himself. *I'm* insane, I'm as crazy as she is! He closed his eyes and clenched both of his fists. Preparation for trial. What was she going to do, crawl up on the wheel and mount him?

The motion of St. Katherine's fingers stopped and she pulled her hand away.

"If you survive the trial," she said, "you will be my consort." Then, "Open your eyes, Minor Danzig. Look at me."

Mixer opened his eyes, stunned to hear his birth name. How could she know that?

"My name is Mixer," he said, looking at her. "I've seen

survivors of your trials, and they didn't look like consorts to me. They hardly looked human."

St. Katherine slowly shook her head. "They only survived in the crudest sense of the word. In truth, they all failed their trials, failed miserably."

"Did you 'prepare' all of them, too?"

"Yes."

"You did a piss-poor job, then. And I'm fucked." He moved his head from side to side. "Let's get this over with."

St. Katherine smiled, leaned over, and kissed him on the mouth. Then she pressed something on the side of the wheel and stepped back.

The wheel began to move. Mixer tensed, disoriented at first. He had expected the wheel to spin, but it didn't.

Instead, it angled upward, his head and arms rising while the lower end of the wheel dipped toward the floor, moving smoothly, steadily, until he and the wheel were vertical. The straps held him in place, but he could feel the strain on his arms as gravity tried to pull him to the floor. He coughed, struggling a moment for breath. Fucking great, he thought, I'm being crucified.

He was at the head of the room, facing St. Katherine. Two more large, metal wheels emerged from the wall behind him, one on either side; another slid out above him, suspended directly over his head.

"Your own wheel will remain stationary," St. Katherine said. "The others will turn, producing and casting the energies for the trial."

Her explanation meant nothing. All Mixer could think was that at least he wouldn't get dizzy. But what did it matter? He stared at St. Katherine, waiting for further explanations of what would be done to him, but she didn't offer any more.

The door opened again, and women filed into the room. Four in simple gray robes entered first, followed by six in lush, layered outfits like St. Katherine's, but in different colors. The six were followed by a dozen more in gray. What? Full-fledged Saints and novitiates?

The six Saints—Mixer recognized St. Lucy among them—sat in a row on the floor just a few feet in front of him, silent, gazing steadily at him. The novitiates sat behind them in four rows, just as quiet.

St. Katherine reached into the layers of her clothing, withdrew her hand, and held up a bundled neural net. She shook out the net, held it spread in front of her, then turned and displayed it to the Saints and novitiates.

"The Neural Shroud," she said.

Oh, fuck me, Mixer thought. He expected her to keep talking, mouthing ritual words and phrases, but she said no more, only bowed her head once. All the Saints and novitiates bowed their heads in return, and then St. Katherine turned and faced Mixer, holding the neural net up between them. Her face was crosshatched by the fine wires and nodes, and her skin seemed to shine behind the net.

She stepped forward and draped the net over Mixer's head, face and shoulders, the nodes tinging against the metal of the exoskeleton. The net was surprisingly light, but the fine wire dug into his flesh, not quite breaking the skin. A panic attack a lot like he had in elevators kicked in, sending a jolt to his heart and a flush to his neck and face. He managed to keep from crying out by breathing slow and deep and reminding himself that a lot worse was still to come.

St. Katherine took a step back. "You are to be torn to pieces on the wheels," she said, "just as my namesake, Saint Catherine of Alexandria, was to be torn to pieces on the wheels. For you, however, the pain and destruction will be mental, not physical. The three wheels around you will turn and generate holy energies, then transmit them into your brain through the Neural Shroud. Your mind, not your body, will be torn to pieces.

"But do not despair, Minor Danzig. An angel came to Saint

Catherine of Alexandria and broke the wheels and spared her. Perhaps an angel will come during your trial, in one form or another, and spare your mind from the ravages of the wheels. If so, you will have been shown worthy." She paused, breathing deeply. "Worthy to be my consort for life."

St. Katherine's face seemed to glow, and Mixer thought she looked even more beautiful than before. His heart was banging around inside his chest, but he could not take his eyes away from her face. My mind's already gone, he thought.

The Saint smiled at him, a smile filled with passion and hope. Or was it his own desperate hope he saw in her face?

St. Katherine stepped to the side wall, pressed a panel with her hand. The wheels beside and above him began to slowly, slowly spin. St. Katherine walked toward the front row of Saints and stood before them. She said nothing, just looked at each of them in turn, then swung around to face Mixer and the spinning wheels. She lowered herself to her knees, placing her hands on her thighs, her gaze and smile fixed on Mixer.

Mixer suddenly became very calm. All the panic left him. He thought of Sookie, and he wondered if she'd become calm and unafraid just before the Chain Killer had murdered her. He hoped so. Then he thought of Paula, and a wave of grief rolled over him. He was going to miss her. Or would he? Even if he lived through this, he probably wouldn't even know who she was.

The wheels were spinning more rapidly now, and tiny sparks of blue and white electricity danced around their rims, glittering at him. The sparks grew, joined one another, formed thin, flickering strings of electric fire leaping toward him. Mixer gazed at the blue and silver fire above and around him, transfixed.

Then he realized a chanting had begun, and he looked out at the Saints and the novitiates seated before him. Their eyes were wide open, and they were all staring directly at him, lips parted, a long and deep, wordless chant welling from their throats. The sound wavered, sliding back and forth around itself. Mixer was mesmerized by the chanting, transfixed by the dancing strings of electricity surrounding him.

No, he was paralyzed. That's what it was. Paralyzed.

A single flash of electric blue fire arced from the wheel above him and struck one of the net nodes, stinging him. Suddenly his calm vanished, and the panic returned.

Mixer lost his breath for a moment. More flashes arced from the wheels to the net. Mixer could feel them firing along the net wires, jolting into him at the nodes, like cold, sharp needles. He twisted, pulled at the arm and wrist straps, knowing it was hopeless. *Oh fuck me*, he thought, *fuck you all!*

The wheels spun even faster, and flares of energy scattered from them, arcing into the nodes. Mixer felt a shaking in his head, like his mind was being electrocuted.

Pain skittered along his face and neck, tiny lines of it burning his skin. He hadn't expected that. Everything was going jittery inside him, his thoughts, even his vision, jumping around, flickering in and out. But he was also aware that something strange was happening to his right arm. He managed to turn his head and look at it.

His right arm—the exoskeleton, really—was twisting and straining against the straps, almost of its own accord, like a metal-sheathed snake. Mixer could just hear the high whine of the exo's motors working, shifting back and forth. The strangest thing, though, was the electricity coming from the wheels: it seemed to be focusing on his right arm and hand, on the exoskeleton, most of it now guided and pulled away from his head, funneled to and spread out along the exo. The electricity swam along the metal surface, and as the wheels continued to spin faster and pour out more energy, more of it flowed to the exoskeleton.

The pain in Mixer's head seemed to ease, but his right arm was on fire. He could see just enough to realize that now almost all the energy from the three wheels was funneling into the exo, flashing and glowing, making the metal shine and burn. *Shine and burn, shimmer and shake*, Mixer thought. Where the hell had that come from?

There was a bright, silent explosion of sorts, three of them, actually, one from each of the three spinning wheels, and the energy gouted from them like fountains. Some of it washed over his head and face, tingling his thoughts and shimmering his vision, but most poured into the exo and his right arm. He didn't notice anything different for a few seconds; then the pain blossomed in his arm and he screamed.

His arm *was* on fire. He couldn't even see it anymore, hidden by the flames of blue and white energy that surrounded it, swirling and heaving like an electric beast. This was, he realized, the moment when his mind should have been torn to pieces. Instead, it was his arm and hand.

More explosions, this time loud and bright, and Mixer screamed again, the pain in his arm unbearable, tearing him apart. His face was starting to burn now, too, the net wires burning into his skin. White and blue crashed all around him; he couldn't see anything, just wild shadows in front of him, leaping and flying. The Saints, he thought, they're going crazy. Or they're burning up along with me. Good, man. Burn, you crazy fuckers!

Then even the dancing shadows were gone, and there was nothing but painful silver-white light all around him. *I'm dying*, he thought, *I'm fucking dying*. Orange and red flared up behind his eyes, and he thought he felt his arm burned and torn away from his body. Mixer screamed one final time; his vision burst, and then he was gone.

THIRTEEN

IT WAS TIME for Carlucci to talk to the slug, and it was the last thing he wanted to do. So he set up an appointment for that night, then left the station to play pool.

When he stepped out of the buildings, he was hit by a wall of damp and heat. The clouds were thick and heavy, a sick brown-orange overhead, and he could barely tell where the sun was behind them—a pale, slightly brighter disk shimmering high above the buildings. It was going to rain soon, he was sure of that, but he had his raincoat, and he decided to walk.

A few blocks to Market, another block south, then up a few more blocks to Bricky's. "X" marks the spot, Carlucci thought to himself. The only sign anywhere was a tattered piece of cardboard in the window with the word POOL handwritten in faded black ink. The windows were so grime-coated, all Carlucci could see through them were vague, shifting lights and shadows. He pulled the door open and stepped in.

Inside was cooler and quiet. A time warp. The place probably hadn't changed in seventy-five years. Maybe even a hundred, Carlucci thought. Fifteen tables, low overhead lights above each, no other lights in the room except for a few beer signs behind the bar and a small orange-shaded lamp on

Bricky the Fifth's desk. Most of the tables were occupied, but there were a few open. Players looked at him, but no one nodded or waved or smiled. Those who knew him knew he was a cop; they accepted him, because Bricky did, but that didn't mean they'd be friendly.

Bricky the Fifth sat behind his desk smoking a cigarette, watching Carlucci. He was tall and gaunt, short hair almost hidden by the red 49ers hat he always wore. He was only about forty, but looked at least ten years older. A year ago his son, Bricky the Sixth, had been gutted with a linoleum knife in front of the pool hall, two days after his wedding. There would never be a Bricky the Seventh.

Carlucci walked over to the desk and asked Bricky for a rack. Bricky nodded without a word, pulled out a tray of balls from a shelf behind the desk, and pushed them toward Carlucci, then made a note in pencil in an old spiral notebook.

Carlucci took the balls to an open table near the front corner, went to the bar for a bottle of Budweiser, then returned to the table and racked up the balls. He spent a few minutes picking out a cue, took a long drink from the beer, then placed the cue ball on the table and stroked it into the balls.

Carlucci spent the next hour playing alone. No one stopped by the table, no one said a word to him. He wasn't very good, but he enjoyed it, and it relaxed him. When he couldn't play his horn, he liked to play pool. His session with the slug would be awful, and he needed to relax and skim out before going.

Though he was near a window, he couldn't see any more of the streets than he'd been able to see of the pool hall from outside. He could hear the rain start, though, about ten minutes after he arrived. Surprisingly, the rain got stronger as he played, and gave no signs of blowing over. There hadn't been a good long rainstorm in months. People coming in off the street dripped water, and Bricky gave them towels to dry off; he wasn't going to let his tables get wet.

Carlucci nursed his beer through the hour; it went from ice-cold to warm, but he didn't mind. As he played, bits and pieces of the cases flashed across his thoughts, but he pushed them all aside, tried not to think about Chick Roberts or anyone else. He focused all his attention on the colored balls clacking and moving smoothly across the green felt.

After an hour, Carlucci took a break from the table. He got another Budweiser, then sat on a stool by the table; he stared at the now motionless balls, listened to the rain still coming down outside, drank from the bottle, and thought about the last few days.

Three cases: Chick Roberts; the mayor's nephew, William Kashen; and Robert Butler. Or rather, three murders, and all one case. Not on the books, not in the files, not for anyone else, but all one case for Carlucci. The more time that passed after his lunch with Diane, the more convinced he became that they all *were* connected in some important way. Carlucci felt caught between them, pressed and torn in several directions at once, and what he was afraid of more than anything else, was that he was going to get fucked over by the whole mess. His career would be shot, or his life would go to shit, or he'd end up dead. The chances of coming out of this clean, he thought, were pretty fucking close to zero.

Options.

He could walk back to the station, work up a letter of resignation, effective today, and walk away from it all. He had the years, he'd come away with full pension and benefits. He'd have to go through a review, but he'd be able to lie his way through it; the committee would want to believe his lies, and they'd approve his resignation; probably they'd even drop a citation or two on him.

Carlucci didn't like that option one bit. It stank, and he would stink along with it.

He could just push forward with the nephew's case, forget he knew anything about Chick Roberts, not let the connections lead him anywhere; *avoid* the Chick Roberts case; hold back and let Hong and LaPlace drive the investigation of the other two cases, just stay out of their way. With any luck, they'd eventually dead-end, gradually pull back, and finally quit without solving them. Or somehow solve the damn things without blowing anything open, no spillover into *anything* else.

He didn't like that option much better. Too much could go wrong. And what about Paula Asgard?

Third option? He could push forward as hard as he could with everything, eyes open, knowing the whole fucking mess could blow up in his face.

Carlucci smiled to himself, shaking his head, and finished the beer. He didn't like *any* of his options. And what the hell was Tremaine's interest in all this?

He got a third beer, picked up his cue, pushed away all those thoughts again, and went back to playing pool.

It was still raining when he left Bricky's. Carlucci stood in his raincoat with his back against the pool hall windows, trying to keep out of the downpour. He had three more hours until his session with the slug, and now it was time to go see Brendan. He scanned the street, searching for a phone. Nothing on this side, but he spotted one across the street, just outside a pawnshop.

When he saw a break in the traffic, he dashed out into the rain and across the street, horns blaring at him as he juked in and out of the cars. Up the curb, across the sidewalk; then he ducked under the hood of the phone. He shook off the worst of the water, ran his card through the box, then punched in his code and Brendan's number.

Brendan answered almost immediately. "Chez Prosthetique," he said, a joke almost no one but Carlucci would understand.

"Brendan. This is Frank."

Brendan coughed, then said, "Funny, I thought you'd be calling soon."

"Can I come over?"

"Now?"

"Now."

Brendan hesitated, muffled the phone, and said something to someone else in his apartment. He came back on. "Give me fifteen minutes."

"Is it all right?"

"It's fine, Frank."

"See you in a bit, then."

"Right." Brendan hung up.

Carlucci put the phone back in the slot and looked out at the rain. If he walked, it would take about fifteen minutes, just right, but he would be drenched. Or he could stand here under the hood for ten minutes, then hope to flag down a cab or bus. Fuck it, he decided. He stepped out into the downpour and started walking.

When he reached Brendan's apartment building, Carlucci wasn't as wet as he'd expected. His raincoat had kept off the worst, and the rain had lightened up, though it had never quite stopped. Biggest rainstorm in weeks, and the gutters were flooding. Carlucci took the few steps up to the building entrance and pushed Brendan's bell. He identified himself, and Brendan buzzed him into the building.

Brendan lived on the second floor, his apartment in the back with views of the neighboring brick buildings, thick bushes, and the airwell. Carlucci knocked on the door, and Brendan pulled it open. Brendan and a young woman were standing barefoot in the front room, both wearing jeans and both naked from the waist up. A strange sight. The woman, who was probably in her thirties, was a Screamer; her lips had been fused together, and Carlucci caught a glimpse of the nasal tube in one nostril. He also couldn't help thinking that she had damn nice breasts. And of course Brendan had only an eight-inch stub protruding from his left shoulder where an arm should be.

"Frank, this is Mia. Mia, Frank."

Carlucci nodded. Mia nodded in return, then pulled a sweatshirt on over her head. She sat on the edge of a chair and buckled sandals onto her feet.

"Something to drink?" Brendan asked.

"No thanks, I've had enough."

"I haven't." Brendan padded out of the room and into the kitchen.

Carlucci took off his raincoat, looked around for someplace to hang it, but Mia got up from the chair to take it from him. She carried it down the hall and into the bathroom; Carlucci watched her hang it from the shower. "Thanks," he said when she returned. She smiled at him and nodded. At least he thought it was a smile.

Brendan came out of the kitchen with a tall glass of vodka over ice in his hand, and a towel draped over his stub. "Dry yourself off," he said. Carlucci took the towel from him and started with his hair. Mia came up to Brendan, took a deep sniff of the vodka, brushed her fused mouth against Brendan's lips. Then she nodded one more time at Carlucci and walked out of the apartment.

"Sit down," Brendan said. He carried his drink to the recliner across the room and dropped into the chair, splashing the vodka without quite spilling any. Carlucci took the only other seat in the room, a worn, overstuffed chair beside a table stacked with books; on top of one of the stacks was an old telephone. The front room had the view of the building next door: cracked brick and crumbling cement and metal grilles and shaded, glowing windows. Dusk was falling early with the clouds and the rain.

"She's a Screamer," Carlucci finally said.

"What clued you in?"

"You don't have to be sarcastic."

"You don't have to state the obvious." Brendan paused, drank deeply from the vodka; it would be the cheapest he could find. "She doesn't talk much, she doesn't smoke, and she doesn't mind fucking a gimp," Brendan concluded.

Carlucci didn't say anything. He'd had this kind of conversation with Brendan too many times, and it never went anywhere. They had known each other for twenty years, and they were still good friends of a sort, but Brendan had never been the same after he'd lost his arm. He had lost it five years earlier because of a fuck-up by his partner, Rossi, who was drunk at the time. Brendan began drinking too much himself, afterwards, and it wasn't long before his wife left him. He hadn't seen her in two or three years, hardly saw his two sons. He could have had the best artificial arm available, but he refused any kind of prosthetic, taking a perverse pride in his stump. He'd stayed on the force a while, behind a desk, and soon became a liaison to the slugs, doing most of the main interviews himself. No one liked the job, but Brendan was good at it, which was why Carlucci was here. Even that, though, hadn't lasted, and two years ago Brendan had resigned. Between disability and pension payments, he had enough money to keep himself in his cheap apartment and a steady supply of even cheaper vodka. Carlucci saw him once or twice a month. Miserable evenings, every one, but Carlucci couldn't abandon him.

"You've got a session with a slug," Brendan said.

Carlucci nodded. "I want your advice," he said. "I haven't had a session with a slug in over ten years." He shook his head. "Only had a couple, back when we were first bringing them into the department. Disasters, both of them. Then we got the liaison position going, and I've managed to avoid them ever since."

"You had people like me to do the scut work," Brendan said with a faint smile.

Carlucci nodded.

"But you can't do it this time."

"No," Carlucci said. "I need a private session."

Brendan nodded. "The mayor's nephew." It wasn't a question.

"Sort of," Carlucci said. "You up on the case?"

Brendan finished off his drink. "I'm a drunk, not an illiterate," he said. "Yes, I'm up on the case. Or as much as I can be from the news, and we both know how that is." He reached down beside his chair and brought up a half-full vodka bottle, refilled his glass. "What does 'sort of' mean?"

"There's more involved than just the mayor's nephew."

Brendan shrugged. "Robert Butler, sure. That was an easy connection to make. Partners in sleaze. I'm surprised none of the reporters have seen it yet."

"A couple have," Carlucci said. "We've killed it." He didn't see any reason to mention Tremaine's interest. "But there's more to it than Robert Butler."

"What, then?"

Carlucci shook his head. "I can't, Brendan."

Brendan studied him, sipping thoughtfully at his vodka.

"I just want your advice for dealing with the slug," Carlucci said.

Brendan remained silent, watching him. Carlucci finally looked away and stared out the window. Shadows moved behind a window shade in the building next door, two large shadows that seemed to be dancing with each other.

"Don't do it," Brendan said. Carlucci turned to look back at him, and Brendan was shaking his head. "You're roguing it, aren't you? Chasing ghosts." He continued to shake his head. "It's not worth it, Frank. Anything goes wrong, they'll bury you, they'll fucking launch you into the sun."

"It's not that simple."

"Oh fuck, it never is."

"Just help me with the slug, Brendan."

Brendan drank again from his vodka, then set it beside him.

"Shit, I know you. Frank Carlucci, bull moose, bull elephant, bull whatever. Bullshit. I can't talk you out of it, can I?"

"Nothing's decided yet," Carlucci told him.

Brendan smiled. "That's what you say. Hell, might even be what you think." He breathed deeply once, and the smile disappeared. "All right, Frank. I can't help you much, but what I can . . . Which slug you seeing?"

"Monk. He was the first slug put on the case."

Brendan nodded. "Good. He's one of the best."

"What do you mean?"

"Jesus, Frank, you too? Man, everyone thinks the slugs are all the same, a bunch of freaks who mainline all that brain juice and sit around all day doing nothing but think. I mean, yeah, that's what they are, but they're not interchangeable. Some are better than others. Monk is fucking acute. He makes intuitive leaps that are just incredible. Sometimes they're insane leaps that are dead wrong. Most times, though, he's razored right in on it, and you have no idea how the hell he got there." He paused. "When's the session?"

"Tonight." Carlucci was fascinated, listening to Brendan. He hadn't noticed so much excitement and life in the man in months. Years.

"All right," Brendan said. "First thing you want to do is cancel the session, reschedule it for tomorrow. Or better yet, if time isn't that critical, wait a few days."

"Why?"

"Monk'll be pushing to get everything he can and be ready for you with his best analysis. Cramming himself full of every bit of information he can scrounge up. An extra push for the scheduled session. Which is good. But if you cancel and reschedule, he'll have a day or two free of pressure to swim around in all that info, maybe pull in a little something extra from here or there. Time to allow other possibilities to emerge, different connections to make themselves known. A chance for Monk's real strengths to manifest. Trust me, it's the smartest thing you can do."

Carlucci nodded. "All right. That's why I'm here. What else?"

Brendan shrugged. "It's hard, Frank. When you actually get in there and start talking to him, there's no formula, you just have to go with your gut. But don't try to guide Monk. Let him take you where *he's* going. That's what he's there for. Don't be surprised if his questions and replies don't seem to track. They don't, at first, if ever, because he'll be jumping all over the place, and you won't have any idea how he's getting from one thing to another. Just go with it."

He paused, looking at his drink, but didn't pick it up. He turned to Carlucci. "One last thing, Frank. Don't expect any pat answers. You may get answers that don't seem to mean anything at all. He might give you some names, or places, or just a few phrases that don't make sense. It won't do you any good to ask Monk to explain them, because he won't know what they mean, either. The intuitive leaps I was talking about. He'll give you as much explanation as he can. You'll just have to follow up whatever he gives you, fucking run it down, and hope it pays off." He shrugged. "With Monk, it probably will. It may not be what you want, it may not go where you want to go, but it'll take you to the heart of things." One final shrug. "That's all the advice I can give you, Frank. It's not much, but there it is. You'll do fine."

Carlucci nodded, thinking Brendan should still be on the force, working with the slugs, doing *something* with his life besides drinking it away. "Thanks, Brendan. I appreciate it." He stood. "I should get going."

"Wait," Brendan said. His expression fell. "Don't go yet, Frank." He pointed at the telephone beside Carlucci. "Call the station and cancel the session. Then stick around, have a drink with me. Just a little while."

Carlucci stood looking at Brendan for a few moments. Another drink wasn't what either of them needed. Christ. He finally nodded. ''All right, Brendan. For a little while.'' He sat down again and picked up the phone.

FOURTEEN

THREE NIGHTS, AND nothing. Paula was exhausted, but she couldn't stop. She'd canceled one gig with the Black Angels, and she'd left the theater early last night and tonight. She wasn't sure how much longer she could keep this up. Amy had helped her when she could, but most of the time Paula had been on her own, skimming the streets of the Tenderloin at night, searching for Mixer.

She was halfway through night four and doing no better; what little hope remained was fading rapidly. She had strayed a few blocks into the Asian Quarter for a break, and now stood in front of one of her old haunts, Misha's Donuts and Espresso. Amy was supposed to meet her here at two. Paula punched the door aside and walked in.

Misha's hadn't changed. Haunting metallic echoes and tones washed through the room from the sound system—"ambient industrial," Misha called it. Ion poles sparked among the tables; booths around the edges were on platforms about four feet above the floor. Plasma tubes provided the lighting, deep reds and oranges glowing and flowing through them.

The place was nearly full. Paula worked her way to the counter, picked out two sour-cream-filled donuts, got a large black coffee, and sat at a small empty table set between an ion pole and a metallic stick tree. Sparks from the ion pole jumped across the table to the tips of the tree branches. The ion pole activity was supposed to make her feel better. It didn't.

She had taken only two bites from the first donut and a sip from the coffee when Jenny Woo slid onto the chair across the table from her, banging her elbows onto the tabletop. Her long, straight black hair was woven through with silver metal strands, which caught some of the sparks from the ion pole.

"Hey, Asgard." Jenny Woo flashed a split-second smile, but her expression was hard.

"Hello, Jenny." They didn't like each other at all, and neither tried to hide it. Jenny and Chick had had a brief but intense affair about a year ago, which ended when Chick got hit by another of his periodic bouts of impotence. All of Chick's affairs ended in impotence. Karma. Paula almost smiled, thinking about it.

"Why is it," Jenny Woo asked, "that I keep seeing you lately? Three, four times the last few days. You following me, dinko?"

"Why would I be following you?" Paula had seen Jenny a couple of times herself, and had assumed Jenny was following *her.* She pushed the plate toward Jenny. "Have a donut."

Jenny Woo leaned back in her chair. "What I asked myself," she said. "I come up with only one answer, and I don't like it. Chick."

"Chick."

"Yeah." Another flashing smile. "You know. The *dead* guy."

"I see you're torn up about it," Paula said.

"He was a good fuck, until he couldn't. After that, he wasn't good for anything." She raised a single eyebrow at Paula. "Which is what got him killed, really."

Jenny leaned forward, and Paula could see she was about to say something else, when Amy came up to the table.

"Hey," Amy said. "Am I interrupting anything?"

"Yes," Jenny Woo said. "Come back in five minutes."

Amy glanced at Paula, then turned back to Jenny Woo. "I know you, don't I?"

"Not like you think you do," Jenny said.

"And I don't like you," Amy concluded.

"No, you don't." Jenny smiled again, this time holding it for several beats. "Now flash, and leave us alone for five minutes, like I said."

When Amy looked at her, Paula nodded. Amy shoved her hands into her jeans pockets, then walked away.

"She with you on this?" Jenny asked.

"There is no 'this,' "Paula said. "She's helping me look for someone. It's got nothing to do with you or Chick."

Jenny Woo leaned forward again. When she spoke, her voice was quiet but firm. "Chick was an ambitious little shit who thought he had a lot more shine than he did. He didn't know his limitations. He didn't understand how dark things were until someone put a few holes in his head. Too late, then." Jenny shook her head. "Don't make the same mistake, Asgard. Leave it. Chick's dead, you can't change that, and getting dead yourself won't help anyone." She stood up. "I don't want to see you again."

Paula pretty much felt the same, but she didn't say anything. Jenny Woo started to turn away, then quickly swung back to face Paula.

"You *are* looking for someone," Jenny said. "Mixer. The trial of Saint Katherine, that frigid bitch."

"You know something," Paula said, trying to keep the desperation out of her voice.

"Oh yes," Jenny Woo said. "I know something."

"What?"

Jenny Woo shook her head, this time with the first genuine smile Paula had seen on her face. A nasty smile. "I never give information away, sweetheart. There's always a price. And there's not a thing you've got that I want." She paused, still smiling. "I like it this way, knowing that you *don't* know."

Paula wanted to get up and strangle Jenny Woo, or smash a chair over her head. She remained seated, silent. Karma would get Jenny Woo one day, she told herself. Except Paula didn't really believe in Karma. How could she, in this god-damn world?

"Goodbye, Asgard." Jenny was still smiling. She turned and marched away, pushing out the door and onto the street.

Paula sat without moving, staring at her coffee and donuts. No fantasies of Jenny Woo coming back and telling her what she knew about Mixer, no fucking chance of that. Shit. Paula just didn't know what to do.

Amy reappeared in front of her. Paula had forgotten. Amy sat in the chair, frowning. "Jenny Woo, right?"

Paula nodded.

"You know what she does?" Amy asked. "What she boot-legs?"

Paula nodded again. "Yeah, I know. Body-bags. Chick was in on it, too." She paused. "So was Mixer, at the 'retail' end." She shook her head.

"Great," said Amy. "And you're killing yourself looking for him."

Paula shrugged. "What can I do? He's my friend." She sighed. "Jenny Woo said she knew something about Mixer, about the trial. She refused to say what."

"I've heard something, too."

"You have?" Paula felt a tightening inside her chest. "What?"

"Nothing too specific. A contact on the nets says something went wrong with the trial. He didn't know what happened, didn't know if Mixer was alive or dead or what. The Saints are trying to keep a lid on, but he got the impression there was going to be some kind of public announcement in a day or two. And they never, *never* go public about their trials."

"Jesus," Paula said. "Is that good or bad?"

"No idea," said Amy, shaking her head. "But it probably isn't any worse than what we've been looking at."

Amy was right. They'd been expecting to find Mixer dead or completely wrecked, and there wasn't much that could be worse than that. "Worth hitting the streets again," Paula said.

"Maybe so," Amy replied. "But you're on your own tonight. I've got other business. Only reason I came down here was to tell you what I'd heard."

"Thanks, Amy. You've been a wonder, really."

Amy smiled, then said, "You know, chances are still shit for finding him, even if something good's happened. You haven't heard from him, which probably means they've still got him wrapped up, even if he isn't dead. They just might be gearing up to run through the trial again. Or, hell, who knows what else? Don't expect too much."

"I know, Amy, but I've got to have a little hope. I was just about down to none, and I can't keep going without it."

"Yeah." Amy stood. "I've gotta go. Luck to you, Paula."

"Thanks."

Amy left, and Paula watched her walk out of Misha's. She felt better than she had in days. She pulled the donuts back and reached for the coffee. A good shot of caffeine and a couple solid hits of carbos and she'd be ready to go back out onto the streets.

By dawn, what little new hope had pumped through Paula was pretty much shot. Exhaustion, she told herself—too many days without enough sleep. She felt like shit again.

She dropped onto an old concrete bench across the street from a shock shop. If she let herself, she could fall asleep here, become ripe meat for the street scavs. People moved all around her, and she closed her eyes, tried to imagine herself being ripped apart. Then she sensed someone sit beside her on the bench.

"Hello, Paula."

Paula opened her eyes to see Tremaine sitting next to her. The rising sun reflected off the shock shop window across the street, then off the left lens of Tremaine's glasses, obscuring his eye.

"You've been following me," she said.

"No," Tremaine replied, shaking his head. The shimmer of reflection shifted from one lens to the other and back again. "Or rather, yes, but only the last few minutes. I was in the Asian Quarter, on the edge, and I saw you sort of drifting back and forth between the Asian and Euro. You seemed lost. Wiped." He paused. "You know, Paula, you look terrible."

"Thanks a lot."

"Well, you do."

"Yeah. I *feel* terrible. Lack of sleep and food will do that to you." She shrugged. "I've been looking for someone."

"Mixer?"

A shot of fear sliced through her. "How did you know?"

"I was there, remember? At The Final Transit when your friend came in and said something about Mixer and Saint Katherine."

Paula looked askance at him. "You have a damn good memory."

"It helps in my business."

"Yeah, you're right." She turned away and looked at the shock shop. An old woman in heavy, flowing robes was closing up. Jesus, Paula thought, she must be roasting in those robes. Things had cooled down some with yesterday's rainstorm, but it was still warm, even this early in the morning. "Yes," she finally said, still not looking at Tremaine, "I've been looking for Mixer."

"You haven't found him."

"No."

"A close friend?"

"Yes."

"How close?"

Paula heard something familiar in his voice, and she turned to look at him. "Not that kind of friend. But a *close* friend."

Tremaine nodded.

"Chick Roberts was the one who was that kind of friend."

"I know," Tremaine said. His expression seemed to convey a real sympathy, which surprised her for some reason.

"Aren't you going to ask me again about him being killed?" Paula said.

Tremaine shook his head.

They sat without speaking for two or three minutes, watching the sun come up orange and crimson between the buildings, its outline shimmering through the haze.

"Let me take you home," Tremaine finally said.

"What do you mean?"

"I've got a car outside the Tenderloin. Just a few blocks away, a short walk." He paused. "You look like you could do with some sleep."

Paula looked at him, still trying to decide what kind of person he was. She didn't know yet, she just didn't know. But she nodded anyway. "Sure," she said. "Take me home. Why the hell not?"

The old Plymouth ground to a stop in front of her apartment building.

"Thanks for the ride," Paula said.

"Sure," Tremaine said. He put his hand on her shoulder. "You *are* exhausted. Get some sleep." He took his hand away.

"I will." Paula had been half expecting Tremaine to invite himself up to her apartment, and she'd been dreading having to tell him to fuck off, but now it didn't look like he was going to do that.

"Let me buy you dinner tonight," Tremaine said. "You could probably use a good meal, too."

"Yeah, probably I could." She shook her head. "But I just might sleep through the night as well." There was something about this guy, something she liked. She smiled at him. "Make it tomorrow?"

"Sure. Tomorrow it is."

"Call me," Paula said. "I'm sure you know my number."

Tremaine nodded, and Paula got out of the car. She closed the door and stood on the sidewalk, watching as Tremaine and the old Plymouth pulled away from the curb, surprisingly sorry to see him go.

FIFTEEN

CARLUCCI HAD ARRANGED to meet Paula at noon by the Civic Center pond, a large oval four feet deep at its center, the water covered by a thick layer of green and brown muck. She was waiting for him when he arrived, pacing at the water's edge; after the morning rain, the overflow channels were draining slowly toward the streets, and she stepped over them as she paced back and forth.

As he approached, she saw him and stopped pacing. The skin beneath her eyes was dark and puffy, and the rest of her face was pale. For the first time since he'd met her, she looked her age, maybe even a little older.

"Hello, Paula," he said, putting out his hand.

"Hello, Lieutenant." She shook his hand, her grip firm in spite of the way she looked.

"Come on," Carlucci said. "Call me Frank."

"Okay. Frank."

"You look terrible."

She half smiled. "People keep telling me that. Think there's something to it?"

"Want something to eat?" he asked, gesturing at a cart nearby selling sausages and giant pretzels.

"God, no." Paula shook her head. "Coffee, though, I could use."

Carlucci nodded. There were a couple of coffee carts on the other side of the pond. "I'll buy," he said. "How do you want it?"

"Black," said Paula. "As black as you can get it."

Carlucci walked along the edge of the pond, stepping across the overflow channels, rolling up his shirt sleeves as he went. The heat was stifling again, as if they were back in July or August. Where the hell was fall?

He bought two large coffees from the girl running one of the carts; she couldn't have been more than thirteen, and she was pregnant. Carlucci gave her a tip that was double the price of the coffee.

When he got back to Paula, he handed her one of the coffees and they stood together sipping at them, gazing out at the muck-covered pond. Something heaved under the muck, out near the middle, and Paula laughed.

"I wonder what lives in there," she said. "I think everyone's afraid to clean off the crap and find out."

"Fish, or snakes," Carlucci suggested. "Turtles, maybe."

"Mutant alligators," Paula said. She looked at him. "I'm glad you called. I wanted to talk to you, but I didn't think calling your office was a good idea."

"I didn't give you my home number?" When Paula shook her head, Carlucci frowned. "Sorry. I should have. I thought I had."

"Why *did* you call?" Paula asked.

"I need to tell you some things." Carlucci hesitated, staring down into his coffee. "It's an incredible mess. It's not just Chick's murder anymore. There's a lot more involved."

"Like what?"

Carlucci shook his head. "Christ, I don't know. I mean, I know some of it, but I don't know what I should be telling you. Too much firepower, too damn many things that could blow up in my face."

"Are you dropping it?" Paula asked.

"No. I half wish I was, but no." He looked out at the pond and drank from his coffee. "There's no more screwing around. What I've done up to now has been pretty much risk-free, checking into a few things here and there. I've found a lot, but none of it good." He shook his head again and looked back at Paula. "Nothing's going to be risk-free any longer. Not for me, not for you. You've got to know that."

"But you're not going to tell me what's involved."

"I don't know. I keep thinking it's better for both of us if I'm the only one who knows." Damage control, Carlucci thought, if everything goes to shit on me. But he didn't say it.

"Look, that's up to you," Paula said. "But I'm not sure I can help much if I don't know what the hell's going on."

"I know. I'll think about it." He paused. "What I really need now is to talk to Mixer."

Paula gave a choked laugh. "Good luck."

"What is it?"

She slowly shook her head. "I've been looking for him for days."

"Why?"

"You know who the Saints are?"

"I've heard of them," Carlucci said. "Some women in the Tenderloin, they take on the names of old Saints, right? Most of what I've heard sounds a little crazy."

Paula gave him something like a smile. "Then most of what you've heard is probably true." The smile faded. "They take people off the street and put them on trial. 'Trial' meaning some kind of torture like the historical saints were put through." She paused, breathing deeply. "About a week ago they picked up Mixer. Saint Katherine was to put him on trial a few days ago." She turned away from him. "The survivors of Saint Katherine's trials end up with scrambled eggs for brains. I look like shit because I've been spending nights in the Tenderloin looking for him, hoping I could find what's left of the bastard before the scavengers pick him clean."

"No sign of him?" Carlucci asked.

"No," Paula said. "A friend told me last night that she'd heard something went wrong with the trial, but nobody knows *what*. No one knows what happened—if he's dead, if he's still alive, if he's fucked up, nothing." She looked back at Carlucci. "I've got a little hope, but not much. I wouldn't count on him for anything, if I were you."

"You think there's any connection between Chick's death and the Saints picking up Mixer?"

"I doubt it. The Saints live in another world, and I don't think it's got much in common with ours. They don't do anything for anyone but themselves."

"Is there anything I can do?"

"What do *you* think?" Paula said. Then, "Sorry." She drank the rest of her coffee and walked over to a trash can on the sidewalk. The can was overflowing, and Carlucci watched her standing in front of it, crumpling the cup in her hand, squeezing it over and over. Finally she shoved the crushed cup into the other trash, wiped her hands on her jeans, and walked back.

"Something else I need to tell you," she said. "One of the names I gave you last week. Jenny Woo."

"Yes."

"Something there, I think. She's worth an extra look. She thought I was following her, and she warned me off. Told me getting dead like Chick wasn't going to do anyone any good." She paused for a moment, then went on. "She and Chick were bootlegging body-bags. Anyway, she gave me the impression she knew exactly why Chick had been killed."

"All right," Carlucci said. "Anything like that will help." He took a business card from his wallet, jotted down his home number, and handed the card to Paula. "Any time, day or night, you need to call me, do it, all right?"

Paula stuck the card in her back pocket and nodded. "One other thing," she said. "You know who Tremaine is?"

Carlucci nodded, his gut tightening.

"He's poking around in this. He came to see me, wanted to talk to me about Chick."

"What did you tell him?"

"Nothing. What *should* I tell him?"

Carlucci shrugged. "I don't know if it really matters. That guy, if he's got a story, and puts it all together, nothing will keep him from sending it out over the nets."

Neither of them said anything for a few moments. Then Paula sighed heavily. "I've gotta go," she said.

"Mixer . . ." Carlucci started, but he didn't finish. She knew better. "Let me know if you find him."

Paula nodded again, then turned and walked away without another word. Carlucci watched her cross the plaza, hands jammed into her pockets, head down. She turned a corner and was gone.

Tremaine. I should talk to him, Carlucci thought. He probably knows more about what's going on than anyone.

Carlucci looked into his coffee cup, which was still half full. His stomach rebelled at the thought of any more coffee right now. He stepped to the edge of the pond and poured out what was left in the cup. *Drink up*, he said silently to whatever was living beneath the muck. *Drink up*.

Carlucci stood at the mouth of an alley across from the outer edge of the Tenderloin. One more meeting before returning to the station. He checked his watch. Fifteen minutes before Sparks was supposed to be there. Just about right. Sparks would be early.

He hesitated before entering the narrow passageway. The sun had broken through the clouds and haze and glared down on him; sweat dripped down his neck, rolled down his sides under his shirt. Steam rose from the alley floor where the sun sliced in. Sometimes, like now, Carlucci wished he still carried a gun. At least it wasn't nighttime.

He started into the alley. His first few steps were through the rising steam, but he was soon past it and into shadow, his shoes splashing through shallow rain puddles. Above him hung fire escapes and huge sprays of flowering bromeliads; water dripped on him, almost like rain.

Halfway along the alley, on the right, were two concrete steps leading up to a metal door. Carlucci climbed the steps and pushed open the door, which swung inward with an echoing screech. He stepped inside and closed the door behind him.

He had expected darkness, but dappled light came in through broken windows and large cracks in the walls, strangely illuminating the huge, empty, high-ceilinged room. An old machine shop or storage facility, Carlucci guessed. Cooler than outside, a welcome relief. The floor was a mix of broken concrete and dirt, scattered with wood and metal debris. A dark, open doorway broke the solid interior wall across from him, and Carlucci stood in the cool shadows, listening and watching the doorway.

A minute or two later, he heard a harsh coughing, and Sparks appeared in the doorway. Sparks stopped for a moment, blinking, then came into the room. He coughed again, shaking his head. Sparks was tall and gaunt, his eyes dark, his cheeks hollow; a slice of light from outside cut across his neck, revealing the jagged lines of needle marks. Dermal patches were everywhere on the streets, but some people still needed those needles, straight shots to the veins, the heart.

"Carlucci," Sparks said. "You're early."

"So are you."

Sparks smiled. "Have you got anything for me?"

Carlucci worked his way across the rubble until he was just a foot or two from Sparks. Sparks was younger than Carlucci, but looked much older. He'd been a hot-shot demon once, freelancing for the cops in addition to several big corporations, hacking his way through life and getting rich, until one night his nervous system had taken a huge hit from a defective black-market head juicer. His career as a demon was over. His life was over. His career as a junkie had just begun.

Carlucci took a small wad of bills from his pocket and handed it to Sparks. "More later, if you can get me some whisper."

Sparks pocketed the money, then broke into a long coughing fit, doubling over for a minute or two before it eased. He straightened, coughed a few more times, then sighed heavily. "I'm dying," he said.

"I know," Carlucci replied.

"Can you get me into a hospice?" Sparks asked.

"I don't know." Carlucci turned away, unable to maintain eye contact. "I'll try, Sparks." He turned back to face the old junkie. Not that old, really, but old for a needle freak. "I'll try."

Sparks nodded, then said, "What do you want?"

"Chick Roberts." Carlucci paused for a few seconds as Sparks closed his eyes, locking in the name, then opened them again. "Jenny Woo." Another pause, Sparks's eyes closing, opening. "William Kashen." One final pause. "Robert Butler." Carlucci stopped, trying to decide whether to throw in Mixer. He wasn't completely sure where Mixer fit in, and he was afraid of complicating things. Gut feeling said to leave it there, so he did. "How are they connected?" he finished up.

Sparks made a sound that might have been a laugh. "Three of them are dead." Another cough. "Yeah, I'll see what I can come up with. I'll be in touch." He started to turn, then shifted back around, looking at Carlucci with his head cocked. "There's something to do with New Hong Kong in all this," he said.

Without another word, Sparks turned and walked back

through the doorway. Carlucci remained where he was, feeling that their conversation, their meeting, whatever it was, wasn't quite finished. But Sparks was gone, and there was nothing more to say.

Carlucci walked back across the room, opened the door, and stepped out into the alley. The heat struck him hard, and he was dizzy for a moment. The plants overhead dripped steadily on him. Fuck this city, Carlucci said to himself. He took the two steps to the alley floor, turned, and headed for the street.

Amy was sitting on the steps of Paula's apartment building, head back against the brick, eyes shaded by pixie-specs. Paula's stomach dropped and turned in on itself when she saw her. She walked up the steps, and Amy stood.

"Have you heard something?" Paula asked.

Amy nodded. "The Saints made an announcement on the local net." She took a piece of paper from her jeans pocket. " 'A pilgrim who took the name Mixer was put to Saint Katherine's Trial,' " she read. " 'The trial was a glorious event, producing holy immolation never before seen in the trials. Clearly, Mixer was a chosen, a prophet, whose dying cries provided profound revelations to the gathered Saints and witnesses. He passed the trial superbly, in spirit if not in flesh, and will be remembered as a glorious martyr in the family of Saints.' " She stopped, looked up at Paula. "That's it."

"He's dead." Paula looked down at the piece of paper in Amy's hand. "Mixer's dead."

Amy nodded, but didn't speak.

Paula could hardly move, could hardly breathe. She turned her head slowly, squinted against the glare of the sun that seemed so hot and huge in the sky. The street and buildings were bleached out all around her. She turned back to Amy.

"I'm tired," she said. "I'm going to lie down for a while."

Amy nodded. "I'm sorry."

Paula gestured at the piece of paper in Amy's hand. "Can I have that?"

"Yeah, sure."

Paula took the sheet from Amy, folded it carefully, and tucked it into her pocket, next to the gravity knife. "Thanks." She went to the building door, unlocked it, and stepped inside.

Several hours later, Paula climbed the stairs of her apartment building again, Tremaine just behind her. Her legs felt heavy, her breath was short and halting. Even her sense of hearing seemed to go in and out—one moment their footsteps were loud and echoing in the stairwell, Tremaine's breathing clear and close, and the next a swirling filled her ears and she could hear nothing at all.

Tremaine was coming up to her apartment, and she knew where it all was headed, and she was half certain it was a terrible idea. She had no one to blame but herself.

They'd eaten dinner at Mai's, good food and even better wine—an expensive bottle of Chardonnay bought by Tremaine. A long, relaxing meal, followed by coffee and mint ice cream, then a walk through the noise and energy of the Polk Corridor. The sexual tension was strong, almost suffocating, and it was crazy to try to deny it was there. She didn't tell him about Mixer. She wasn't sure why.

Tremaine had suggested going somewhere for a drink, and Paula had said, Why not my apartment? It was quiet, they could be alone, talk, have some peace. You sure? Tremaine had asked. She hadn't been, but she'd said yes anyway, her heart pounding against her ribs.

And now, here they were, at her door. Paula unlocked the dead bolt, stuck another key in the main lock, punched in her security code, then turned the key. The lock clicked and she pushed open the door. The only light on in the apartment was a small fluorescent over the kitchen sink. Paula brushed her hand along the wall and turned on the overheads, which lit up the large room that served as kitchen and entry. She held the door wide, and Tremaine followed her in.

The kitchen half of the front room looked normal, with table and chairs, stove and refrigerator, but the other half was a mess, stacks and piles of boxes and bags and crates, all the stuff she'd kept from Chick's apartment—tapes, discs, books, sound system, video sets and cameras, recording and mixing equipment, his guitars. Paula stood staring at it for a long time, hardly aware of Tremaine beside her, noticing it all for the first time in days. Ever since she'd moved it here in Nikky's van, she'd been able to ignore it. Now, having invited Tremaine into the apartment, knowing what was going to happen, she felt like Chick's things were everywhere, overwhelming the place.

"What's wrong?" Tremaine asked.

Paula shook her head. "All this." She waved at it, afraid it was going to move and grow. "Chick. All this stuff is his. I haven't been able to do anything with it." And there was Mixer, too, dead like Chick, but again she didn't mention him.

There was a long silence, and Paula continued to stare at the clutter, not moving. She didn't know what to do or say.

"Do you want me to leave?" Tremaine asked.

Paula turned to look at him. He would, she realized. If she asked him to, he would turn around and walk out. "No," she said. "No." Her heart was beating harder again; she could feel it in her throat. "Stay."

Tremaine nodded, reached out and lightly brushed her cheek.

Still unsure, feeling sick to her stomach, Paula led Tremaine into the dark bedroom.

Shadows and dim light, the smell of sawdust and sweat. Tremaine's weight above her, his body slick and heavy, dipping and thrusting. Paula wanted to push him away, wanted to scramble out of bed, wanted to cry. She could not stop thinking of Chick.

Tremaine was warm, gentle, caring with her, but it didn't matter. It was a mistake, Paula thought, a terrible mistake, and it was way too late.

She saw Chick sitting by the open bedroom window, smoking a cigarette, blowing the smoke out into the night. She saw him sitting at the kitchen table, barefoot, wearing blue jeans and shirtless, drinking coffee, smiling at her. She saw him onstage beside her, wailing away at his guitar, hair sticky with sweat. And she felt his mouth on hers, his lips and tongue and fingers on her skin and inside her.

Paula squeezed her eyes shut, fighting back the tears, and held onto Tremaine with everything she had.

Paula woke, feeling strangely groggy. It was still dark. She was alone in bed. Had Tremaine gone? She glanced at the tiny glowing clock face next to the bed. Three-thirty. Would he have left without saying anything?

The apartment was quiet, but not silent, and she thought she heard faint sounds—tinkling, a click, a slight scraping. She was too exhausted to get up, and she was only half awake. She turned over, the bed creaking, and faced the wall. Was she even half awake? Paula put her hand out and pressed it against the wall. What did that prove? Where was Tremaine?

Time seemed strange, stretching out and closing in, spotted with fragmented dream images. Chick was dead, and now Mixer was, too. Then she heard the toilet flush, and the present seemed to lock back into focus. A few moments later she felt Tremaine get back into bed, settle in.

"Are you awake?" he whispered.

"No," she answered. She felt his arm wrap slowly around her, holding her. She closed her eyes and drifted back into sleep, unsure whether things were somehow all right, or were terribly wrong.

PART THREE

SIXTEEN

CARLUCCI SAT WITH Andrea and Christina on the back deck in the fragmented shade of a tattered umbrella. Christina had cooked breakfast for them and they'd eaten outside, and now they were drinking coffee and talking. It was rare that all three of them had a free day together. Gazing out over the lush, overgrown garden, Carlucci thought of how he needed to get out there and do some weeding and pruning; and there was his appointment tonight with the slug. But for now he intended to do nothing but sit and talk and enjoy the company of his family.

There was a thump and scrabbling at the fence, and Tuff's face appeared, golden eyes wide. As he perched atop the fence, he seemed unsteady. Christina got up, hurried to the fence and picked him up, cradling him in her arms and bringing him back to the deck. "Poor guy," she said, sitting down and holding him on her lap.

"Why?" Carlucci asked. "What's wrong?"

"Didn't I tell you? I was talking to Harry, and he said Tuff was having kidney failure." She shrugged, holding Tuff closer. "He's just getting old." She pressed her face against the gray cat's face, and Tuff tried half-heartedly to squirm away.

Carlucci felt bad for the old guy, and he found himself almost unconsciously reaching out and taking Andrea's hand in his; he was thinking of Caroline again, who would never have the chance to grow old.

Andrea smiled at him and squeezed his hand. Then, their thoughts running on similar tracks, she said, "I forgot to tell you. Caroline called last night, and she's coming over for dinner next weekend."

Carlucci returned Andrea's squeeze, smiled, and said, "Good. I wish we could see her more." Meaning more than one thing. He turned and stared at Christina, a terrible ache going through him—grief for Caroline and fear for Christina, fear of something taking her away as well.

The side gate squealed, and a few moments later McCuller came around the corner of the house. Carlucci wanted to tell McCuller to get the fuck out of his yard. He didn't want the man in his house, his yard, even his neighborhood.

McCuller approached the deck, smiling and looking too damn comfortable in his expensive suit. "I tried the front door," he said, "but there was no answer." He shrugged. "On the off chance, I came around."

"Lucky us," Carlucci said.

McCuller's smile tightened briefly, but he turned to Andrea and softened it. "Good morning, Andrea, good to see you again. Sorry to intrude."

Andrea forced a smile. "Hello, Marcus."

"Christina," McCuller said, turning to the young woman.

Christina nodded, but didn't say anything, didn't attempt to smile. She just held Tuff closer to her, as if trying to protect him.

McCuller turned back to Carlucci, no longer smiling. "Be ready at seven o'clock this evening. A car will be here to take you to a meeting."

Carlucci shook his head. "I have a session scheduled with a slug tonight."

"Cancel it. Your meeting's with the mayor. His personal car and driver will pick you up and take you to his house." McCuller put his right hand in his pocket, fingers of his left hand flexing. "Quite a privilege."

"Sounds more like a commandment," Carlucci said.

"If you choose to look at it that way."

"Why are you here, Captain? Why not just call?"

"The mayor asked me to make sure you got the message personally. This meeting is important to him, and he didn't want any . . . miscommunications."

"All right," Carlucci said. "I've received the message. I'll be ready."

McCuller seemed ready to say something else. But he shook his head, as though whatever he had in mind was pointless. Then, "I'll see you, Frank. Andrea, Christina." Without waiting for a response from any of them, he turned and walked away, around the corner and out of sight, the side gate squealing once more, rattling shut.

Carlucci stared at the spot where McCuller had stood, trying to ease the tension in his neck and head.

"Frank?" Andrea said. "Frank, he's gone."

Yeah, he thought, but it was too late. The man had soured his day, and Carlucci knew that no matter how hard he tried, it would stay that way.

At seven that evening, Carlucci stood on the sidewalk in front of his house, waiting for the mayor's car. He waved to Harry and Frances, who were sitting on their front porch next door in the last of the sun, drinking iced drinks, Tuff at their feet. It was hot and muggy, and Carlucci was already uncomfortable in the suit and tie Andrea had insisted he wear.

Shit, he said to himself, seeing the large, dark gray limo come around the corner. He didn't need this. What the hell would Harry and Frances think? The limousine pulled in to the curb, and before the driver could get all the way out, Carlucci was at the rear door and opening it for himself. He got in and quickly closed the door. The driver got back behind the wheel, closed his own door, and pulled the limo out into the street without a word.

The air inside the limousine was uncomfortably cold and dry, and Carlucci tried to open the tinted windows, but none of the controls worked. He did not want to ask the mayor's driver for anything. The guy probably earned twice what Carlucci did.

The journey was silent, seemed almost motionless at times, and Carlucci felt cut off from the world. No wonder the mayor didn't have a clue, traveling through the city like this, and living up on Telegraph. Or maybe the man knew exactly what he was cutting himself off from. Carlucci wondered if the mayor ever looked out the windows of the limo and watched the city go past him.

Carlucci did. Crossing the Panhandle, he looked out on the mass of tents and shacks erected on what had once been open park land; smoke rose from open fires, and shadows of people moved across the dwellings, stretched and flickered on fabric, wood, metal. Further on, they passed the fenced-in enclave of the University of San Francisco; through the chain-link Carlucci could see the outlines of the bunkers.

They drove through the Japan Center, heading north, passing between shiny, brightly lit buildings and glass-covered walkways, colorfully dressed men and women walking in complete security. They continued northward, avoiding the Tenderloin, then finally cut through Russian Hill, headed toward Telegraph. Crossing Columbus, they had to work slowly past a series of police barricades surrounding a block of burning buildings. Something heavy and hard crashed against the side window, but the glass didn't break, didn't show even a hint of damage, and the driver kept on as if nothing had occurred.

At the base of Telegraph Hill, they passed through a heavily fortified checkpoint, then started up the steep, winding road.

At the top, just below the ruins of Coit Tower, the driver turned into a long drive as a metal gate swung out of the way and quickly closed behind them. As soon as the limo came to a stop, Carlucci opened the rear door, but this time the driver didn't even try to get out of the car.

Mayor Terrance Kashen's house didn't stand out from those surrounding it, but then all the houses, condos, and apartments on Telegraph were worth small fortunes, especially those here at the summit, built on what used to be public park land. In the growing twilight, Carlucci could see the shimmering glow of a Kronenhauer Field surrounding the house and grounds. But he couldn't see much of the house itself from the drive—most of the structure extended out from the hillside, facing north and slightly west, with what he imagined must be stunning views. Maybe even of the sunset, which was now blazing the sky and clouds with bright crimson and orange streaks, though the sun itself was no longer visible.

The front door opened and Mayor Terrance Kashen appeared, wearing both a smile and a dark silk suit with apparent ease. Carlucci walked up the stone path and shook the mayor's outstretched hand.

"Thanks for coming, Frank." The mayor stepped back to let Carlucci into the house.

"I didn't have much choice, did I?"

Kashen's smile broadened, and he closed the door. They were in a glass-walled, glass-floored entry, a pale creamy light diffusing from the glass. "There's always a choice," the mayor said. "It's just a matter of consequences."

He led the way from the entry, passing through a shimmering curtain of metallic fabric, then over a footbridge crossing a brook that flowed out of the right wall and into the left. Then they were in the main room: huge and jutting out over the hillside, three walls of glass, with the view every bit as spectacular as Carlucci had expected: Alcatraz, with its flame towers ablaze, directly in front of them; stretching away to the north, far on the left, the Golden Gate Bridge, spans alight, orange flickers in the deepening twilight. As they approached the windows, the city itself appeared below them, glittering silver and gold and red. More lights bobbed out on the bay—private security cutters circling two large luxury yachts. The last remnants of the sunset lit the western sky with wide slashes of deep purple and crimson.

Kashen gestured toward one of two small leather couches that faced one another, next to the main window. "Have a seat, Frank." Carlucci sat, just back from the window, with the full view of the city below and facing the Golden Gate. Kashen remained standing. "Can I get you something to drink?"

Carlucci shook his head. Drinking with the mayor didn't seem like a good idea. The mayor nodded once in return, then sat on the other sofa, facing Carlucci. He settled back, crossing his legs.

"I'm told you're a good cop," Kashen said. "One of the best we've got." He paused. "An honest cop."

"Is that good or bad?" Carlucci asked.

The mayor smiled. "I'm also told you're insubordinate. Would that be true, do you think?"

Carlucci shrugged. "I just try to balance out those who spend too much time on their knees."

Kashen hesitated a few moments, then said, "Like Captain McCuller?"

Carlucci didn't respond. He wasn't going to get drawn in that deep.

"Well," the mayor said. "There's something to be said for both kinds of people. The world needs both kinds."

"I don't think so," Carlucci said.

The mayor smiled again. "Okay, Frank. The *political* world needs both kinds."

Carlucci wasn't sure he agreed even with that, but didn't think it really mattered. He wondered how long it was going to take Kashen to get to the point of this meeting. Or would all of this be part of the point?

"How old are you, Frank?"

Not a question Carlucci had expected. "Fifty-two."

"Really? You're in good shape for fifty-two. Well, perhaps 'shape' is the wrong word. You do look good for your age, though. Younger. I would have guessed mid-forties, maybe late." He paused, as though waiting for Carlucci to say something. Like what? Carlucci thought. Thank you? The mayor went on. "Fifty-two," he repeated. "If you had a choice, Frank, living another thirty years or so, your body slowing down, gradually falling apart—or living another hundred, hundred and fifty years, without aging, or aging so slowly you hardly notice it, which would you choose?"

At first Carlucci didn't think the question was serious, but as he watched the mayor studying him intently, waiting for his response, he realized the question *was* serious. What the hell was all this about?

He thought about the choices for a minute, then asked, "Would my family be able to live longer as well, or would it just be me?"

Kashen seemed puzzled at first. "Would that really make a difference?" Then, "I can see that with you it would. You're an interesting man, Frank." He pressed something on the square table beside the couch, and a moving hologram came to life above a well in the table. Four figures moved about just above the table, playing badminton—the mayor, his beautiful, younger wife, and a teenaged boy and girl, presumably the mayor's son and daughter. After watching the hologram for some time, Carlucci realized that it was no more than about fifteen seconds of movement, repeated over and over.

"My family," the mayor said. He turned back to Carlucci. "I understand your older daughter has Gould's Syndrome."

Carlucci nodded, wondering if the man was deliberately trying to cause him pain. "Yes, she does."

"It must be terribly hard on you, knowing you'll probably outlive your own daughter."

"Harder for her," Carlucci said, a sharp edge to his voice. What the fuck was it with this man?

Kashen nodded. "Yes, I imagine so." He pressed the table again and the hologram snapped off. He looked at Carlucci. "One of my own family members is already dead," he said. "My nephew."

All right, Carlucci thought. Here it is, finally.

"We've been coming down hard on you," the mayor said. "On you and LaPlace and Hong." He paused, nodding to himself, stretching his arms out along the back of the couch. "I want to apologize. It's been unfair. As I said earlier, you're a good cop, and I know you've been doing your best." He uncrossed his legs, recrossed them. "I reacted the way I did because William was my nephew. He was family. The way you feel about your family, I'm sure you understand."

Carlucci wanted to shake his head. He didn't think there was much similarity between the two families. But he sat motionless, listening.

"The pressure's coming off," the mayor said. "You'll be able to do your job just as you would with any other case. You won't have Captain McCuller or Chief Vaughn or me coming down on you anymore. We won't be demanding you do anything you wouldn't normally do." He made a dismissive gesture with his hand. "No more crazy overtime, no more extraordinary measures or expenses. We'll even take most of the slugs off, no sense wasting them. Treat this just as you would any other case."

There was a long pause, but Carlucci didn't know what to say. He felt certain Kashen wasn't quite finished yet. Carlucci continued to sit and wait. He wasn't going to ask anything, he wasn't going to make it any easier for the bastard.

"Okay, look," Kashen said. "The truth is, my nephew was something of a scumbag, wasn't he? You're on the case, you've been looking into his history, you know what he was involved with. I'm not going to pretend I just recently discovered what the son of a bitch was up to. I've known. He'd been in one illegal or immoral scam after another, and he was probably chest-deep in one more, and that's what got him killed. He probably had it coming. He was a scumbag. A rich one, but a scumbag nevertheless, and probably got killed by other scumbags.'' He paused, glancing away for a moment before looking back at Carlucci. ''What I'm getting at, is, you don't need to go out of your way to solve this damn thing. It's just not worth it.''

Finally, finally, Carlucci thought. ''You're not asking me to bury the case, are you?''

The mayor stared directly at Carlucci, his gaze steady and hard. ''No,'' he said. ''Of course not.''

Bull*shit*. That's *exactly* what he was asking. Carlucci didn't say anything.

''Just don't kill yourself over it.'' Kashen waved his hand again, the same gesture. ''Like the session you've got scheduled with the slug. Nobody likes them, nobody likes to go through those damn interviews.'' He shook his head, grimacing. ''Just cancel. Don't put yourself through it.''

Yes indeed, Carlucci thought. He knew just what the mayor wanted. ''Too many people know about the session,'' he said. ''This is the second time I've postponed it. If I cancel now, right after I've had this meeting with you, it's going to look bad. Like you *are* asking me to bury the case.''

The mayor seemed to think about that, and he nodded. ''You're absolutely right, Frank. Don't cancel.'' He paused. ''It's a private session, isn't it? No one else present, no one else listening, no recordings?''

''Yes. They almost always are. The slugs prefer it that way.''

''Then no one would know if you just went through the

motions, showed up, asked the slug a few innocuous questions, then got the hell out.''

''That's right. No one would know. Just me and the slug.''

Kashen nodded, smiling slightly. ''Well. You do what you think is best, Frank. I trust you.''

''What about LaPlace and Hong?''

''Tell them just what I've told you. Take the pressure off.''

Yeah, right, and dump on a different kind, a worse kind. ''Is that all?'' Carlucci asked. He wanted to get out of this man's house.

The mayor nodded and stood. Carlucci pushed himself up from the couch and followed him back through the main room, across the water, and into the glassed entry. Kashen opened the front door, let Carlucci out, then came out onto the porch with him. The limo was waiting in the drive, the driver standing beside the front door.

''Thanks for coming out to see me, Frank.'' The mayor put out his hand, and the two men shook. ''I feel good about this meeting. I'm confident we understand one another.''

Carlucci nodded. *More than you think.* ''Yes,'' he said.

Carlucci started down the walk, when Kashen stopped him. ''You never answered my question, Frank.''

Carlucci turned back to him. There was something here he didn't understand. Almost like some kind of offer. But what? ''You never answered mine,'' he replied.

''About your family? Whichever you would prefer. With or without.''

''Then it's not really a choice, is it?''

The mayor smiled and shook his head. ''You're right, Frank. It's not.'' A brief pause, then, ''Good night, Frank.''

Carlucci turned away from the mayor and continued down the stone walk toward the limo.

It was nearly midnight by the time they met at Hong's family flat in Chinatown. Carlucci arrived first, LaPlace less than five minutes later. All of Hong's family—wife, father, three kids, and his two widowed sisters—were still awake, talking and playing cards and drinking tea in the enormous kitchen. Kim, Joseph's wife, offered to cook for them, but they declined, and after a few minutes of obligatory visiting, Carlucci, Hong, and LaPlace left.

They walked two blocks through the heart of the Chinatown night, nearly as bright and colorful and loud as the Tenderloin after dark. The smells of cooking food and incense, cigarette smoke and spiced perfume filled the air as they passed restaurants and stores, groceries and herb shops, gambling clubs and bars. They entered Madame Chow's Mahjongg Parlor and climbed four flights of stairs in the back to a small room with a single window, a table and four chairs, and an overhead light. Carlucci could barely get his breath. An ancient uncle of Hong's served them tea, then left them in private. Carlucci, Hong, and LaPlace sat at the table, just a few feet from the window, which let in the flashing and blinking colors of the street.

"Bet we're not going to like this," LaPlace said, breaking the silence. Hong lit a cigarette and stared at Carlucci, but didn't say anything.

"You'd win that bet," Carlucci finally said. He stared out the window, watching the colors shift and flicker, reflecting off glass and metal across the way. He thought about opening the window, letting in fresh air, but decided against it. He looked back at Hong and LaPlace.

"McCuller came by my house this morning with a message. A car would show up to take me to the mayor's house for a meeting. It did, and I went, and we had the meeting. Just me and the mayor and his million-dollar view."

"Fuck," LaPlace said. "More pressure to solve his nephew's case. Just what we need."

Hong shook his head slowly, taking a deep drag on his cigarette. "No," he said, speaking through the smoke. "It's worse than that, isn't it? Something different.''

Carlucci nodded. ''Yes, it's worse than that.'' He paused, glancing from one to the other. ''He wants us to bury it.''

''What the fuck?'' LaPlace took off his glasses as if he could hear better without them, and stared at Carlucci. ''He said *what*?''

''Not directly. He's not about to stick his ass out like that. But he made it clear. He apologized for all the pressure that's come down from him and McCuller and Vaughn, said it would stop, that he knew we were all good cops doing our best, that he got carried away because it was his nephew, but he knows his nephew was a scumbag who probably just got what he deserved.''

''And he wants us to bury it?'' LaPlace asked.

''He said we should treat it like any other case. No extra measures, no extra time, no more spending a fortune on expensive lab work, all that. He said we shouldn't kill ourselves over it.''

''Oh, terrific,'' LaPlace said. ''That's subtle.''

''Yes. He even told me to cancel my session with the slug.''

''That would be a little obvious, wouldn't it?'' Hong said.

''I told him that. He agreed, suggested I go through the motions, ask a couple of pointless questions and burn out. Private session, no one would know.''

No one spoke for a minute or two. Hong finished his cigarette and lit another.

''So if we catch the guy who whacked his nephew,'' LaPlace finally said, ''it causes big problems for the mayor.''

''Apparently,'' Carlucci agreed.

''So why the *fuck* did he come down so hard on us to solve the damn thing in the first place? Two weeks with this shit.''

''He didn't know,'' Hong said.

''What?''

''That's my guess, too,'' Carlucci said. ''The mayor didn't know that solving his nephew's murder could dump him in the shit. He was doing the political thing, for PR, his family and all that.''

''But somebody's clued him in,'' LaPlace said, nodding. ''So what the fuck is going on, and what the fuck are we going to do about it?''

They were all silent again for a while, drinking their tea and thinking. None of them had any immediate answers, and it wasn't going to be easy to come up with the right ones.

''So what the fuck has that goddamn mayor got into?'' LaPlace said. Then he shook his head. ''We're probably better off not knowing. But what happens if we tank this case, after all the screaming about it from the mayor himself, all over the papers and the tube? Demotions? Or we just look like fucking morons?''

Carlucci shook his head. ''Probably the mayor will make some kind of statement; he's checked into it, we've done a superb job on an impossible case, praise for the department, praise for us, probably citations, he's disappointed but understanding. We'd be fine.''

''All right. More important, what happens we catch the guy, and the mayor takes it in the balls because of it? They can't fire us for doing our jobs—so what happens, somebody cuts off our legs or kills us?''

Carlucci didn't answer. What the hell could he say? He didn't know what would happen. But he was damn sure the mayor wouldn't go down without taking as many people with him as he could, one way or another.

Hong started to light another cigarette—though his last one was only half gone—then stopped, looked at Carlucci. ''There's something else, isn't there? Some other thing happening in the middle of all this that Pete and I don't know about. Something *you* know.''

Carlucci nodded. They had a right to know. Maybe not *what* it was, but at least that it was out there waiting to blow up in their faces.

"There's another case," Carlucci said. "Someone killed about a week before the mayor's nephew. The case got buried but good. There didn't seem to be any connection to the nephew, but now it looks like there is."

LaPlace put his glasses back on and looked at Carlucci. "You buried a case, Frank?"

"No. Someone else did. It doesn't matter who, someone who had no choice. I only found out about it by accident."

"And you've been poking at it," Hong said.

Carlucci nodded. "This whole thing is a lot messier than it looks. I don't know who's involved, or *why* all this shit is happening, but it's turning into a fucking nightmare." He paused, then said, "One other joker in this deck. Tremaine's been digging around in all this. I have no idea why. Frankly, I don't know whether that's good or bad."

Again there was a fairly long silence, broken only by the clinking of tea cups on saucers and the muted sounds from the street outside.

"I've never tanked a case before," LaPlace said.

Hong said nothing, just stared at the window, smoking.

"I know," Carlucci said. "Probably the smartest thing for us to do is let the nephew's case slide, go through the motions, don't follow up shit, and let the case die from lack of oxygen. It wouldn't really be burying it."

"And what about that other case, the one you're poking at?" Hong asked.

"I'd have to let that go, too. They're too damn connected. Anything I did might blow open the nephew's case."

"Why *are* you poking at this other case?"

"Personal reasons."

"But you would drop it?"

"Yes." It was one thing to risk his own career, another thing to risk theirs as well unless they were with him on it.

"Fuck." LaPlace got up from the table and went to the window; the colored lights flickered across his face.

"If we *don't* tank the case," Hong began, "we'd need to make it look like we were. Nothing obvious, nothing anyone else would notice, but something for the mayor to see. He wouldn't want us to be obvious. Maybe back off a little, make a statement or two about the case bogging down, something like that. Frank has his session with the slug, says nothing came out of it, even if the slug gives him gold." He put out his cigarette, breathing deeply. "We need to look like we're still working on the case, so we do it for real, and we keep everything we come up with to ourselves."

LaPlace remained at the window, but now he was looking at Hong, listening to his partner. "And what about Frank's other case?" he said.

Hong turned to Carlucci. "You'd have to bring us in on that one, too, Frank. If they're connected, it's got to be both, or none."

Carlucci looked back and forth between the two men. He hadn't been sure which way they would go on this, and he wasn't completely sure he was happy with the way it appeared to be headed. But it made him feel good, somehow; these two men, no matter how this all worked out, pumped him with something like hope.

"You're saying you're willing to jack the mayor on this and go after the case? Both cases?"

Hong turned to look at LaPlace, who shrugged. "We're not stupid, Frank. If it gets too scorched, we can always back off and pull out, can't we? None of us wants to get killed."

"Maybe," Carlucci said. "That's what I keep telling myself with this other case. But we can make mistakes."

No one spoke for a while. There was a strange tension in the air, a feeling they were on the edge. If they went ahead with the two cases, they would remain on the edge, an edge that would get narrower, and sharper.

"Ruben," LaPlace said, breaking the silence. "He's the one

who buried this other case, isn't he? He's looked like shit for almost a month.''

Carlucci didn't answer. He didn't really need to.

''I don't want to tank anything,'' Hong said.

LaPlace breathed in deeply once, then slowly let it out and nodded. ''I'm with Joseph.''

Carlucci sat thinking. He didn't want to back away from any of this either, but he was afraid of what they were letting themselves in for. They still didn't know what was at stake here, so it was hard to guess how far the mayor and whoever else would be willing to go.

''All right,'' Carlucci said. ''I'll bring you in on this other case. But. I'll tell you all about it, I'll let you know everything I find out, and I'll ask for your advice, your judgment. But I've got to keep digging into it on my own. Just me. With the mayor's nephew, all three of us are *supposed* to be working on it. This other case is supposed to be buried. *Nobody* should be looking into it. If all three of us start screwing around with it, somebody's going to notice something. I've got to stay solo on it.''

Hong and LaPlace looked at each other, then both briefly nodded and turned back to Carlucci. ''We're in,'' Hong said. He took out one more cigarette and lit it. ''So tell us about this other murder.''

''All right.'' Carlucci ran his hand through his hair. ''Just some guy,'' he began, recalling Ruben Santos's words. ''Some part-time rocker, petty thief, ex-junkie. His name was Chick Roberts.''

SEVENTEEN

MIXER'S ARM WAS on fire. He twisted his body, tried opening his eyes, but they seemed welded shut. Red and orange flares erupted behind his eyes—the flames consuming his arm? Mixer opened his mouth, tried to cry out, but no sound emerged.

Then he felt something cool and wet on his forehead, cool fingers brushing at his face, something pressed against his neck. A patch? Finally, a whisper in his ear.

"Ssssshhhh, ssssshhhhh. You're fine, Minor Danzig, you're just fine. Now sleep."

Mixer thought he could feel the sleep pulsing into him, into his neck, and he had no choice, and it was fine with him; he had no objections at all. . . .

The next time he woke, his arm was still on fire, but it wasn't so bad. There was other pain, though, in his face, his back, a tremendous pounding in his head. He still couldn't open his eyes. His mouth, too, was stuck closed, but he managed to pry his lips apart. A short, harsh, coughing sound, scratching at his throat. He tried swallowing, tried again, finally got it. Then, "Is . . . is anyone th-th—?" Another cough.

"Sssshhhh, Minor Danzig." The same voice as before.

Cool, dry lips were pressed to his forehead, his cheek, his lips. His right arm was aflame, impossible to move, but his left was free and he moved it, brought it up near his face. The lips pulled back, but his hand met hair, an ear, soft skin. Then other fingers locked with his.

"Soon, Minor Danzig." Was that St. Katherine's voice? "You are healing well."

"My . . . eyes," he whispered.

"Your eyes are fine. The lids were badly burned. They're healing now. Tomorrow the bandages come off." The fingers squeezed his, massaging, reassuring. "Tomorrow you will see."

"My arm," he said.

There was a long silence, another squeeze of fingers. "Your arm," the woman's voice said. "Tomorrow you will see."

He woke again. Everything seemed darker, quieter. Night? Strangely, he was almost completely without pain. Even stranger, he was afraid. The world seemed to have disappeared.

"Saint Katherine?" He barely managed a whisper. "Saint Katherine?" Louder this time. Then, one final time, straining. "Saint Katherine?" He reached out with his left hand, moved it from side to side, feeling nothing, panic ratcheting up inside him. "Where are you?"

Then he heard a rustling, felt fingers taking his hand again, *two* hands taking his.

"I'm here," she said, voice sleepy. "It's all right, I'm here."

Mixer sank back, relaxing, the panic sliding away.

He felt a patch being pressed against his neck. "I . . . " he started, then forgot what he wanted to say. He squeezed the fingers holding him. Everything was fine.

• • •

Awake once more. The pain back, but easier now. St. Katherine at his side—he was certain now that it was she. The bandages still covered his eyes, but he saw a bright flash of light through them. A few moments later he heard thunder crash and roll, shaking glass. Then he noticed the sound of rain, heavy and steady.

"Hot thunderstorm," St. Katherine said. "It's pouring outside." A slight pause. A sliding sound, the room growing dimmer still. "Now, keep your eyes closed, let me take off the bandage."

She raised his head with one hand, worked at the bandage with the other. Mixer fought the urge to open his eyes, kept them shut until he felt the last of the bandage come away, the air cool and soothing on his eyelids.

"Beautiful," St. Katherine said. "They've healed beautifully. Go ahead, Minor Danzig. Open your eyes."

Mixer did, blinking. The light in the room was dim, a heavily shaded lamp in the corner. Window blinds closed.

The room was small, sparsely furnished. His bed, medical equipment, two small tables, two chairs. Bare walls that hadn't been painted in years. The only person in the room was St. Katherine, standing on his left. She was just as beautiful as he remembered.

He looked at his right arm and hand. He expected them to be heavily bandaged, but he couldn't be sure—plain white cloth was tented over them. The arm felt heavy. He could just see a patch of metal around his shoulder. The exo?

Mixer turned to St. Katherine. "My arm," he said.

St. Katherine stood, came around the bed to the other side. "We did everything we could," she said. "We saved it. Remember that, Minor Danzig. We saved it." She lifted the tented cloth, revealing his arm.

Mixer's arm was a confused mash of metal and scarred flesh and a few small, still-healing sections of raw skin. He could not believe that it didn't hurt more than it did, and he wondered what they'd pumped into him to keep the pain bearable.

"The exoskeleton fused to the arm," St. Katherine said. "To the skin, the muscle, in some places even the bone. Impossible to remove it without taking too much of the arm with it. Maybe up in New Hong Kong or some rich hospital they could do something else, but not here."

Mixer tried to lift the arm, managed it a few inches. Tried flexing his fingers, strange digits of metal and flesh. They, too, moved slightly.

"We had a choice med-tech work on the arm, the exo. You'll have movement, fingers, wrist, elbow, but it will be restricted." She reached for his face, turned it gently toward her own and gazed into his eyes. "A stiff, awkward arm, Minor Danzig, but you still have it."

Mixer lowered the arm, his shoulder exhausted from the effort of holding it up, and smiled at St. Katherine. "Got no complaints about the arm," he said. "Looks pretty fucking rabid to me."

She cocked her head, not quite smiling. "Is that good?"

Mixer gave a short laugh and closed his eyes. "Yes, that's good."

"How long has it been?" Mixer asked later that day.

"More than a week," St. Katherine replied. She handed him a strawed glass of ice water. Mixer held it in his left hand, got the straw in his mouth, and sucked hard. He was so thirsty, constantly thirsty. A med tech had come in and taken out the IV's and catheter. Solid food was on its way, St. Katherine promised.

"We kept you completely sedated to aid the healing, and to let us work on the arm."

"Why did you save me?" Mixer asked. "Why didn't you just let me die?"

St. Katherine turned away, and didn't speak for a long time. When she turned back around, there were tears in her eyes.

Real tears, Mixer realized. Which made him feel strange.

"Because you survived the trial," she finally said. "Because you broke the Wheel. And because I love you."

Mixer slept, woke, slept some more. During his waking periods he began moving about, working out the stiffness in his limbs, his neck, everything. He ate and drank, used the toilet across the hall from his room. He stood at the barred window and looked out at the Tenderloin, the alleys and streets six or seven floors below him; at night there were drum fires in the alley, flames casting shadows up the building walls. Off to the right, he could just see the edge of the Core, the four square blocks of hell in the center of the Tenderloin, which reminded him of Sookie again. She'd had metal fused to her own arms and legs by the Chain Killer before he'd murdered her. The pain came and went, and he asked St. Katherine to cut back on the meds. She did.

There was no mirror in the room, no mirror in the bathroom, and he finally asked for one. His vague reflection in the window looked wrong, somehow. When St. Katherine brought him into a larger bathroom one floor below, with a large mirror above the sink, he saw why.

The spikes were gone from his forehead, burned and melted away; scarred, nearly smooth flesh remained behind. His eyebrows were just now growing back, stiff and coarse. Beard and moustache, too, had begun. His hair was uneven, stuck out from his head.

"I like the look," he said. And he did. He looked like someone else, which matched the way he felt.

"That's good," St. Katherine said, standing beside him. "Better if you are not recognizable."

"Why?"

They looked at each other's images in the mirror, reflected gazes meeting.

"Because you're dead."

• • •

They sat at the table of a small kitchen on the same floor as the larger bathroom. St. Lucy served coffee and joined them.

"Saint Lucy is my primary adviser," St. Katherine said. "Also our medical expert."

Mixer stared into St. Lucy's eyes. A stunning, deep blue, unlike anything he had seen before. "Are your eyes real?" he asked.

St. Lucy smiled softly. "Yes, they're real. They're not the eyes I was born with, but they're real." Her smile faded. "They're New Hong Kong eyes."

There was something pained in her voice, in her expression, and Mixer knew better than to ask any more about it. He turned back to St. Katherine.

"So why am I supposed to be dead?"

"We made . . . an announcement. Over the nets. You died a martyr. Something like a Saint yourself." She looked away, apparently uncomfortable. "A great trial, providing us with profound revelations."

"Why?" Mixer asked again.

"For your protection," St. Lucy said.

"We did something terrible," St. Katherine said, still not looking at him. "*I* did something terrible."

"It was a joint decision," St. Lucy put in.

St. Katherine shook her head. "You advised against it. *My* responsibility." She finally looked back at Mixer. "I came looking for you, Minor Danzig. For the trial. I came looking for *you*." She laughed harshly. "I entered into a contract, a contract of the damned. For money and . . . other considerations, I agreed to find *you* for my next trial. You were expected to go the way of all the others. You were to die, or lose your mind." The tears reappeared, welling in her eyes. "You did neither, Minor Danzig."

Mixer didn't know what to say. He looked back and forth

between the two women. "Why do you call me Minor Danzig?" Not the question he really wanted to ask. "It's the name I was born with," he said, looking into St. Lucy's incredible blue eyes. "But it's not my name any longer. My name is Mixer."

"You've been reborn," St. Lucy said, smiling again. "It's only right that you reclaim the name you were given at birth." Then she gave a brief, graceful shrug. "You will need a new name, when you go out into the world again."

St. Lucy glanced at St. Katherine, then got up from the chair and walked out of the kitchen, leaving the two of them alone.

"Who wanted me dead?" Mixer asked.

St. Katherine wiped tears from her eyes. "I'm confused," she said, shaking her head, not quite looking at him. "I sacrificed my principles . . . no, not sacrificed. Sold them, for money and other things." She now looked directly at him. "But doing that brought me *you*, one who has broken the Wheel and passed the trial. The first, the only one ever. The one man proven worthy to be my consort. Selling out my principles brought you to me, so perhaps it was meant for me to do, perhaps it was the right thing, perhaps I was guided."

Mixer just shook his head. He finished his coffee, got up, and refilled his cup from the glass carafe on the stove.

"Perhaps . . ." St. Katherine said.

"No," Mixer said. "It was wrong. I think *all* your goddamn 'trials' are wrong. Murder, is what they are. You believe it's your calling; well, that's for you to figure out. But doing what you did to me, for money, contracting out, even for you it was wrong. Doesn't matter how it all turned out. Blasphemy, babe."

He stood with his hip against the counter, watching her. He held the coffee in his left hand, though it was awkward. His right arm was too heavy, and still hurt. St. Katherine remained silent a long time, returning his gaze. Finally she nodded.

"You're right, Minor Danzig. It was blasphemy, and I'll have to atone for that."

"Who wanted me dead?" he asked again.

St. Katherine sat up straighter in the chair, more confident and self-assured. Back to normal, Mixer thought. Was that good? She gave him a half smile.

"A woman named Aster," she said. "But she's not important, she was just a courier. She was working for someone else."

"Who?"

"She wouldn't tell us. What we did may have been blasphemous, but we didn't do it stupidly. Lucy and I weren't about to take the risk without knowing who was buying us." She finished her own coffee and joined Mixer by the stove, refilling her cup and emptying the carafe. "Wasn't easy tracing her, but we have hot demon resources. Angelic demons, of course," she said, smiling. "Took us nearly three days, but we found it."

"*Who?*"

"The trace led back to two sources," St. Katherine said. "First, the mayor of this great city, the Honorable Terrance Kashen. And then, through him, we were fairly certain, to New Hong Kong."

Jesus Christ, Mixer thought. The mayor. The New Hong Kong connection didn't surprise him; there had been hints from Chick before he got himself killed. But the mayor. Fuck these people. What the hell was going on?

"Do you know why?" Mixer asked.

St. Katherine shook her head. "We never got even a hint."

Mixer sighed deeply. "So, you were paid to kill me, and when I didn't die, when my brains didn't get scorched, you covered your asses and put out the word that I was dead."

"No," St. Katherine said, firmly shaking her head. "We could have let you die, and then it would have been the truth. We saved your life. You would have died without medical help. Lucy said it. We did it for your protection. So the mayor or whoever else won't come after you again."

"And you announced it over the nets."

"Yes."

He thought about Paula and Carlucci, Tia and Miklos and Amy, other people he knew, some friends, some not. They all must now think he was dead.

"Who knows I'm still alive?"

"Saint Lucy and I. The doctor, who is my sister. And the techs, but they don't know who you are. The other Saints and all the novitiates think you're dead. You *looked* dead when we carried you away."

Mixer shook his head. "But I'm supposed to be your consort now, right? I survived the trial. So how does that happen if I'm dead?"

A wry smile crossed St. Katherine's face. "I haven't worked that out yet."

Mixer looked out the small kitchen window. They were still several floors above the street. The day was bright and hazy, the sun glaring down through the sick mustard sky. What the hell was he going to do?

"I love you," St. Katherine said.

Mixer turned back to her, remembering now that she'd said it once before. "You don't even know me."

She smiled. "It doesn't matter. Besides, I *do* know you. I've been at your side for days, nursing you, watching you, talking to you, even when you couldn't hear me. I know you, Minor Danzig. And I do love you."

Mixer studied her face, looked into her eyes, and realized it was true. In her own way, whatever that was, whatever that meant to her, St. Katherine loved him. He thought it should frighten him, or repulse him, but for some reason it didn't. Mostly he felt uneasy, a little confused. He remembered thinking as he was strapped to the wheel that he could fall in love with someone who looked like her. She was still stunningly beautiful, and there was something compelling about her, the way she was with him. But she had tried to kill him. She had saved him, but she had nearly killed him. Could he ever care for someone who had done that to him? Someone as crazy as St. Katherine? He didn't know, and that disturbed him as much as anything else.

"Am I a prisoner here?" he asked.

"Of course not," she replied. "But you're still healing, you don't have much strength." She paused. "And it's going to be dangerous for you. It would help if the beard were longer."

"People think I'm dead. My friends think I'm dead."

St. Katherine nodded. "And you had better be certain who your friends are, and careful who you see." She paused. "Stay a few more days, Minor Danzig. Rest, and be cautious."

Mixer nodded. "I'll stay. And don't worry, I'll be careful." He smiled. "I've already died once. I don't want to do it again any sooner than I have to."

EIGHTEEN

PAULA WAS FEELING reckless. Chick was dead, Mixer was dead, why not go all-fire? She was still uncertain about Tremaine, and she wanted to get away from that as well. Fuck Jenny Woo and the Saints and whoever killed Chick, fuck 'em all. Jenny Woo had thought Paula was following her? Fine, she'd do it for real, see if she couldn't find out what the hell was going on.

She thought about calling Carlucci and letting him know what she was doing, but he'd just try to talk her out of it, and she didn't want to be talked out of anything right now. Instead, Paula left a message for Bonita, canceling another Black Angels gig that night, and headed for the Tenderloin.

Paula had her own ways into the Tenderloin, at least one into each of the Quarters. Two—into the Euro and Arab Quarters—were expensive and unpleasant, and she avoided them. Her two ways into the Asian Quarter would take her right into the heart of where she wanted to be, but would be a hell of a lot more likely to alert Jenny Woo. The Latin Quarter was too far away, so she decided on the Afram.

The sun was setting, streaking dark, heavy incoming clouds with deep orange and red, and the heat of the day still shimmered in the air, baking up from the street and off the dark brick and stone and concrete all around her. It was probably going to rain sometime tonight; Paula could feel it weighing down on her.

She walked to the farthest reach of the Polk Corridor, then crossed into the DMZ between the Polk and the Tenderloin. DMZ was a bad name for the strip. After dark it got crazy, and by midnight was more of a free-fire zone than anything else. Now it was marginal, lights coming on and going off in windows, street traffic noisy and snarled, sidewalks jammed. Paula felt probing hands and fingers when she was bumped, saw crazed eyes staring at her, smelled panic and desperation in the air. A Black Rhino thundered down the street, clearing traffic as it ground up the pavement in its path, smashing vehicles aside. Paula leaped into the empty street in its wake, just in front of a pack of trailing Tick-Birds, ran behind it for a block, then cut up toward the Tenderloin, only two blocks from the Nairobi Cafe, her way in. She hurried along the two blocks, nervous energy pushing her close to a run. She'd have to settle down or she'd drive herself crazy.

She stopped across the street from the Nairobi Cafe, looking at the windows filled with lush tropical trees and plants and birds. A huge boa constrictor was wrapped around one of the trees, two feet of tail end dangling from a branch; a large, pop-eyed green lizard sat below the boa, flicking its tongue, eyes shifting with jerky movements. Paula crossed the street and pushed through the front door, still walking way too fast.

She was more than halfway to the rear of the cafe when she realized something was wrong. People turned to stare at her, and the noise level dropped, though the place didn't actually go silent. As she walked among the tables, she realized she was the only white person in the place.

The Nairobi customers were always mostly black, but never exclusively, and though she'd never seen any Asians in the place, there were always whites, usually a few Latinos. Neither, right now. Blacks at every table, at the bar, a lot of them looking at her. Shit. Shockley's Raiders had re-formed recently, pounding around the city, making things jittery again. She'd bet they'd made some hit in the last day or two that she hadn't heard about. Shit.

Paula kept going. No one tried to stop her. Maybe it wasn't smart, but she was already closer to the back than the front. When she reached the end of the bar, she walked around it and into the short hall leading to the bathrooms. She passed the women's room, the men's room, then hesitated before the curtained doorway at the end of the hall. Fuck it. Paula pulled the curtain aside and walked through.

The room in back was small and dark. Orange lamps in the corners, a few chairs, a desk with a computer. A big-boned man sat at the desk, staring at her. A woman sat in one of the chairs, smoking a cigarette.

Paula walked up to the desk, laid down two twenties, and said, "Paula Asgard." Her voice sounded perfectly calm, which surprised her.

"Your money's no good here, white girl." The man behind the desk made no move toward the money or the keyboard. "*You* are no good here."

"Paula Asgard," she said again, pointing at the computer. "I'm in there."

The man behind the desk shook his head. "Nobody white is in there," he said. "You pick up that money now, and go back out the way you came in."

Paula still had too much nervous energy, pumped up now with adrenaline, and it made her stubborn. And maybe stupid, but she didn't care. Her heart was beating hard, but she didn't care about that, either.

"Samuel Eko is a friend of mine," she said. "You call him upstairs, tell him I'm here."

"He's not your friend anymore, sugar," the woman said.

Paula turned to her. "Yes, he is. Samuel will always be my

friend.'' She swung back to the man behind the desk. ''You call him.''

There was a long silence, no one moving. Finally the man behind the desk stood. ''Wait,'' was all he said; and then he went out through the curtain.

Paula remained standing in the middle of the room, hands in jacket pockets, right hand gripping the hilt of the gravity knife. She kept her gaze straight ahead, at the unoccupied desk.

The woman put out her cigarette, gave a short laugh, then lit another. ''You've got balls, sugar. Too bad you're about to get them cut off.''

Paula didn't respond. She thought of Samuel Eko, hoping he was upstairs, reachable. She had known Samuel even longer than she'd known Chick. His sister, Angie, had been the percussionist in Heatseeker, the first all-woman band Paula had joined. When Angie had been killed, Paula and Samuel had become close friends, sharing their grief.

The curtain was pulled aside and Paula turned to see the big-boned man come into the room with Samuel Eko right behind him. Samuel was a tall man, well over six feet, almost thin, and one of the darkest men Paula had ever know. He approached her, smiling, and put his long arms around her. Paula hugged him back.

''Let's go,'' Samuel said. With one arm over her shoulder, he led the way to the door in the back corner of the room. He opened the door, and stepped back to let Paula go first.

''So long, sugar,'' the woman said.

Paula entered the passage, which led to the Afram Quarter proper, and Samuel Eko followed, shutting the door behind them. The passage was long and narrow, with an occasional door on one side or the other, and lit by bare incandescents spaced every twenty feet.

''You're a crazy woman,'' Samuel Eko said.

"Probably," Paula replied. "What did I miss? Something with Shockley's Raiders?"

Samuel nodded. They walked side by side, little space between them; Samuel had to duck at each light.

"They burned down an apartment building on Fillmore this morning. Killed eleven people."

"*That's* what the smoke was." She'd seen it from her apartment when she got up; smelled it, even.

"Same old shit."

They reached the end of the passage and Samuel pushed the door open. They stepped out into the Tenderloin, the sky now dark above the buildings, no stars visible through the thick clouds.

"Where you headed?" Samuel asked. They stood on the sidewalk, and Paula was certain that people on the streets were staring at them.

"The Asian Quarter."

"Why didn't you just go in there?"

"I should have."

"I'd better go with you," Samuel said.

Paula laughed. "Yeah, you'd better." It was only a few blocks, but Paula didn't want to do it alone. The streets didn't look much different than the Nairobi; Paula saw only one other white, a man walking with two black men. A real different feel from what she was used to here. They started walking.

"Sometimes I think we're never, absolutely *never*, going to get along," he said.

"Who?"

"Whites and blacks. Asians and blacks. *Anyone* and blacks. Hell, anyone with anyone else. Every time things seem to get better for a while, something like this happens. Two years ago it was the crucifixions on the Marina Green. Before that, it was those black crazies burning down all those Cambodian houses and stores. Five years ago it was the Tundra riots and the Mission fires. It's always something."

They stopped at an intersection, waiting for a traffic knot to unsnarl. All-percussion music was coming from a bar just down the street; the strong smell of spiced coffee made Paula want to stop at Kit's, a sidewalk cafe next to the bar, and have coffee with Samuel, but she knew it was impossible. Traffic cleared, and they crossed the street.

"You know my father came from the Sudan," Samuel Eko said.

"Yes," Paula replied. "And he met and fell in love with a Namibian beauty who made him the happiest man alive, who became his wife and the mother of his three sons and two daughters."

Samuel shook his head. "And I'm the only child of his still alive. Sometimes I think I'd like to go back to the Sudan. A simpler life."

"Starvation's always a simpler life," Paula said. "That doesn't make it better."

Samuel shrugged. "I know. I know it's fantasy. But I tell you, Paula Asgard, sometimes I need a little fantasy just to get through the day."

"I understand, Samuel."

They approached the Asian-Afram boundary. Most of the Quarters merged gradually into one another, with transitional areas of a block or two. Not here, though. The demarcation was sharp and obvious, as if a line had been painted in the street. Paula half expected to see checkpoints, with armed border guards. Maybe someday.

They stopped at the boundary and Samuel hugged her again. "Take care, Paula. You're rooting around in something risky, I can tell."

"Yeah? You a psychic, now?"

Samuel smiled. "You've got the feel."

"I'll be careful, Samuel."

"And, Paula? Best if you don't come back to the Afram Quarter for a while. Maybe a long while."

Paula breathed deeply, and nodded. "Goodbye, Samuel." She turned and strode into the Asian Quarter night.

Paula was more at ease on the streets of the Asian Quarter, and within minutes of saying goodbye to Samuel Eko she felt almost normal again, though still keyed up. As always, the streets and sidewalks were crowded, the vehicles hardly moving faster than people on foot. It was so bright that only by looking up, through the message streamers and strings of light, up past the balconies and hanging plants and signs, only by staring up at the dark and heavy clouds overhead, could she convince herself that it was night and not midday.

It took her four hours to find Jenny Woo, and then Paula almost walked right into her. First, Paula had tried Jenny's apartment above Hiep Quan's Tattoo Heaven, then a couple of nearby clubs, then the Foil Arcade, followed by run-throughs at a dozen sleazy bars and pits, finishing up at Master Hawk's Orgone Parlor. No Jenny Woo. She went back to Hiep Quan's, and almost walked into Jenny as she came out the door next to the shop.

Paula spun around and walked quickly away and into the crowd moving along the sidewalk, not looking back, then swung around the corner and pressed herself against the building wall.

Paula worked her way back to the corner, came around it, and looked toward Hiep Quan's. Jenny Woo wasn't in sight. She must have gone the other way. Paula pushed out into the crowd and hurried through it, searching for Jenny.

A pocket of foil dealers surrounded her, scattered when she growled at them. Club barkers reached for her, gesturing into shifting lights and dark shadows. A rat pack streamed past, keeping to the gutter, the leader chanting. Paula squeezed between people, jostled others, sidestepped a quartet of gooners.

Half a block ahead, she saw Jenny Woo dart into the street, zigzagging through traffic, shoving her way through two pop-

sellers to reach the opposite sidewalk. Paula hurried forward, but stayed on this side of the road. Another block, and Jenny turned the corner, forcing Paula to cross the street. But she caught a light, used the crosswalk, and almost immediately picked her up again.

Two more blocks, another turn, and they were edging the Core, which made Paula nervous. She had to stay further back, because the crowds had thinned, and now they were moving along an alley half a block from the Core itself. Twice, when she crossed another alley, she could see the ruins of the Core over the barriers: the quiet, collapsing buildings, the crumbling brick and twisted metal, the broken glass and the dark holes. She shivered despite the warmth of the night.

Ahead, Jenny Woo ducked through a doorway. Paula stopped for a minute, then slowly moved forward, past plated-over windows, bricked-in doorways, until she reached the spot where Jenny had disappeared. A deep alcove, and an unmarked, heavy wooden door. Paula was feeling reckless, but she didn't feel stupid. She didn't try the door. Instead, she backed away, and looked around the alley, searching for a place where she could hole up and watch the doorway.

There was none, so she had to retreat to the end of the alley and the street. She stationed herself at the corner of the building across the alley, which gave her a view not only of the doorway, but of the Core barrier and the upper reaches of the Core itself, half a block away. She kept her hands in her jacket pockets; the feel of the gravity knife didn't give her much comfort.

Paula knew she was safe, but part of her kept imagining some subhuman monster emerging from the Core, clearing the barrier and sweeping down on her, capturing her and hauling her back over the barrier and into the depths of the Core, where unimaginable things would be done to her. She'd never been in the Core, didn't know anyone who had, but the stories were always there, too damn many for all of them to be false.

The side of the building across the alley seemed to open up, a huge section of metal and brick and wood sliding to the side with a tremendous rumble and creaking. A van worked its way out of the opening, shifting back and forth twice before it could get into the narrow alley, pointed toward Paula. Once it was clear of the opening, the section of wall slid back into place. The van came slowly up the alley, with just enough side clearance to allow people to press up against the building walls on either side of it. Paula hung back and watched the unmarked van. As it neared, she recognized the driver—Jenny Woo. Paula pulled back farther, back into the crowd. The van inched out of the alley, then forced its way into the slow traffic and moved down the street, headed away from the Core. Paula followed.

Following the van was almost easier than following Jenny Woo on foot had been. Paula could stay farther back and still keep the van in sight, and in the crowded streets of the Asian Quarter the van didn't make any better time than Paula did. It was only two in the morning, so the sidewalks were still jammed, and sometimes she had to push her way through knots of people, but it wasn't much of a problem.

Just five blocks from the alley, near the fringes of the Asian Quarter and along the perimeter of the Tenderloin, the van pulled off the road and dipped down a concrete ramp leading to the basement level of a brick building. Paula ran forward, then cautiously leaned over a pipe railing to look down. A wide metal door rolled up into the wall, and when there was just enough room, the van shot forward and into shadowed darkness. The door immediately reversed direction, and seconds later clanged shut.

Paula had lost Jenny Woo. The van would emerge from the other side of the building, *outside* the Tenderloin, and there was no way Paula could get to one of the Tenderloin exits she knew and get out to catch the van as it appeared. Even if she could, outside the Tenderloin she'd never be able to follow on foot.

A hand gripped her shoulder. Paula spun around and pulled away in one motion, hand going into her jacket and pulling out the gravity knife, charging it with a squeeze.

It was Tremaine.

Her heart was pounding, and strange feelings swirled around in her stomach. She didn't know what the hell to think or feel.

"I wasn't following you," Tremaine said.

Paula wasn't sure whether or not she believed him.

"We're both following the same person," he added.

"Who?" she asked, still not sure.

"Jenny Woo."

"Then we've both lost the same person."

Tremaine shook his head. "Not if we move now. I know where she's coming out. Are you with me?"

A bang decision. Why not? She had nothing to lose, did she? "Sure," Paula said. She cut the knife's charge and tucked it back into her jacket pocket.

Tremaine had a way out of the Tenderloin in the building next door, through a bubble courier office and a travel agency. His battered Plymouth was parked at the curb just a few feet away. Half a block down, Paula could see the van coming up another ramp, then turning away from them and heading down the street. The night was much darker outside the Tenderloin, the streets nearly deserted.

Tremaine seemed to be in no hurry. "I'm pretty sure I know where she's headed," he said. He unlocked the passenger door for Paula, then got in the driver's side, started the engine, and pulled out into the street. Two blocks ahead, the taillights of the van turned a corner and were gone from sight.

"So where's she going?" Paula asked.

"Hunter's Point."

The spaceport. Which almost certainly meant New Hong Kong. "She going up herself?" Paula asked. "Or delivering?"

"Delivering."

"Delivering what?"

Tremaine gave Paula a half smile without looking at her. "I don't know everything."

They turned briefly onto Market, then swung onto Fourth. The Marriott was a blaze of colored lights, surrounded by security guards and the shimmer of portable Kronenhauer Fields. But just past it, long abandoned, was Moscone Center, a low, dark shadow on their left, broken windows reflecting jagged strips of light. Paula thought she could still see the taillights of the van ahead of them, but she wasn't sure.

"What *do* you know?" she asked.

Tremaine didn't answer immediately. Rain started falling, light at first. Tremaine raised the windows, leaving small gaps for fresh air. They drove under the freeway, barrel fires burning against the concrete supports. The roadway was cracked and potholed, and the Plymouth bounced and creaked across it. When they emerged from under the freeway, the rain was a torrent.

"Before we talk about that," Tremaine said, "I want to be clear about something. The other night, what I did, what *we* did, had nothing to do with this." He looked at her a moment, then returned his attention to the road. "That was personal, not business. That was between you and me, and nothing to do with my story, or Chick Roberts." He twisted his head and neck and Paula could hear bones cracking, like knuckles. "I'm not saying this very well, am I? I'm having a lot of trouble with this." He glanced at her again, then looked away. "I like you, Paula. I think I like you a lot, and I want to spend more time with you, so I don't want you to think that all that the other night was just trying to get to you about this story."

They were crossing Mission Creek now, and Paula could smell the stench of stagnant water through the narrow openings in the windows. She wanted to believe him. Of *course* she wanted to believe him. And, she guessed, she mostly did.

"Okay," she said. But she didn't know what else to say.

They drove along slowly, in silence. Dark warehouses, small, low buildings on either side, a few street lights, everything streaked with the heavy rain. More barrel fires under shelter. Paula hoped the Plymouth was in good shape; this wasn't a part of the city she wanted to break down in.

"Then tell me," she said to him. "What *is* all this about?"

Tremaine shook his head. "You won't like this, but I can't really say much about it. It's a story I'm working on. I don't talk about my stories, not until they're done. It's pretty much all one way. I ask a lot of questions, but I don't answer many. I want to ask you about Chick Roberts. You can talk to me about him or not. I can tell you a few things, but you won't think it's enough."

"Tell me what you can, then," Paula said.

"Will you talk to me about Chick?"

"I don't know." She was lying. She would tell Tremaine what little she knew, but she didn't want him to know that yet.

Tremaine nodded once. He slowed, swung around a huge pothole, then picked up speed. They crossed water again, Islais Creek Channel. Two enormous ships were docked nearby, and their lights reflected like flashing, multicolored scales off the water. Paula wondered what it would be like to board one of those freighters and head out onto the open sea.

Tremaine took a hard left, and Paula looked ahead. There were no taillights, no signs of the van. "Did we lose her?"

"No. I'm taking a different way in. Too easy to be spotted following her this time of night."

There were small houses on either side now, interspersed among warehouses and other commercial buildings. Almost everything was dark. Then suddenly, as they got closer to the spaceport, more lights appeared, on the street and in buildings, and people were out. Shops were open, and the sound of machinery grew louder. Trucks and vans and cars moved along the road.

At the gates to Hunter's Point proper, Tremaine showed the guards a pass, and they let the car through. Just ahead, moving slowly in and out of the bright cones of light from overhead lamps, was Jenny Woo's van. The rain stopped, like a dam closing, leaving a bright sheen on the ground and dripping from all the vehicles around them.

"There it is," Paula said.

Tremaine nodded. He didn't follow the van. He swung around the perimeter of the large parking lot, then drove along the high, shielded fence. Paula kept her gaze on the van, which approached another gate, this one in the shielded fence and leading out onto the tarmac.

"We'd never get through the gate," Tremaine said. He pulled the Plymouth right up to the fence so they were facing the tarmac, turned off the lights, and cut the engine.

Far out on the tarmac, a ship stood in its gantry, outlined by bright lights. Other than that, the tarmac was bare. Paula looked over at the gate. Jenny Woo's van pulled away and drove out across the open pavement. It came to a stop about two hundred feet from the ship.

The ground opened up beside the van, and four people in gray overalls, standing on a platform, rose up from the opening, the platform stopping at ground level. Jenny Woo got out of the van, went around to the back and opened the rear doors. The four people stepped off the platform and began unloading the van.

They unloaded a huge, long crate shaped almost like a coffin, all four of them lifting the crate at the same time, then carrying it to the loading platform. They returned to the van, unloaded a second crate, then two more. Jenny Woo closed the van doors, got back in, and headed back to the gate. The four people and four crates on the platform descended slowly back into the ground, which then closed over them.

"What the hell is in those crates?" Paula asked.

"I don't know," Tremaine said.

She looked at him. "But you have an idea, don't you?"

He nodded. "I think people are in those crates."

"People?"

Tremaine nodded again.

"Alive, or dead?"

"That's the question, isn't it?"

Jenny Woo's van reached the gate, quickly passed through, and headed out of Hunter's Point.

"Are we going to keep following her?" Paula asked.

"No. She'll take the van back to the Tenderloin, then go home." He shrugged. "I have someone here, just outside Hunter's Point, who'll be picking her up in case she doesn't. And someone back in the Tenderloin. But she's done for the night." He paused, staring out at the tarmac. "I need to see what's inside those crates. I've seen the manifests, but they're identified as hydroponic equipment." He looked at Paula, then reached under the seat and pulled out a thermos and a ceramic mug. "Can I buy you a cup of coffee?"

Paula smiled and nodded. "Sure."

Tremaine poured coffee into the mug and handed it to her. Apparently he was going to drink straight from the thermos. Paula sipped at the coffee, which was hot and surprisingly good, though stronger than she liked. She imagined it eating away at her stomach.

"Are we waiting for something?" she asked.

"No. I just want to talk." He drank from the thermos, looked out at the tarmac and the ship again. "There's something happening here, and it's got to do with the recruiting vans, some of them, anyway, and New Hong Kong, and medical research they're doing up there. And there's something to do with the mayor, and the mayor's nephew getting himself killed. And, I'm pretty sure, something to do with Chick."

"I don't know why he was killed," Paula said, shaking her head. "I really don't."

Tremaine nodded. "I thought maybe you didn't. But you

might know something, what he was up to, who he was working with, anything like that.''

Paula shook her head again. ''He was bootlegging body-bags. With Jenny Woo, and Mixer. Some other people I didn't know. But he'd been doing that a long time. And it wasn't something to get killed over.''

''Probably not. But something was.''

''I don't know. Chick didn't tell me about his 'business dealings,' and I didn't ask. I didn't *want* to know, because I didn't like any of it. Last couple of weeks before he was killed, hell, he didn't seem any different. I hadn't seen too much of him because he had so much going, but Chick did that a lot.'' She paused, looking at Tremaine. ''He'd been fucking Jenny Woo, but that was over, months ago.'' She sighed, looking out the windshield, sipping her coffee. ''Christ, what else? He was always fucking up, and this time it got him shot in the head.'' She turned back to Tremaine. ''Why do *you* think he was killed?''

Tremaine shrugged. ''I think he stumbled across something, and whatever it was, I think he was trying to sell it. And someone killed him for it, either the people he was trying to sell it to, or the people he'd taken it from. That's my best guess. I was hoping you'd know more.''

Paula leaned back against the seat and closed her eyes, the ache starting up in her chest again. Why had she loved the goddamn fuck-up all these years? Screwing other women until the guilts twisted him up. Periodic bouts of abusing one drug or another. The smoking and the filthy bathroom and kitchen, and the irresponsibility he'd never grown out of.

But Chick had saved all the letters she'd ever written to him. And when she and Chick were together and they were ramped and on, they were something out of this fucking world—on stage, in bed, or just sitting together listening to music with the rain pouring outside. The best times of her life had been spent with Chick.

Paula opened her eyes and sat up, staring out at the tarmac and the gantry. "Take me home," she said.

When the Plymouth pulled in to the curb in front of Paula's apartment building, Tremaine didn't ask to come up, and Paula didn't invite him. They sat for a while in silence, the engine idling.

"Tremaine," Paula said. "What is that, first or last name?"

"Neither," Tremaine said. "Well, that's not true. It *is* my last name, but it's the only name I use on my stories. It's the only name I use anywhere."

"Isn't there something else I can call you? I feel weird calling you Tremaine. If we're going to be spending more time together, there must be something. Like a first name?"

Tremaine smiled. "Yes, there's a first name."

"So what is it?"

"Ian."

Paula smiled back at him. "That's a name that'll do." She got out of the car, closed the door, then stuck her head in through the open window. "Goodbye, Ian. Call me. Or I'll call you."

He nodded. "Goodbye, Paula."

She backed away, and Tremaine put the car in gear and pulled out into the street. Paula was tired, and didn't want to move. She stood on the sidewalk, watching the Plymouth drive away.

A cough sounded behind her, and Paula turned. A figure emerged from the building shadows, left hand outstretched.

"Got a buck, lady?"

The man's voice was harsh and croaking. His hair was ragged, almost choppy, his beard scraggly, and his face was smeared with burn scars between the ragged clumps of hair. The man's right hand was heavily bandaged, and the arm hung awkwardly at his side. He was a wreck, but there was something familiar about him.

With her right hand in her jacket pocket, fingers gripping the gravity knife, Paula dug into her jeans with her other hand, pulled out a couple of bills. A five and a one. She took a couple of steps forward, held out the bills, then set them in the man's outstretched hand. The man's fingers curled around the money; then he nodded and said, "Thanks, lady," and turned away.

The eyes. That was what was so familiar, his eyes. Paula watched the man shuffle down the street. Mixer. They were like Mixer's eyes, she thought, and another ache drove through her chest. Chick and Mixer. Jesus. Paula turned away from the man and climbed the steps to the building's front door.

NINETEEN

CARLUCCI SAT IN the basement dark, listening to Miles Davis. Soundtrack pieces from an old movie called *Siesta.* He'd watched the movie once, but it was too damn weird for him; the music, though, was great. He watched the pulsing colored lights of the sound system, the shimmer of the street light pooling in through the tiny, high basement window. His trumpet lay on the sofa beside him, untouched for the last hour. All he wanted to do was listen to Miles blow.

The basement door opened, light slashing down the stairs. Christina stood in the doorway, a shadow outlined by the hall light.

"Dad?"

"Yes?"

"Sorry to bother you, but there's someone at the door for you."

"That's all right." He sat forward, blinking. "Who is it?"

"I don't know, she wouldn't say. A woman."

"I'll be right up." He picked up the remote and shut down the system, then climbed the stairs.

On the front porch stood a woman in dark robes, beautiful blue eyes gazing at him. "Frank Carlucci?" she said. Her hair was damp, and Carlucci could see wet sidewalk and street behind her.

"Yes."

"I'm Saint Lucy."

Carlucci looked at her, at her robes, her soft leather boots, her long hair, those stunning blue eyes. She didn't look crazy. "Saint Lucy," he finally repeated.

"Yes," the woman said. "One of the Saints."

"And you want to talk to me."

St. Lucy nodded. "It's about Minor Danzig."

"Who?"

"Sorry. Mixer."

Mixer. Carlucci took a step back. "Come on in. We can talk inside."

St. Lucy shook her head. "No, just come with me, please. Mixer is alive, and he wants to talk to you. I'm to take you to him."

Mixer alive. Was it true? Or just a scam to lure him somewhere? Looking at St. Lucy, he couldn't quite believe she was lying. Which meant nothing, he knew. He also knew that she wouldn't be answering too many questions from him. It was either go with her now, or not.

"Will we be going into the Tenderloin?" he asked.

St. Lucy hesitated a moment, then nodded.

"All right," Carlucci said. "I'll go with you. You want to come inside and wait for a minute? I've got to get a couple things, let my family know I'm going."

"I'll wait here," St. Lucy said.

Carlucci left the front door open. Andrea and Christina, in the kitchen, looked up at him as he came in.

"I've got to go out for a while," he told them. "I have no idea how late I'll be."

"Where's the woman?" Andrea asked.

"Waiting on the porch. She wouldn't come inside." He

glanced back through the doorway, but couldn't quite see St. Lucy.

Carlucci went into the bedroom, opened the closet, and took out his shoulder holster; he worked his arms into it, then reached up onto the top shelf for his 9mm Browning, tucked it into the holster. Finally, he put on his slick-skin raincoat.

He returned to the kitchen, kissed Andrea and Christina goodbye, then joined St. Lucy on the front porch, locking the door behind him.

"You want me to drive?" he asked.

"No," she said. "We'll take the streetcar."

Carlucci nodded, then he and St. Lucy stepped down from the porch and headed down the street.

Carlucci never felt quite comfortable in the Tenderloin. He wasn't afraid, he just thought he stood out, that everyone on the street looked at him and knew he was a cop, knew he didn't belong. He *didn't* belong. He'd known cops who did seem to fit into the Tenderloin—Tanner, Koto, Francie Miller—but he wasn't one of them. The last time he'd been inside the Tenderloin was three years ago, when they'd brought out the Chain Killer.

It was sensory overload for Carlucci. The lights, the flashing and sweeping signs, the message streamers swimming through the air, vehicles of all kinds jammed into the roadways, and the swarming mass of people. Most parts of the city were crowded, but there was nothing like this anywhere else.

Carlucci and St. Lucy were in the Euro Quarter, but close to the Asian so that he caught occasional glimpses of a Red Dragon in the air a few blocks away, smoke pouring from its nostrils. Directly above them here in the Euro, tensor wires were strung across the streets from building to building, at the fourth floor and higher. Carlucci watched the flashes of color shooting across them.

St. Lucy took his arm, guided him into a narrow alley that

wasn't as crowded as the street. Half a dozen barrel fires were burning, several people clustered around each one. A dogboy crawled past them, barking, the metal tail wagging through his pants. Parrots squawked from a mass of bromeliads on a landing three floors above. Two squealing girls on bicycles careened along the alley, bumping against people and the alley walls.

St. Lucy stopped before a wooden door, took a set of keys from inside the folds of her robes, and unlocked the door. She opened it, stepped quickly inside, and pressed her hand against a wall plate. She pulled Carlucci in after her, then shut the door and locked it.

They were in a bare entry. St. Lucy led the way down a hall, then up a stairway. The plaster walls were cracked, covered with a mosaic of paint and peeling wallpaper. Light came from dim, bare bulbs in ceramic wall sockets up near the ceiling. On the third floor they left the stairwell, entered another hall. St. Lucy stopped just outside an open doorway, and gestured inside. Carlucci approached the doorway and looked in.

Sitting at a table in a small kitchen was a bearded wreck of a man, his forehead and upper cheeks swirled with burn scars. He was holding a thick ceramic mug with a hand that was a hideous and fascinating fusion of metal and flesh. The man raised the mug to his mouth, the movement stiff and unsure, then returned it to the table.

"I'll leave you alone," St. Lucy said. She touched Carlucci's arm, then walked away, along the hall, down the stairs.

"Hey, Carlucci," the man said.

"Mixer?" There *was* something familiar about the man's voice, something about his face despite the beard and scars.

"Yeah, it's me. Hell of a disguise, isn't it?" He raised his mug. "Want some coffee?"

Carlucci shook his head. For some reason he was reluctant to enter the room. "People think you're dead."

Mixer nodded. "Come in and sit down, for Christ's sake. It's not catching."

Carlucci entered the room, walked to the table, and sat across from Mixer. Close up, he could see it *was* Mixer sitting in front of him; but close up, Mixer looked even worse. Especially the hand, scarred flesh fused to metal, both flesh and metal bent and distorted in places they shouldn't be. Mixer was wearing a long-sleeved shirt, and Carlucci had the impression the damage extended up along his arm.

"Does Paula know you're alive?"

Mixer shook his head. "Other than Saint Katherine and Saint Lucy, you're the only one."

"Jesus, Mixer, what the fuck happened?"

Mixer made a sound that might have been some kind of laugh. "The Saints happened. Saint Katherine, especially." He looked away and breathed deeply once. "Saint Katherine's Trial. Total burn, man." He held up his right hand and stared at it, the metal and flesh melted together like cooled lava. "I was wearing an exoskeleton. It kind of got fused to me." He finally looked back at Carlucci. "But I survived. And I'm alive."

Carlucci nodded. "And you're not a spikehead anymore."

Mixer smiled. "Yeah, how 'bout that?" He got up from the table, took his mug to the stove, and poured himself more coffee. There was an amber bottle beside the stove, and he uncapped it, poured some into the coffee. He turned to Carlucci, holding up the bottle. "How 'bout a drink?"

"What is it?" Not that it mattered, really.

"Bad Scotch."

"Sure," Carlucci said. He noticed that now Mixer's right arm hung limply at his side, and that he had switched to doing everything with his left. Mixer brought his own mug to the table, got another from the cupboard, hooked the handle with his left thumb and grabbed the bottle with fingers and palm, brought mug and bottle to the table, and set them before Carlucci. He poured Scotch into Carlucci's mug, then sat down heavily.

"How bad's the arm?" Carlucci asked.

"Bad," Mixer said. "But it gets better every day. They're trying to replace or repair some of the exo motors so they can help out more." He held the arm up for a moment, then dropped it back to the table. "It's what saved my life apparently."

Mixer left it at that, and Carlucci sipped from the mug. Mixer was right, the Scotch was bad; it burned his lips and tongue. But it also burned going down his throat and into his stomach, and Carlucci thought maybe that was good.

"The Saints announced you were dead." When Mixer nodded, Carlucci said, "Why?"

"They were paid to kill me."

After a long silence, Carlucci again asked, "Why?", meaning something different this time. And then, "Who?"

Mixer gave out the choking laugh sound again. "Yeah, those two questions are tied together, aren't they?" He drank from his coffee, then reached across the table for the Scotch and added more to his mug. "The mayor paid them," he said. "Not directly, of course, but they found out who it was." Mixer shrugged. "Why? I don't know, but I've got an idea."

"Which is?"

Mixer shook his head and drank again before continuing. "I don't really know anything, you gotta understand that. Which is why I never thought I had this kind of trouble. I don't know what it's about. But I can put Chick and the mayor's nephew together. I had connections to both, Chick was a friend, and they're both dead." He shook his head again. "I think maybe somebody decided I know more than I do." Mixer winced, put his hand to his shoulder and rubbed, twisting head and neck.

"You all right?" Carlucci asked.

"Christ, I'm alive. No complaints."

"That's another question," Carlucci said. "Why *are* you still alive?"

Mixer breathed deeply twice. "I survived the trial," he said. "Never happened before. The trial always leaves the accused dead, or a mental washout. I survived."

"But the Saints announced you did die in the trial."

"Most of the Saints think I did. Apparently I looked dead when they hauled me away. Saint Katherine and Saint Lucy are the only ones who know I'm alive. They saved my life. They got a doctor for me, nursed me. Saint Katherine and Saint Lucy saved my life."

"It was Saint Katherine's trial?"

"Right."

"And who took the contract to kill you?"

"Saint Katherine and Saint Lucy," Mixer said, smiling.

"Then why the hell did they save your life?"

"It's complicated." After a long pause, Mixer shook his head. "No, I'm not going to try to explain it. It doesn't matter."

"But they announced that you had died."

Mixer nodded. "For my protection. And theirs. We're all better off if the mayor and his pals think I'm dead."

Carlucci sipped more of the bad Scotch. He needed it. "All right, then. What *do* you know about this?"

Mixer drank, shifted in the chair; he slid his right arm slowly back and forth across the table, making a harsh, scratching noise. "Body-bags, to start with. Chick and I bootlegged them. We were in it with Jenny Woo and Poppy Chandler. The mayor's nephew provided a lot of the big financing."

"Body-bags," Carlucci said, shaking his head. He pictured a man completely wrapped in neural nets, twitching and twitching, eyes rolled back, foam spattering from his mouth. "Nice business," he said.

Mixer looked away, seemed to gaze out the kitchen window. There was nothing outside to be seen except grate-covered windows and crumbling brick across the way. "Yeah," Mixer said, "it's a fucked business. It's what we did.'' He turned back to Carlucci. ''But it's not something to get killed over.''

''So what is?''

Mixer shrugged. ''Chick had something going with Kashen, or had hooked something from Kashen, I could never be sure. The nephew, not the mayor. Chick didn't talk about it, except to say he'd finally gone nuclear, and was going to make enough money never to have to do a deal again. He was going to retire.'' Mixer shook his head. ''Well, he retired all right.''

''And you don't know what he had?''

''No. Something to do with New Hong Kong, something to do with the mayor. It was all messy. Kashen and his uncle, that was a wonky deal, too. Kashen couldn't stand his uncle, but they were connected, they were logged into each other. Kashen was doing something for him, something to do with New Hong Kong. But the way Kashen talked, he was getting ready to screw over his uncle somehow.'' Mixer shrugged again. ''I think Chick was mixed up in all that. And Chick . . . man, that guy never knew when he was in over his head, and he always was. He wasn't nearly as smart as he thought he was, and it finally got him killed.'' He raised a ragged eyebrow at Carlucci, a distorted gesture with all the scarring. ''*That's* what I know,'' he said. ''Which shouldn't be enough to get me killed, but it just about did.'' He drank again, then held the mug out toward Carlucci. ''I plan to know a hell of a lot more.'' He lowered his mug, then raised his right arm, rotating it slightly and wincing. ''I've already paid for it, and I'm going to know just what the fuck I've paid for.''

''How are you going to do that?'' Carlucci asked.

''I don't know yet. Saint Katherine and Saint Lucy will help me, and they have a lot of strange contacts. And there's something else. You know who Tremaine is?''

Tremaine again. Carlucci nodded.

''He's digging into this mess,'' Mixer said. ''He's been asking Paula about Chick. I got a feeling he might know more about what's going on than any of us.''

Wouldn't be the first time, Carlucci thought. ''I think I want to talk to him,'' Carlucci said.

''Yeah, so do I. Might not be too hard. He's been seeing Paula, I think.''

''What do you mean?''

''Like, personally. You know.'' Mixer gave a harsh laugh. ''Like maybe they're slippin' 'n' slidin' between the sheets.'' He closed his eyes for a few moments, then opened them. ''I don't know,'' he said, somber now. ''I think it started, he was asking her about Chick, and something happened between them. Sparks or something.''

Sparks. Carlucci hadn't heard from Sparks yet, and he should have by now. If Paula and Tremaine were spending time together, what did that mean? Anything?

''I need to talk to Tremaine,'' he said to Mixer.

''I'm going to see Paula soon, let her know I'm still alive. I'll let her know you want to talk to him. I'll let her know *I* want to talk to him.'' He brought the mug to his lips, then looked down into it. ''Fuck the coffee.'' He set the mug down, poured Scotch into it. He looked at Carlucci. ''More?''

Carlucci finished off the Scotch in his mug, then held the mug out to Mixer. Mixer poured. ''Tell Paula not to mention to Tremaine that I'm looking into Chick's death. Just that it's to do with the mayor's nephew.''

''Okay.''

They drank a while in silence. Mixer was obviously in pain, but didn't say anything.

''Is there anything you need?'' Carlucci eventually asked. ''Something I can do for you?''

''No,'' Mixer said. ''What I need you can't give me.'' He paused, shaking his head. ''Shit, I feel like an old man. Not just physically.'' He raised his right arm and gestured at his head with metal and flesh, not quite touching it with his fingers. ''In here, too. I feel older inside.''

"Wiser?" Carlucci asked.

Mixer smiled. "No, just older."

Mixer had survived the trial, he was still alive, but Carlucci wondered if he would ever really recover. "Are you all right here?" he asked. "They're not holding you? Against your will?"

"No, I'm fine. I know it sounds weird, but Saint Katherine and Saint Lucy are doing everything they can for me."

It was hard to believe, but Carlucci didn't doubt Mixer. There was a lot more going on here than he understood. He knew that much. He also knew it was time to go.

"Is there anything else?" he asked Mixer.

Mixer shook his head. "This was just about Chick, at first," he said. "That's all. Paula and I wanted to find out who killed him, and why. But there's more now. I want to see this whole fucking thing blown open. I want to know what the fuck is going on, and I want to see people pay. Anything I find out, I'll let you know. I want you to do the same."

Carlucci stood up from the table, shaking his head. "I can't promise that, Mixer."

"I know. Do what you can, though. Yeah?"

Carlucci nodded. "I will." Then, "I've got to go."

"Downstairs, Saint Lucy's waiting. She'll make sure you get out okay."

"If I see Paula before you do . . ."

Mixer shook his head. "Don't tell her you've seen me. I need to do that thing myself."

"All right." Carlucci started to leave, then turned back to Mixer. "Take care of yourself."

Mixer smiled and nodded.

TWENTY

MIXER HAD PUT it off for days, but now he finally went by his apartment. It was only a couple of blocks from where he was staying with St. Katherine and St. Lucy, but it seemed much farther; he felt he was walking into the past. He still had his keys—the Saints had saved his things after the trial—and he used them and his code to get into the building. He passed on the elevator and climbed the three flights of stairs to the fourth floor.

He didn't need his keys to get into his apartment. The door was wide open. Christ, he thought, nobody had even bothered to shut the door, not even his neighbors. How long had it been like this? Days? A week?

Inside, nothing. The place had been picked clean. Bits of trash lay on the floor, in the corners, but nothing else. No furniture, no books, no music, no clothes. In the kitchen was some rotting food, but no plates, no pots or pans. Even the refrigerator and stove, which came with the apartment, were gone. He was half surprised no one had ripped the cupboards from the walls and hauled those away.

In the bathroom, too, everything was gone, medicine cabinet cleared out; even the toilet paper had been taken. Mixer sat on the closed lid of the toilet, staring out at the empty apartment. Everything he owned was gone. Vanished. He wondered if it had been the mayor's ferrets who'd cleaned out the place, or scavengers descending on it once word got out that he was dead. Maybe both. It didn't really matter.

New life, he said to himself. St. Lucy was right. No more Mixer. Minor Danzig reborn.

He sat, not moving, trying to imagine what it would be like.

Mixer followed Paula for hours. He wasn't sure why. Afraid to go up to her and tell her he was alive? Everything seemed different, changed; maybe he was afraid *she* had changed, too, changed so much she wouldn't, or couldn't, be his friend anymore. He'd wanted her to be more than a friend, though, after Chick died. Even before that. He'd never been able to tell her. That was all impossible now; he knew that. Probably always had been. Now there was Tremaine, and St. Katherine. Crazy, all of it. He didn't know what he wanted.

He'd picked her up late afternoon coming out of her apartment building and followed her to the Lumiere. He bought a cup of coffee from a window cafe, drank it, then sat down near the corner across from the Lumiere, where he had a view of the entrance. He set the empty cup in front of him and settled in.

Two hours later, when Paula came out of the theater, Mixer had collected several bucks in change. I must look bad, he thought. He pocketed the money, dumped the cup, and took off after Paula, staying half a block back. She went to her apartment, stayed inside for fifteen minutes, then came back out and headed into the heart of the Polk Corridor as the sun was setting.

Paula stopped in front of Christiano's and leaned against the building. Mixer had to hang back, crouched beside a phone box. Looked like she was waiting for someone.

Not for me, Mixer said to himself. Paula thought he was dead. But he wasn't, and he needed to tell her. There was way too much unfinished; there was still Chick between them, and Chick's death, if nothing else.

If nothing else. *Jesus, Mixer, what the hell are you thinking?* He hadn't spoken a word to her, and already he was assuming that everything between them was dead and gone. Maybe the goddamn trial did fry his brain.

Paula *was* waiting for someone. Tremaine, of course. Mixer saw him before Paula did, coming down the sidewalk, wire-rim specs flashing the lights of the night. Mixer rose to his feet to get a better view. If Paula was singing for Tremaine, it wasn't because of his looks. That had always been part of it with Chick, Mixer was pretty sure of that. But not with Tremaine.

When Paula saw him, she smiled and pushed off the wall. Mixer hadn't seen her smile like that in years, and it made his chest ache. She and Tremaine spoke to each other, then went into Christiano's.

Mixer felt suddenly hungry, and for more than just food. But food was something he could take care of. He crossed the street, walked past a target alley, and bought a falafel from an old Arab woman cooking on basement steps. As he ate, he wandered up and down the Corridor, never getting too far from Christiano's.

The street seemed to be on downers tonight. The air was heavy with heat and humidity, but it was more than that. People moved like they were in slow motion. Even a string of bone dancers shifted aimlessly along, arms and legs flapping limply. Weed hawkers called out to him, but they weren't trying very hard. The stunner arcade was half empty. The stagnant energy in the Corridor was dragging Mixer down, and he was already more than low enough.

He was only half a block away when he saw Paula and Tremaine come out of Christiano's. They stood for a minute on the sidewalk, looking around, talking, then headed in Mixer's direction. He pulled back into the entryway of a bone-slotting club and turned his face from the street until they had passed him. Then he moved back out onto the sidewalk and followed.

Paula and Tremaine didn't hold hands, or put their arms around each other, or kiss, anything like that, but there was something intimate about the way they walked together—the way Paula leaned her head toward Tremaine to say something, the way Tremaine touched her shoulder, the way he looked and smiled at Paula, and the way she laughed. It all made Mixer feel strange and drifty.

They stopped and looked in the window of a dinkum store, both laughing at something Paula pointed to. Half a block later they stood and watched a kinetic oil painting in the window of an art gallery. When they finally went into a spice and espresso bar, Mixer had had enough. He didn't wait for them. Instead, he turned back and walked in the direction of Paula's apartment.

Three things could happen, he figured. They could both come back to Paula's place; or they could go to Tremaine's; or they could each go their own away. The odds were good Paula would be coming home, one way or another.

Mixer still had keys to her place, more useful now than the ones to his own apartment. He unlocked the main building door, stood in the lobby for a few moments, then climbed the stairs and walked down the hall to her apartment.

He stood in front of her apartment door for a minute, keys in hand. He pocketed the keys. It would be too much for her, he decided. To come home and find a stranger inside her apartment. It would be bad enough to find him sitting in the hall.

Mixer sat on the floor, his back against her door, and waited.

TWENTY-ONE

PAULA WAS JUST as nervous this time, climbing the stairs to her apartment with Tremaine just behind her, but it was a different kind of anxiety. There was more excitement in it, as well as a stronger, different kind of fear. And, as before, she could not completely stop thinking of Chick.

They reached the third floor, and had just started down the hall when Paula sensed something wrong. She slowed, stared ahead, and saw a shadow, a form in front of her door at the end of the hall.

"What is it?" Tremaine asked.

"I don't know." She continued forward, saw that it was the form of a man; then, as they drew closer, recognized the man who had scrounged money from her the other night. She stopped a few feet from him. "What the hell are you doing here?"

"Don't you recognize me?" the man said. His voice didn't seem as harsh as it had that night. His head was tilted forward and to the side so that she saw mostly hair and beard.

"Yeah, I recognize you. I gave you money the other night, outside. And that's where you should be. Outside."

The man leaned forward and pushed himself slowly to his feet. His right arm, which had been bandaged before, was now bare—metal and scarred flesh twisted and melted together, almost shiny in the hall light. He turned to face her. "You still don't recognize me, Paula?"

His voice. She knew the voice. Paula stared at him, and her heartbeat kicked up, pounding away inside her. And the eyes, she knew those eyes, too. But it couldn't be. He was . . .

"Mixer?"

The man smiled without saying anything.

"Mixer?" she said again. And then she knew it was him, and she ran forward and threw her arms around him, hugging him tightly to her. "Jesus, Mixer, you're alive!"

"Yeah, Paula, I'm alive. But you're killing my arm."

She let him go, looked into his face, feeling the tears pooling up in her eyes, then put her arms around his neck, pressing his bearded face against her skin. "Mixer, I can't fucking believe it." She let go again, wiping her cheeks with the back of her hand, staring into his wrecked face. "Jesus, look at you." She shook her head, looking down at his arm. "Is that the exo?"

Mixer nodded.

"What the hell happened?" Then, "The Saints announced you were dead."

"I am," he said.

Paula didn't know what to say. Then she remembered Tremaine, and she turned around, saw him standing a few feet away. "Ian, this is my friend Mixer. Mixer, this is Tremaine."

"I know who he is," Mixer said. He smiled. "Ian?"

"You can just call me Tremaine."

"I will," Mixer said.

"Come on," Paula said. "Let's go inside where we can sit down and talk."

"I think I should go," Tremaine said.

"Oh, no," Mixer replied, shaking his head. "I need to talk

to Paula, but I need to talk to you, too. You're not going anywhere."

Tremaine smiled. "I'm not?"

"No."

"Jesus," Paula said. "What the hell is all this?"

Tremaine shrugged, still smiling. "It's fine. I'm happy to stay. I'd like to know what Mixer wants to talk to me about."

Paula sighed and looked back and forth at the two men, who seemed to be having a good old-fashioned stare-down. She unlocked the door and let them inside, half-tempted to pull the door shut behind the men and lock them in. But she was too damn happy to see Mixer alive, and so she followed them in, turning on the apartment lights.

They all stood silently just inside the door, the kitchen on their left, the piles of Chick's things on their right. Paula waved at the kitchen table. "Sit down, both of you," she said. "Anyone want anything, coffee, tea, something to eat? Mixer?"

Mixer walked over to the table and sat in one of the chairs, laying his injured hand and arm on the table. "I could really use a drink."

Tremaine sat across the table from Mixer, and the two men continued to stare at each other.

"Tremaine?" Paula asked.

"I'll have whatever Mixer's having."

How accommodating, Paula thought. She went to the refrigerator, opened the freezer, and pulled out a bottle of Stolichnaya vodka. She looked at the bottle, her gaze unfocused, the cold seeping into her hand, making it ache. It was the only booze she had in the place; it was what Chick had liked to drink more than anything else. She got two small tumblers from the cupboard, took them to the table with the bottle. "Help yourselves," she said. She went back to the refrigerator and poured herself a glass of orange juice, then joined the two men at the table. Mixer was already draining his glass; he poured another.

"What happened?" Paula asked. "Are you okay?"

"Yeah, yeah, I'm fine," Mixer said, nodding. He laughed. "What happened? I'll tell you." He took a drink, stared into the small glass. "Chick used to drink this stuff, didn't he?" He looked at Paula, who nodded. "Well. I'm sure it'll do the job." He set the glass down, glanced at Tremaine, then turned back to Paula.

"I went to a wham-wham, remember? I'd pumped myself full of neutralizers, and they kept me from caving in to whatever they'd gassed into the place, but they made me a little misted, too, I think. I don't know. I was looking for someone, and I got into a little trouble with two freaks, and someone bailed me out. A woman. I wasn't thinking straight, like why were the two freaks afraid of her? By the time I figured it out, it was too late. She'd collared me, and I was gone."

"Saint Katherine," Paula said.

Mixer nodded. "That was her. There was this and that, a few days, and then the trial." He polished off his vodka, coughed, and poured some more. "Let's just say I survived, and this is what it did to me." He held up his right arm, rotated it. "Still pretty fucking rabid, isn't it?"

"But the Saints announced over the nets that you had died."

Mixer dropped his arm to the table with a thump. "It's complicated. But if I want to stay alive, I'd better stay dead. You can't tell anyone you've seen me, you can't tell anyone you know I'm alive." He turned to Tremaine. "You too."

"I understand," Tremaine said.

"Do you?"

"Who knows you're alive, then?" Paula asked.

"Two of the Saints. The rest think I'm dead. You and Tremaine." He paused, staring at Tremaine. "And Carlucci."

"You've seen him?" Paula asked, wondering why he was

looking so intently at Tremaine.

"Last night." Still staring at Tremaine.

"Frank Carlucci?" Tremaine asked.

Mixer nodded. "Yeah, that Carlucci. And he wants to talk to you."

Tremaine smiled. "Really? I've made several interview requests, but I've always been turned down. And now he wants to talk to me. What about?"

"Something about the mayor's nephew. Bill Kashen."

"He thinks I know something about the murder?"

"Apparently."

Paula watched the two men, feeling there was some kind of strange contest in progress, some cat-and-mousing. But what was it all about?

"How do you know Carlucci?" Tremaine asked, glancing back and forth between Paula and Mixer.

Paula didn't say anything, remembering Carlucci's warning. No one was supposed to know he was digging into Chick's murder.

"Remember the Chain Killer a few years ago?" Mixer said.

Tremaine nodded.

"I got mixed up in that whole mess. By accident. I got to know Carlucci through a friend of his."

"Louis Tanner."

Mixer nodded. "That's the guy. See, you always know more than anyone expects. That's why Carlucci wants to talk to you. He knows you've been digging into stuff with the mayor, the mayor's nephew."

There was a long silence, and Paula was still afraid to say anything, afraid to give anything away. She didn't think anything bad would happen if Tremaine knew everything, but she couldn't know for sure. And she had made promises to Carlucci.

"Does Carlucci . . . ?" Tremaine paused, as if unsure he should say anything. The reporter, trying not to give away more than he had to. "Does Carlucci know there's a connection between the mayor's nephew's killing, and Chick Roberts's killing?"

"Is there?" Mixer asked.

"I think so."

Mixer shrugged. "He didn't say anything about it. You'll have to ask him."

There was another silence, and Paula felt extremely uncomfortable. She wanted them both to leave.

"I don't suppose," Mixer began, "that you'd be willing to tell me everything you know about all this."

Tremaine shook his head. "Not a chance."

"You wouldn't happen to know why the mayor would want me dead, do you?"

"What?" Paula asked. "What is this?"

"Do you?" Mixer said again.

"No," Tremaine said. "Are you sure he does?"

"Not anymore," Mixer said, smiling. "He thinks it's done." Then, "Would you tell me if you knew?"

Tremaine nodded. "Yes." He paused. "Maybe you and I should talk sometime. Maybe we can help each other."

"Maybe."

Tremaine stood. Paula noticed that he hadn't touched the vodka. "I think I'd better go."

This time Mixer didn't object. He just said, "Don't forget. Carlucci wants to talk to you."

"I won't." Tremaine turned to Paula. "I don't know what to say. This is going to be difficult for a while, I guess. I'll call you soon, all right?"

Paula nodded, relieved that Tremaine was leaving, and feeling guilty about it.

Tremaine walked to the apartment door, opened it, and left, closing the door behind him.

• • •

"Are you sleeping with him?" Mixer asked.

"It's none of your fucking business," Paula said, furious with him. "That's the first thing out of your mouth, now that we're alone? I've been thinking you were dead, all these days, and that's what you've got to say to me?"

Mixer looked down at his glass. "Sorry," he said. He poured himself another drink, sucked some of it down. He looked up at Paula. "I *am* sorry, for Christ's sake."

Paula put her head into her hands, rubbing at her eyes. "It's all right." She reached out, took his right hand gently in hers, feeling the metal, the alternately smooth and ridged, scarred flesh. "Are you really okay?"

Mixer nodded. "Yeah."

"What *happened*?" she asked, knowing he hadn't told her everything while Tremaine had been there.

"Saint Katherine was contracted to kill me through her trial," Mixer said. "By Mayor Kashen."

"That's why you asked Tremaine."

"Yeah. Do you believe him? That he doesn't know? That he'd tell me if he did?"

Paula hesitated, feeling awkward. "Yes," she finally said.

"Yeah, I do too." He took a sip of the vodka, twisting his face. "Maybe you get used to this," he said, refilling his glass. "The trial scorched my arm and face instead of my brain, and I'm alive, and most of the time my head's all there. Saint Katherine and Saint Lucy took me away, and I guess I looked dead, because all the other Saints think the trial killed me. Saint Katherine and Saint Lucy took care of me. They brought in a doctor, they stayed with me night and day, Saint Katherine in particular. They saved my life."

"But Saint Katherine was supposed to kill you."

Mixer nodded. "Yeah. But I survived, and she believes I've been chosen. Chosen to be her consort." He paused. "She says she loves me."

Paula looked at him, watched his eyes blinking at her, his

chest moving with each breath. "Does she?"

Mixer smiled. "Yes. I know it sounds crazy, and hell, it probably *is* crazy, but the woman loves me."

"And how do you feel about her?" Paula asked.

Mixer's smile faded, and he shook his head. "I have no idea."

"What are you going to do now?" Paula asked.

"I don't know. Stay dead for a while, that's for sure. Try to find out why the mayor wanted me dead. It's all tied up with Chick, somehow. And Tremaine probably knows more about what's going on than anyone else right now. I'll try talking to him again."

They sat at the table a while longer without talking. Paula finished off her orange juice, and Mixer drank one more glass of the vodka. He slid the glass back and forth, then stood. "I've gotta use the head."

While Mixer was in the bathroom, Paula cleared off the table, leaving the vodka and Mixer's glass in case he wanted more. She drank Tremaine's vodka, slowly, steadily, savoring it going down her throat cold and hot at the same time, melting its way down into her stomach. Then she put the glass in the sink and stood with her hips against the counter, looking at nothing. She was exhausted, drained.

She should be feeling ecstatic, seeing Mixer alive when she'd thought he was dead, when she'd spent days grieving for him, combining it with her continuing grief for Chick. And she was happy, she *was*, but she was anxious, too, worried about what was still to come. Mixer being alive didn't end things. In a sense, it only added to her worry.

Mixer came out of the bathroom stretching and grimacing. He looked at the vodka and glass, shook his head. "I don't need any more," he said.

Paula put the glass in the sink with the others, put the bottle back in the freezer. There wasn't much left.

"Would it be all right if I stayed here tonight?" Mixer

asked. "I can hardly walk, and I'm not up to going back to the Tenderloin right now. The booze cuts the pain, but puts me out. I can sleep on the floor, on some blankets."

"Of course you can stay. And you don't have to sleep on the floor, Mixer. There's plenty of room in the bed."

"Are you sure?"

Paula nodded, smiling. "I'm sure." She walked up to him and kissed him on the cheek. "Let's go."

She went into the bedroom, turned on the nightstand lamp, thinking about the night Tremaine had stayed. It had been a night too mixed up with other things and there was no way to judge it, no way to know if it meant anything. She turned to Mixer. "You need help getting undressed?"

"No."

"Good. I'll be back in a minute."

Paula went into the bathroom, peed, then washed up, filling her hands over and over with water, splashing it across her face, rubbing at her eyes. She stared at her reflection in the mirror, at the dark patches under her eyes, at the tiny crow's-feet that were just developing, at the narrow crease in her forehead, thinking about Mixer's ruined face. She shook her head to herself.

Back in the bedroom, Mixer was stripped down to his boxers, sitting on the edge of the bed. Paula undressed, put on a light nightshirt that hung to her knees, then sat in her overstuffed chair, facing Mixer.

"You look awful, Mixer. Your hair looks like shit, the beard's a disaster, and your arm, well, you know what the arm is like." She smiled at him. "And you look just wonderful, absolutely wonderful. I'm so happy to see you alive."

Mixer smiled back at her. "I do look pretty bad, don't I?"

Paula nodded. "And that Saint Katherine woman loves you, anyway. Amazing."

"Yeah. She doesn't call me Mixer, by the way. She calls me by my birth name."

"And what's that?"

"Minor Danzig."

"Minor Danzig. It's a good name. Fits you. But I gotta tell you, you'll always be Mixer to me."

"I hope so," he said.

Paula got up from the chair and approached the bed. "Let's get some sleep."

Mixer nodded. It took them a few minutes to work it out so Mixer would be comfortable. Paula was afraid of rolling onto his arm in the middle of the night, but Mixer said it would be fine. Finally they were both settled in, and Paula turned off the lamp.

Paula lay on her side, gazing into the darkness of the room, slashes of light coming in through the window blinds. She could hear Mixer breathing, could feel the warmth of his body even though they were not touching.

"I slept with him once," she said.

There was a long pause, and Paula wondered if Mixer had fallen asleep. But finally he said, "Tremaine?"

"Yeah."

"And you were going to sleep with him tonight?"

"Probably."

Another long pause. "Do you love him?"

Paula almost laughed, shaking her head. "It's way too early for that, Mixer."

"Yeah, I guess so."

"But I like him." She felt she should say something more, but she didn't know what it would be.

She felt Mixer's hand rest for a moment on her hip, squeeze gently. "I hope it works out," he said. Then the hand was gone.

''Thanks, Mixer.'' Paula suddenly felt like crying, and she had no idea why. ''Good night,'' she whispered.

''Good night, Paula.''

Paula closed her eyes, and squeezed them tight against the tears.

TWENTY-TWO

THE INDIVIDUAL SLUG quarters were all different from one another. Some had a solid barrier between the small interrogator's cubicle and the slug's main quarters, with microphones and speakers so the police interrogator would never actually see the slug. Others had a glass barrier with a removable screen, so the slug could be seen if it wished.

Monk's quarters, however, were entirely different: there was no barrier, no separation of any kind. When Carlucci stepped through the door and into the dim, large room atop police headquarters, his first impression was of a constantly shifting maze. Wide, shiny black panels hung from the ceiling throughout the room, the bottom of each panel no more than a foot above the carpeted floor. All the panels were slowly turning, not in unison, creating and closing off ever-changing pathways through them. Pieces of furniture were placed among the panels—a couch, several chairs, small tables. Carlucci only saw the furniture in glimpses as the panels turned, could only see portions of the huge picture windows with their view of the city, got only hints of the information center far in the back.

The second thing that struck him was the heat—warmer than anywhere else in the building, as warm as outdoors at midday, but far, far drier. Already there was a scratchy feeling with each breath, the air was so dry.

The panels stopped turning. "Have a seat," a voice said, seeming to come from all around him. The voice was deep, booming. The lights dimmed a step or two. Small table lamps came on beside the chairs, then two more came on beside the couch, which was further back in the room, the lamps providing pockets of green-tinted light and casting new, sharper shadows. Carlucci smiled to himself, and sat in the nearest chair, setting his notebook and pen on the table beside it. Did Monk really think he would be awed by this show?

"Something to drink?" the voice asked. A man's voice, Carlucci decided, now with an echo effect. What crap.

"Coffee," Carlucci said. "Black."

Almost immediately a short, thin, elderly Asian man in a black suit appeared, zigzagging his way through the panels, carrying a tray with a clear glass cup of dark, steaming coffee. The man stopped just in front of Carlucci and held the tray out before him. Carlucci took the coffee and said, "Thank you." The man did not respond, only retreated two steps, then turned and walked back the way he had come.

"Don't worry," Monk's voice said. "He'll be going to his own room directly. We will have our privacy."

"I'm not worried," Carlucci said.

"No, I don't imagine you are."

There was nothing for a while, and Carlucci sipped at the coffee, studying the room. Two of the panels to his right, near the windows, began turning again, alternately narrowing and widening his view, but he was too far from the windows to really see much anyway.

Then all the panels began turning again, some more slowly than others, and Carlucci glimpsed movement far in the back, in the information center, a form lurching toward him. He saw two canes, two black-coated limbs half stepping, half dragging between the canes. Glimpses of a bloated torso, shoulders and arms strangely both muscular and bloated, all coated in a glistening black, like some luminescent wetsuit. A bloated and goggled face, head encased in a gleaming, studded helmet. The slug. Monk.

The slug staggered to the small couch flanked by console tables, and dropped heavily into it. The panels slowed, then stopped. He was perhaps twenty feet away, almost completely blocked from Carlucci's view by the panels; all Carlucci could see as the slug settled in was a gloved hand gripping both canes, swinging them up and over to set them behind the couch.

There was only labored breathing for some time, which gradually eased. Then the slug said, "Good evening, Lieutenant Carlucci." No more echo effect.

"Monk."

"You have not done this often," Monk said. Even without the amplification, Monk's voice was deep, authoritative.

"Just twice," Carlucci replied.

"Your friend Brendan McConnel talked with us quite a lot, until he resigned. How is Mr. McConnel?"

"He's fine."

Monk laughed. "No he's not. He's a drunk, and he's fucking a mouthless Screamer. We know what kind of sex he's *not* getting." A pause. "He shouldn't have resigned, he should have stuck with it. He understood us, I believe. I liked talking with him."

Carlucci wanted to respond, wanted to defend Brendan, wanted to tell Monk that he didn't know Brendan at all, couldn't know him, and had no right to judge what Brendan did or didn't do. But Carlucci kept it in. He needed things from Monk.

"Ask your questions," Monk said. "That's what we are both here for."

Carlucci wasn't sure where to start. He opened his notebook and stared at the questions he'd jotted on the tan, lined pages, but somehow they didn't seem right anymore.

"Are you concerned about our privacy?" Monk asked. "You needn't be. I have more detection equipment in here . . . Well, be assured, there is absolutely no way anyone will ever know what is said in here. And we both know Mayor Kashen would very much like to be hearing every word." Monk made a sound something like a laugh. "And they did try to infiltrate with listening devices. You do not need to worry."

All right, Carlucci thought, just ask a question. "You've seen all the feeds. A simple question. Who killed William Kashen, and why?"

"Two questions," Monk corrected, "and neither of them simple." He paused, the fingers of his finely sheathed hand waving like drowsy snakes. "The answer to 'who' is probably irrelevant. An uninvolved professional hired for the purpose, most likely. Apprehending and arresting the man or woman who killed William Kashen would, presumably, close the case, but would not provide you with justice. Would not be able to lead you back to whoever did the hiring. And that, of course, is whom you really want. Answering the 'why' would probably give you the answers you are looking for. But not, once again, justice. You might learn who is responsible, and why, but you probably would not be able to convict, or even bring them to court."

"I'm aware of all the flaws in our justice system," Carlucci said, cutting in at Monk's first pause. "I don't give a shit about them at the moment. I asked you a simple . . . no, change that. I asked you a direct question. Can you help me with that or not? Can you help me with anything concrete related to the case?"

Another laughing sound from Monk, then silence. His fingers, all Carlucci could see of him, had stopped moving.

"Robert Butler," Monk said. "An obvious connection. Too obvious. Did Collier ever get the safe open? I never saw a report."

"Yes. The safe was empty."

"And so is the Butler-Kashen connection. Butler was killed, I *believe*, simply to misdirect. A surmise on my part, understand, with nothing *concrete*, really, to substantiate it. William Kashen was attempting to jack Butler just as he was attempting to jack his uncle, the mayor of this beautiful city, His Honor Terrance Kashen."

"Kashen was trying to jack his uncle," Carlucci repeated, hoping for some clarification.

"Oh, yes. Something which the mayor has only recently learned for himself. Which is why he's now called you off the case."

"I haven't been called off the case."

"Not officially, no. But he's asked you to bury the case nonetheless, hasn't he?"

Carlucci didn't answer. He felt he was on shaky ground, unsure where to step next. Too many dynamics he still didn't understand. What was Monk's role in all this? He seemed more involved, somehow, than Carlucci would have expected.

More of that strangled laughter. "The mayor, His Honor, will get his in the end," Monk said. "You just watch. He's not as crucial to things as he believes, and he will be hung out to dry."

"Hung out to dry by who?" Carlucci asked.

"By *whom*," Monk corrected. "That's a good question. But I don't have an answer to it for you."

Carlucci was certain Monk was lying. But what the hell could he do about it? Nothing. Nothing but wait, dig around, ask more questions, and hope for some inadvertent clue.

"How was Kashen trying to screw over his uncle and Butler?"

"That's far less clear," Monk said. "He was trying to sell something. Information of some kind. Now. Either the buyer got what he wanted and then killed Kashen—perhaps to shut him up, perhaps to avoid a very high payment—or Kashen's source for the information discovered that Kashen had 'borrowed' it from them, and called in the loan. With Kashen's life as interest.''

''Very clever,'' Carlucci said.

''Sarcasm is more effective if it's subtler,'' Monk said. ''It doesn't sink in immediately, and then the subject is never quite sure about the intent. Much more disturbing that way.''

''Anything else?'' Carlucci asked.

''Much more. We have hardly begun.''

There was another long silence. Carlucci tried to remember what Brendan had told him. Let Monk go, let him wander around. Try not to guide him. Shit, not much chance of that.

''Your daughter,'' Monk said.

''What?''

''Caroline. She has Gould's, yes?''

''What the fuck does that have to do with this?''

''Nothing,'' Monk admitted. ''I'm just talking, trying to get to know you better. It will make the session more productive.''

''More productive for who?''

There was a slight hesitation, then, ''For both of us. Gould's, yes?''

Carlucci sank back in the chair, closed his eyes. Christ, he was tired. ''Yes, she has Gould's Syndrome.''

''A drastically shortened life,'' Monk said. ''A terrible shame. A terrible waste.'' There was a pause. ''Would it help, to compensate, if you could greatly extend the life spans of the rest of your family?''

Carlucci opened his eyes and sat up. ''What is all this?'' he asked. ''Someone else asked me something like that a few days ago.''

''Who?''

''I don't remember.''

''I'll bet you don't. It doesn't matter, it's nothing. It's in the air. A universal fantasy, a twenty-first century Grail. That's all. It was just a question.''

No, Carlucci thought, there's something more than that. But

what? Monk wasn't going to tell him.

"The Tenderloin," Monk said. "Part of the answer is there. With the Saints."

"The Saints?"

"You know who they are?"

"A little."

"Insane women," Monk said. "They can't have any answers. I don't know why I said it." Monk's voice sounded genuinely puzzled. "Perhaps they do, somewhere. But you won't be able to talk to them, you can't reach those women."

"You're a lot of help," Carlucci said.

Panels moved, turned edge on so he had a full view of Monk. Monk shifted on the couch, and the glistening black coating seemed to undulate over him. His goggled, helmeted head rose, craned forward. Pale, fleshy lips moved. "You want some real help?"

It sounded like a challenge. Carlucci nodded. "Yes, I want some real help."

Monk seemed to weave slightly, as though he had difficulty remaining upright. The lips formed an unpleasant smile.

"Chick Roberts," Monk said. "How's that for real help?"

Carlucci hesitated a moment, then asked, "Who's Chick Roberts?"

"You called up the case," Monk said. "A case that bypassed you, but you called it up. Came across the roadblock, and let it go. You didn't pursue it. Not officially. Later that day, you contacted Sergeant Ruben Santos, the officer in charge of the case, arranged to meet him outside the department building."

"We talked about the mayor's nephew."

Monk laughed. "You talked about Chick Roberts. No, I could never prove it, but I know you talked about Chick Roberts. You later called Paula Asgard, told her you checked into the case, that it was dead-ended, and that she should forget about it."

"Yes," Carlucci said. "The case was a dead end."

"The case was being buried."

"That's your interpretation."

"Yours, too," Monk insisted. "You told the girlfriend to forget about it, but *you* didn't, did you? You've been investigating it on your own, haven't you?"

"No," Carlucci said, trying to remain calm and assured. "I let it go. It wasn't my case."

Monk shook his head. "No, no, no, Lieutenant Carlucci. You kept investigating, you discovered that the Chick Roberts case is connected to William Kashen's."

"It is?"

Monk sighed heavily. "This obstinance does not help the session," he said. "We make far better progress if we work together. If we are completely open and honest."

"What a crock," Carlucci said. "This is supposed to be *my* interrogation, *my* investigation."

"You think so?" Monk said, smiling.

"What the hell are you after?"

Monk slowly shook his head and lay back on the couch, the bloated limbs and body sliding and shifting. Carlucci wished he could see the thing's eyes, not just those damn goggles. Monk's fingers flicked across something on the console beside him and the panels turned back, once more obscuring him from view. The panels weren't in exactly the same position, though, and Carlucci could see a strip of his body, another of his neck and face. He wondered if it was intentional. He watched Monk's gloved fingers pull some of the coating away from his neck, the fingers of his other hand applying a series of dermal patches to the bare skin. Then the coating was worked back.

"I'm just trying to help you," Monk eventually said.

"Then tell me, what's the connection between the Chick Roberts and the William Kashen killings?"

"The mayor wants them both buried," Monk said. "That's a hell of a connection."

"I don't know that that's true."

"It's true. You know it's true."

Carlucci rubbed at his eyes, his temple. He felt like the entire interrogation had gotten away from him. He didn't know what questions to ask. "What else?" he finally said. "What's the *real* connection?" When Monk did not immediately reply, Carlucci said, "What the hell is all this about? Why are these people killing each other? What is at stake here?"

Nothing from Monk. Gloved fingers tapped at the console. What was he doing? His head shifted, goggles and helmet, staring at something.

"The spikehead might have known," Monk said. "But the spikehead is dead."

"Mixer," Carlucci said.

"Yes, Mixer. There's the connection to the Saints."

"I don't understand," Carlucci said, though he understood perfectly well. "Mixer's dead?"

"The Saints put him on trial. And he died. They killed him. Yes, Mixer's dead."

So the slug didn't know everything. Carlucci wanted to tell him, wanted to rub that freakish face in it, but he said nothing. "Why was Chick Roberts killed?" he asked.

"I don't have the answer to that, either," Monk said.

Again, Carlucci felt certain the slug was lying. He wanted to order all the feeds sent to one of the other slugs, and set up another session, see if one of the other slugs would be able to give him something else, but he knew it was impossible. That would be pushing the mayor too far. He wished he understood where Monk stood in all this. There was something crucial there, something Carlucci didn't know.

He picked up his coffee, started to drink it, but it was lukewarm. A bad temperature. What had Monk given him so far? Nothing. A couple of small things. Butler's murder as diversion. Something about this longer life stuff. Nothing particularly useful, not even in a cryptic way. The entire session had gone nothing like Brendan had led him to expect. Monk had been far more active, far more aggressive, than he would ever have guessed.

"Why did you decide to become a slug?" he asked Monk.

No answer. Panels moved, revealing Monk again, and he gave that twisted, thick-lipped smile. "To get laid," he said. The panels shifted, cut him completely from view.

"Do you have *any* answers?" Carlucci asked.

"You haven't asked the right questions. And don't ask me what the right questions are. If I knew, I wouldn't tell you."

Carlucci pushed the coffee cup away, picked up his notebook, and stared at the questions he'd written, stared at the blank spaces between them.

"You haven't given me anything I didn't already know, or had least guessed at," Carlucci said. It was a small lie, mostly true. He felt certain Monk had given him a lot of lies, most of them quite big.

The panels shifted, revealing Monk's face and one arm.

"I'll clue you on something," Monk said. "A big secret." He paused, as though unsure whether or not to continue. "You think we're here for you, don't you? That we slugs are ensconced here in this building for you, pumping ourselves full of reason enhancers and metabolic juicers, deforming our bodies so we can help you solve difficult cases." Monk shook his head, smiling again. "*You* are here for *us*."

Monk pushed himself up, reached behind the couch, and pulled out his canes. "The session is over," he said. He punched something into the console and the panels all began turning again, shifting back and forth as Monk worked up to his feet. Then he lurched away from the couch and headed toward the back of the room. Carlucci kept waiting for him to stop and turn around to say one more thing, take one more shot, but he never did. Monk staggered through the information center, around a corner, and was gone from sight. Then all but two small lights went out, and the room was filled with shifting, leaping shadows.

Carlucci stood, picked up his notebook. He watched the whipping, slashing shadows for a minute, then turned and walked toward the door. As he reached for the handle, he heard an echoing whisper roll through the air. He couldn't be certain, but he thought the whisper said, "*Your life, Carlucci.*" Carlucci waited, but there was nothing else. He pulled the door open and left.

TWENTY-THREE

PAULA ALMOST MISSED it. Of course, she hadn't been looking for it. She hadn't been looking for anything.

It was close to midnight, and she'd just come home after closing up at the Lumiere. Once again, when she walked into her apartment and turned on the light, she stared at the stacks of Chick's things, thinking she had to do something with them. But not tonight. She was too damn tired.

She did open one of the boxes filled with Chick's home-studio discs, some of them just audio, some with video as well. Flipping through the cases, she took out one called *Aphasia Sciatica*, which she didn't recognize. She brought it into the bedroom, powered up system and monitor, put the disc into the player, and sat back in her overstuffed chair to watch.

The disc was filled with speeded-out images of what appeared to be neural surgery, both brain and spinal, backed by lots of atonal screeching industrial music. Twenty minutes into the disc Paula was starting to nod off, kind of bored by the whole thing, when there was a brief blip in the picture and sound. She kept watching for a few moments; then her head jerked and she sat up, realizing something odd had happened. She grabbed the remote and stopped the disc, freeze-framing on the image of a hunchbacked woman, spinal cord exposed, her head twisted around, mouth open, eyes wide and staring at metal strands emerging from her spine. Paula reversed the playback, saw the electrified metal strands whipping about, coiling and uncoiling from the woman's spine as she silently screamed. The blip came and went again. Stop, then play, slow motion now. The blip was longer this time, a clean break in the video. Back again, frame advance, then freeze on the blip.

On the screen was an incredibly complex, detailed drawing, something like the interior topography of a huge insect. At the top of the screen, above a line of ideographs, were the words PART THREE. On both sides of the drawing were columns of dense, tiny text, all ideographs. She guessed the ideographs were Chinese. Not because she knew Chinese, but because she suspected New Hong Kong. Paula dropped to her knees and crawled forward, studying the text, but there was no other English anywhere. Was this what Chick had died for?

Paula got back in the chair and let the disc play at normal speed again. She watched intently for another fifteen minutes, listening carefully to the soundtrack, but there were no other breaks in either the audio or the video on the rest of the disc.

When it ended, Paula stared at the empty blue screen, thinking. "Part Three" sure as hell implied at least two other parts. Where were they? On other discs, of course. They had to be. But which ones? Or were the others taken when Chick was killed? But if they were, how was this one missed?

She went back into the front room, took another of Chick's homemade discs from the box, brought it into the bedroom, and popped it on. She watched it carefully, but when it ended half an hour later, she'd found nothing.

She returned to the front room and stared at the boxes and crates. There were hundreds of discs and tapes in various formats, some commercial, others homemade by Chick or other people. If there were more parts to this, how could she possibly find them without spending weeks searching through everything? She tried to think like Chick, tried to put herself in his place and figure out how *he* would have decided which discs or tapes to put this stuff on, figure out a key, but she quickly realized it was absurd. There was no way to find the other pieces without going through everything, disc by disc, tape by tape. And she'd need help for that.

Then what? Even if she found all the parts to whatever this was, what then? What the *hell* would she do with it? Who could she take it to?

Carlucci? He was digging into Chick's death, he was a cop, a good cop. That made a kind of sense.

Tremaine? He was doing this story, he was trying to find answers, too. No, not Tremaine. She didn't know him well enough yet, didn't know what kind of trust she could put in him. And Carlucci, she wasn't sure about him either, for some reason. There were too many funny things with the cops and Chick.

Mixer.

She went into the bedroom, put the *Aphasia Sciatica* disc in its case. Mixer was the only person she trusted completely.

One in the morning. But Mixer was in the Tenderloin, and in there it was Prime Time. Paula put on her jacket, put the disc in one of the inner pockets, and left.

The Euro Quarter was chaos. A train of Caged Men crawled through the streets, completely jamming up traffic. Chicken-wire cages on wheels were pulled by women in crash suits, two cables over each shoulder, two women to a cage. Inside each cage was a squatting, naked man, fingers gripping the chicken-wire walls. There must have been thirty cages in the train. Thumping drum music pounded from speakers in each cage. The men yelped, they scratched their genitals, they grinned. The women pulling the cages were faceless, features hidden by masks of bone. Horns and sirens blared in futile frustration; if anyone actually tried to get the Caged Men off the street, the women would start shooting.

Movement on the sidewalks wasn't much better. Paula didn't fight the crowds; she moved along with them as they shifted around the Caged Men and the string of dancing foot-followers in their wake. Everyone seemed angry. Paula ducked into Mr. Pink's Bookstop, just to get out of the crush. She hated Mr. Pink's. Perv heaven. Porn never seemed to change much. Paula wandered among the shelves, ignoring the stares of the men, the snickers of other women. How did they know? The cover photos on books and magazines made her queasy; she tried not to look at them, but as she walked along they kept clutching at her gaze. Finally, deciding this was worse than the crush outside, she pushed her way out of the store.

Ten minutes later, the crush eased as the last of the Caged Men rolled past. Paula was sweating, still feeling a little sick from Mr. Pink's. She had to make way for a band of the Daughters of Zion. They were obviously on the prowl, probably hoping to run into a pack of Heydrich's Fists and have a bang-out. Blood and gore and smashed faces. Great.

Eventually Paula found the alley Mixer had directed her to. Not quite as crowded, but hardly empty. Three or four drum fires burned; several people clustered around one, roasting an unrecognizable animal on a spit. A family of Screamers lurched past, two adults and two children all bound together at the wrists and ankles with rope. Paula located the door, pressed the intercom. There was a burst of static, which immediately cleared. "Yes?" A neutral voice, could have been a man or a woman.

"Paula Asgard," she said. "I'm here to see . . ." She caught herself. "To see Minor Danzig."

A long pause, then, "Wait." Another burst of static, then dead air.

"Wait for what?"

No response.

Paula waited, staring at the door. Were they trying to check her out? There were no windows in the door, nothing that looked like a screener. She looked up the wall, but didn't see anyone looking down at her.

"Paula."

The voice came from behind her. She turned to see Mixer smiling.

"Just had to make sure," he said. "Paranoia's our survival strategy right now." He came forward, kissed her cheek, then banged twice on the door. The door swung open, and a tall, stunning woman in long, blood-red robes stepped aside to let them in. The woman closed the door behind them and secured it.

"Paula, this is Saint Katherine. Paula Asgard."

St. Katherine smiled, took Paula's hand. Her fingers were smooth and warm; Paula had expected them to be cold.

"Why are you here?" Mixer asked.

Paula looked at St. Katherine. She didn't know this woman at all. She didn't care if St. Katherine *had* saved Mixer's life. But she felt awkward saying anything. No, not just awkward. Almost afraid. This was the woman who had nearly killed Mixer, who had killed or wrecked others.

"What is it, Paula?" Mixer said.

Paula turned back to him. "Can I talk to you alone?" She paused. "It's about Chick."

There was a long silence, Mixer looking at her; almost smiling, Paula thought. She glanced at St. Katherine, who showed no signs of leaving, and no signs of discomfort. There was something here, Paula realized, something she didn't quite understand, something between Mixer and St. Katherine.

Finally Mixer shook his head. "Saint Katherine and I are together in all this," he said. "Chick, the mayor, the mayor's nephew, all of it."

"I don't know her," Paula said. She turned to St. Katherine. "I don't know you. And so I don't trust you."

St. Katherine smiled. "It's all right. I understand." But she still did not make a move to leave.

"Do you trust me?" Mixer asked.

"I came to you with this. Not Carlucci, not Tremaine," she said, half wishing now she *had* gone to Carlucci instead.

"Then trust Saint Katherine," Mixer said. "Whatever you tell me, if she wasn't here, I'd tell her later."

Yes, Paula thought, something more had happened between them, something since Mixer had come to see her, telling her he was alive. His doubts and fears about St. Katherine were gone.

Paula nodded. She trusted Mixer, more than anyone else. She would trust St. Katherine, too. She took the disc from inside her jacket, held it up. "I've got something to show you."

A basement room, dark except for the colored lights of electronic displays on computers, sound and video systems, communication consoles. Paula sat on a small, hard chair; Mixer and St. Katherine were seated on her right, St. Lucy on her left. They stared at the image on the large-screen monitor. The text was sharp and clear, the ideographs quite beautiful; the diagram was still incomprehensible to Paula.

"The text is Chinese," St. Lucy said.

Paula had met St. Lucy only a few minutes earlier, but already she liked the woman. St. Lucy seemed so normal, so intelligent and grounded; Paula wondered how she could ever have joined the Saints.

"You read Chinese?" Paula asked.

"No. Only a few words and phrases. But I recognize it."

"What about the drawing, diagram, whatever the fuck it is?" Mixer asked, leaning forward.

"It looks medical to me," St. Katherine said.

St. Lucy nodded. "To me also. But . . ." She left it there. Then, "We know someone who should look at the diagram, who might know what it is. And someone who reads Chinese.

Unfortunately, not the same person.'' She turned to Paula and smiled, shrugging gently.

''We need to go through all of Chick's tapes and discs,'' Mixer said. ''You still have them?'' he asked Paula. ''You didn't sell or give any of them away?''

''No. Other things, yeah, but I kept all the music and video. I wanted to go through it, decide what to keep. Which probably would have been most of it. But . . .'' Here was one of the things that bothered her. ''If this is what Chick was killed over, why is it still here? Why didn't they take everything of Chick's when they killed him?''

''I wonder, too,'' Mixer said, ''but I can make some guesses. Chick had this stuff, which he was trying to sell. Diagrams and text, apparently. Something big. Maybe we'll find out what. He found it by accident, or stole it.'' Mixer grinned in the light of the displays. ''We know which was more likely. Now, Chick's not too smart, but he's not completely stupid, either. So he makes an extra copy, splitting it up and scattering the pieces around in his discs. When somebody comes after him, he's still got the original to hand over, trying to save his ass. But they kill him anyway.'' Mixer sighed. ''So what do they do? They've got what they came for. They don't know if there's another copy. Hauling everything out of that place would take a lot of time and be damn conspicuous, and remember, this is a murder that's being buried, *someone's* trying to keep it quiet. And probably the original was in some encrypted format that would be damn hard to copy into readable text like this,'' he said, pointing at the screen. ''But you know Chick, he was a fucking wizard with that kind of stuff. Looking at him, though, you'd never have a clue.'' Mixer shrugged. ''Hell, it's all a guess. But we've got to look through everything and see if there's more.''

''There's a lot to go through,'' Paula said.

''Yeah, I know. But we can get the Saints working on it,

some of the novitiates. No one will know what it is; hell, *we* don't. They'll just be looking for pieces. Everything will be ice."

"And we'll get someone to come in and translate the text," St. Katherine said. "And someone to check out the diagrams. They will be people we can trust, of course."

"And then what?" Paula asked. "If we find the rest of it and figure out what it is, then what do we do?"

No one answered her. No one had any idea.

Paula sat at her kitchen table, drinking the last of Chick's Stolichnaya and staring at what remained of Chick's things. Most of the boxes were gone now, hauled away in several trips on foot by Mixer, St. Katherine, and St. Lucy. His home-studio equipment was still there, along with some books and a couple of boxes of miscellaneous crap, but the music was all gone. Paula was depressed.

She felt like she was losing Chick, losing her memories of him. She'd get everything back from Mixer, but still . . . Chick and his music had turned into something else—murder and money and cover-ups and something big and secret going on up in New Hong Kong. Chick was disappearing.

The hole in her heart seemed to be getting bigger, somehow, and the vodka wasn't filling it. She drank off the rest of the glass and picked up the bottle. Empty.

She got up and walked into her bedroom, dug around in her discs, found the one she'd played over and over since Chick had died, the music video with the footage of the two of them making love here in this room, on this bed. "Love at Ground Zero." She put it on, sank back in her chair, and watched it once again.

As it played, the bluesy music surrounding the slow-motion images of their lovemaking in orange and yellow light, Paula pulled her knees up and wrapped her arms around them, pulling them in tight against her chest, jamming her chin into them. And when the song ended, and she watched the close-up of Chick's face silently saying "I love you," the open pit in her heart expanded, engulfed her, and swallowed her whole.

TWENTY-FOUR

MIXER AND ST. KATHERINE stood in the darkness of the basement room, surrounded by electronics and boxes of Chick's discs and tapes, lit by shafts of pulsing display lights. Faint ether music played on the sound system, whispering from the speakers scattered around the room.

"It's in here," Mixer said. "I know it."

St. Katherine nodded. Her face was ghostlike in the pale amber light. Mixer wanted to breathe his life into it, into her. He didn't know when the change had occurred, but it definitely had. He would do almost anything for her.

"What do we do with it when we find it?" St. Katherine asked. "When we learn what it is."

"What do you mean?"

She looked directly at him, and he thought she might be close to smiling. Or smirking.

"It must be worth a fortune," she said.

Mixer shook his head, trying to read her voice.

"We could give Paula a piece of it. A large piece."

Was she serious? She seemed even closer to a smile now, but he wasn't certain.

"We'll do whatever Paula wants," he told her. "Chick paid for this with his life. I nearly paid with mine. We'll do whatever's right.'' He paused, still trying to read her expression. ''When we know what it is, we'll know what's right. Paula will know what's right.''

Now St. Katherine finally did smile, touched his scarred right arm lightly with her fingers. ''I'm sorry,'' she said. ''I was only giving you a bad time.''

Mixer nodded once. He *could* read her voice. He did know her, somehow, knew she was telling the truth. Knew he could trust her. When had this happened? He wasn't sure, but he was glad it had.

''You loved her,'' St. Katherine said. ''Paula Asgard.''

''I still do. She's probably the best friend I've ever had.'' Sookie might have become the same kind of friend, Mixer thought, but she'd been killed before she'd reached fourteen. She'd never had a chance.

''I mean more than that,'' St. Katherine said. ''You loved her more than as a close friend.''

Mixer nodded, feeling that ache in his chest again. But it was more bearable now, like he could almost take pleasure in it. He watched the volume meters shifting slowly back and forth on the display in front of him.

''Yes, I did. For years. But there was always Chick. He got killed, but there hadn't been enough time. Maybe there never would have been, I don't know. Probably not. Then there was my own 'death.' Now, apparently, there's Tremaine.'' He turned back to St. Katherine, her eyes open and gazing back at him. ''And now there's you.''

''Me.''

Mixer nodded. ''You.''

''Are you sure?''

Mixer shook his head. ''I don't think I'll ever be sure about anything again.''

St. Katherine touched his arm again, his shoulder, his cheek.

"This can wait a couple of hours, can't it?"

Mixer nodded.

Naked, St. Katherine was just as beautiful, just as stunning. Naked, her age showed, which made her more real to Mixer, and even more attractive.

They lay together on St. Katherine's bed, lightly touching, brushing one another. Gray dawn light came in through the blinds, slicing them with shadow. Mixer's breath was ragged, and he could feel his heartbeat pounding up his neck. In the heat of the morning, he was sweating.

"It's been a long time," he said. Trying to explain his anxiety, his awkwardness. "Several years."

"For me, too," St. Katherine said. "Twelve years. Since becoming a Saint." She smiled at him. "I've been waiting for you."

Twelve years. Mixer could hardly imagine that much time anymore. Yet she seemed calm, self-assured. I'm glad one of us is, he thought.

She kissed his arm, nipped at his scarred flesh, and a faint scratch of pleasure shot up his arm, down his body. She seemed to sense it, and nipped him again, gently scraped her teeth along the ridged skin. Mixer closed his eyes, let the pleasure shoot through him, and his nervousness seemed to disappear.

They pulled at each other, kissed and licked and bit and tugged; they clung to one another in the growing heat of the day, their skin slick with sweat. Her taste was bitter and sweet, her smell sharp and biting; she grabbed his hair, pressed his face into her so he could hardly breathe. She shuddered, quaked against him.

Mixer lost himself in her, in her wet, salty skin, her taste and smell and her harsh gasping cries. Struggling for breath, he became dizzy. He was wrapped around her, she was wrapped around him, and they generated heat and sweat and maybe even love. He kissed her deeply, then stared into her golden eyes until she pulled him tight against her once more. Yes, he thought, maybe even love.

TWENTY-FIVE

CARLUCCI FINALLY HEARD from Sparks. On his way into work, on the sidewalk just outside the building, a teenage bubble courier came up to him, stuck a bubble in his hand and popped it. The courier shot off as the message formed in the remains spread across Carlucci's palm: "Home. S." Then the bubble material disintegrated, turning to powder, and Carlucci wiped it from his hand, scattering the particles to the ground.

Carlucci walked into the building, checked in at the front desk, then left through the basement garage, on foot. House call to Sparks.

Home for Sparks was in the DMZ along the western edge of the Tenderloin. Eight-thirty in the morning was way too early for people in the DMZ; the street was quiet, the sidewalks nearly empty. The weather had finally cooled down a bit. Not cool, exactly, but not as hot as it had been; for a change, Carlucci wasn't sweating. The sky was clear, with no sign of rain.

Carlucci walked past a sidewalk cafe, half a dozen puffy-eyed troubadours sucking down coffee, trying to wake up. One of the three women reached out and plucked at Carlucci's arm.

She was young, but missing some teeth. Coughing badly, breath foul. A moniker sewed to her jacket: Sister Ray.

"Want your ding-dong sucked?" she asked between coughs. "Twenty bucks. You can't get it any cheaper."

Carlucci shook his head. It was a horrifying thought. The woman's friends laughed. At him or her, he couldn't tell. He walked on.

He stepped through an open doorway between a cone counter and a music store. Brick walls, metal grating, and plaster high overhead, but plenty of light. Halfway along the corridor, on the left, was another doorway. Carlucci ducked through, then descended concrete steps to basement level and a maze of corridors, not so well lit. The smell, too, was worse. The brick and concrete walls were covered with layers of graffiti and artwork. Doors every twenty feet or so. So early in the morning, it was fairly quiet. Faint Indian music came from behind one door as he passed by; muted laughter came from behind another.

The door to Spark's place was wood, painted solid black. No other decoration. Carlucci knocked. A minute later he knocked again. He stood a little ways back from the peephole, so Sparks could see him. No sound for a minute, then the clicks of locks and bolts. The door opened, and Sparks gestured him inside.

Inside was a single room, with a tiny, one-square-foot window up near the ceiling in the rear wall, too small for anything but a cat or a rat to come through. There was a mattress on the floor, piled with blankets; a hot plate plugged into a cracked wall socket. Two lamps, shaded dirty-white; two bag chairs, and a television; on the screen were two talking heads, but there was no sound. In a narrow alcove carved out of the concrete, a toilet and sink. No tub, no shower. Sparks probably wouldn't use one anyway.

Sparks coughed as he crossed the room toward the bed. He

looked worse than ever. Carlucci knew it wasn't just the bad light. The man was dying.

"Have you found a slot in a hospice for me?" Sparks asked.

Carlucci shook his head, feeling guilty. He'd asked a few people, but he hadn't really looked that hard. "I've checked around," he said, "but I haven't found anything yet."

Sparks nodded, sat stiffly on the mattress, bones audibly creaking. A box of disposable syringes lay open next to the bed, inches away from the hot plate. "Take a seat."

Carlucci sat in the closest of the bag chairs, sinking awkwardly into it. Sparks picked up a bowl, cradled it in his lap. Inside the bowl was a spoon and dark brown goop. Sparks ate a few mouthfuls, then held the bowl and spoon out to Carlucci. "Want some?"

Carlucci shook his head.

"It's chocolate pudding," Sparks said.

Carlucci shook his head again, and Sparks put the bowl back on the floor.

"The whisper you asked for," Sparks said. "Almost impossible to get."

"But you got it."

"I got something. It was a fuckin' bitch." He stared hard at Carlucci. "You'd better watch your ass. Mistakes could get you dead. Just ask Chick Roberts or the mayor's nephew or Rosa Weeks."

"Who's Rosa Weeks?" Carlucci asked. The name wasn't at all familiar.

"Better you don't know, then." Sparks said. "Too much *gnosis* is bad for you."

"Tell me who Rosa Weeks is."

Sparks shook his head, making something like a smile with his pale, thin lips. "You're a stubborn bastard."

"Yeah," Carlucci said. "*Testa dura*. What my father used to call me."

Sparks coughed, spat brown-green phlegm onto the floor.

"Rosa Weeks was a doctor. She gave physicals."

"Yeah? And so?"

"It will become clear, I think. Patience, Lieutenant."

Patience. Patience was something Carlucci had always had plenty of. Sometimes too much. He nodded and waited for Sparks to tell it in his own way.

"Here's the key," Sparks said. "Mixer and Chick and Jenny Woo were bootlegging body-bags. You know that?" Carlucci nodded, and Sparks went on. "You knew Mixer, right?" Carlucci nodded again, and Sparks said, "Another guy who got himself dead. Okay. Body-bags. One out of every ten body-bags was rigged. When they were switched on, a paralytic agent was patched into the wearer's body, and a location beacon activated. Jenny Woo would lock onto the signal, and go pick up herself a live, but quite immobile body. Box it up, and take it home. Well, not home. But someplace private. There, Dr. Rosa Weeks did a complete physical and work-up, then crated them up."

"Crated them up for what?"

Sparks grinned. "A trip to New Hong Kong."

New Hong Kong again. Damn that place. Not much was illegal up there, and no one on Earth could touch them. But there was plenty that was illegal here on Earth, here in San Francisco, and he could do something about that. Maybe.

"Why were they being shipped to New Hong Kong?"

Sparks shook his head. "No idea. You'll have to find that on your own. Course, my advice is, leave it the fuck alone. Forget about it, Lieutenant."

"Did Mixer and Chick know the body-bags were rigged?"

"No. I don't think so. The body-bags were one thing. Jenny Woo had her own separate deal going. But I think Chick found out, through Jenny Woo. From there I think he found out a lot more. Enough to get himself dead. That's what I mean. Ignorance is a lot safer."

"And Rosa Weeks?"

"She's dead, too. Yesterday morning. Probably won't show up on-line for a couple days. It'll come up accidental OD." Sparks nodded to himself. "You just watch."

"Why is she dead?" Carlucci asked.

"Mouth too big, I think. She had a pet to feed that was costing her a fortune, and she tried buying it with something she knew."

More dead people, Carlucci thought. Which was why he couldn't take Sparks's advice and forget about it all. He had to try to figure out what was going on. And he felt he was closing in on it.

"Anything else?"

Sparks nodded. "Yeah. The Saints killed Mixer in one of their fucking trials. Sounds like nothing to do with this, but I got a feeling it ties in somehow. Also, a lot of people picked up in Kashen's recruiting vans end up in the same place as the body-baggers, getting prepped for a trip to New Hong Kong. Some of them, and some of the body-baggers, maybe go up to New Hong Kong in pieces." Sparks coughed, shaking his head. "Not so sure about that info, but it sounds real."

"But you're sure about the body-bags being rigged."

Sparks nodded.

"And you're sure Mixer didn't know."

"Pretty sure. You can't expect much more than that. I'd tell you to ask him yourself, but he's dead. You wouldn't get much of an answer."

I *will* ask him, Carlucci said to himself. He's not *that* dead.

"One more thing," Sparks said. He leaned forward, picked up a syringe from a tray. Carlucci could see that it was already loaded, ready to go. Sparks held the syringe in his right hand, then reached with his other hand for a piece of mirrored glass propped against the wall. "Hold this for me," he said.

Carlucci shifted in the bag chair, crouched forward, and took the mirror from Sparks.

"Hold it up," Sparks said. "So I can see myself, damn it."

Carlucci held the mirror up. Sparks stared into it, stretched his neck, then began tapping at his skin with his left hand. He squinted, pressed his neck, tapped some more. Carlucci kept glancing at the syringe in his other hand. Was he going to have to watch this? Christ.

More tapping, more squinting and grimacing, then suddenly Sparks brought his right hand up and plunged the needle into his neck. He switched his grip, eased back the plunger. Dark blood came back into the syringe and Carlucci turned away.

"Hold still, God damn you!"

Carlucci steadied his hands, the mirror, but didn't look back at Sparks. He was glad there were still some things that made him queasy.

Sparks broke into a coughing fit and Carlucci brought his gaze back around. The needle was out of his neck. Sparks was nodding, waving feebly at him.

"Okay, okay," he whispered. He tossed the empty syringe a few feet away, then took the mirror from Carlucci with slow, steady hands and placed it carefully against the wall. Then he lay back on the mattress, closing his eyes.

Carlucci worked himself out of the bag chair and stood, looking down at Sparks. He took the wad of cash from his pocket, set it on the blanket beside Sparks.

"Frank?" His voice was soft.

"Yes."

"Don't bother about the hospice." Sparks briefly opened one eye, then closed it. "It's too late."

Carlucci nodded, though Sparks couldn't see him. "I'm sorry," he said.

Sparks slowly rolled his head from side to side. "It's all right, Frank. It doesn't matter."

But it does, Carlucci thought. It does.

Later that day, near noon, Carlucci met Tremaine at the Civic Center muck pond, almost exactly where he'd met Paula two weeks earlier. They bought Polish sausages with sauerkraut from a vendor set up near the edge of the pond, and sat on a bench facing away from the scum-covered water. They'd met once or twice before, Carlucci couldn't remember exactly when. Some story Tremaine was working on, some case of Carlucci's.

The Polish sausage was hot, spicy, and greasy; Carlucci was glad he hadn't loaded up on the onions. They didn't talk much as they ate, just a word or two, about nothing, really: the cooling trend, the rat pack asleep in a pile across the plaza. When they were done, Carlucci took the scraps, wrappers, and napkins to a trash can, then returned to the bench. They sat several feet apart, not really looking at each other.

"I've been requesting an interview for two weeks," Tremaine said. "I wonder why you agree to one now."

"I haven't," Carlucci said. "You won't be asking the questions. You'll be answering mine."

"Will I?"

"Yes. This is a police investigation."

"An *official* investigation?"

Carlucci looked at him, but didn't say anything.

"I think I'll just wait for the subpoena," Tremaine said.

"That's a crappy attitude, Tremaine."

"It's a crappy business."

"What, murder? Or journalism?"

"Both. And being a cop," Tremaine said. "All of it."

Neither of them said anything for a while. The sky was still clear, and the sun was shining down on them, not quite hot. The break in the heat was a good change. It brought the crazies out into the open, though, and they were filling the plaza as they woke up, stumbling and wandering around.

"Want some coffee?" Carlucci asked.

Tremaine smiled. "Add some acid to the grease congealing in my stomach? Sure, sounds terrific."

They got up, walked back to the pond and bought coffee

from the pregnant teenager. They circled the pond, and stopped near another bench, but didn't sit. Someone had puked all over it.

"Which murder are you investigating?" Tremaine asked.

"This is *all* off the record," Carlucci said. "Every fucking word. Got it?"

"Got it." Tremaine sipped at his coffee, grimaced. "So, which murder?"

"The mayor's nephew. William Kashen. What did you think?"

"Not Chick Roberts?"

"No. Should I be?"

"You know about Chick Roberts being killed, don't you?"

Carlucci shrugged. "Something. Wasn't my case. Some punk. A drug killing."

Tremaine shook his head. "You don't believe that."

"I don't?"

"No. He was Paula Asgard's boyfriend."

"I don't really know Paula Asgard. Only because she's a friend of Mixer's."

"Yes, Mixer. A dead guy who's still alive."

"Are you trying to tell me the two murders are connected?"

Tremaine shook his head. "No. You already know that. I *know* you do."

"The Chick Roberts case is closed."

"Buried, you mean."

Carlucci started to put his foot up on the bench, then remembered the vomit. He found a clean spot for his shoe and leaned forward, stretching his other leg.

"Why don't *you* tell me what the connection is between the two?" Carlucci said.

"Why don't we make a deal, an information trade?"

"It doesn't work that way," Carlucci said. "No deals. I'm a cop."

Tremaine laughed. "Cops are always making deals."

"What's the connection?" Carlucci asked again.

"You *do* know it's there, don't you?"

Carlucci nodded. He guessed he had to give Tremaine something. "I know it's there. I just don't know what it is."

Tremaine drank some more of his coffee, then dumped the rest of it in the trash can next to the bench, shuddering. "Awful stuff." He paused, then went on. "I can't be sure of any of this, you understand. Not completely. But I believe it."

A few feet away, a trio of trance walkers formed a circle, arms linked, and began humming. The plaza was filling with people on lunch break, but the crowds avoided the trance walkers, giving them plenty of space.

"Chick, Mixer, a woman named Jenny Woo, and the mayor's nephew were all spliced together. They had business. Body-bags. I don't think the body-bags had anything to do with this, that's just how they knew each other."

So he doesn't know everything, Carlucci thought. But then, none of us do.

"Something's going on up in New Hong Kong," Tremaine continued. "That's the real missing piece. And the mayor's tied up with it, the mayor's wrapped up tight inside whatever it is. He was doing something with his nephew, connected to all this somehow. But the nephew got hold of something he shouldn't have had, and was getting ready to sell it. He was getting ready to fuck over his uncle and New Hong Kong both. Now, what I believe happened is this. Chick Roberts got hold of the same thing, probably from the nephew. And Chick tried to cash in. Kashen wasn't stupid, and he'd managed to be discreet. No one knew what he had, except his potential customers. But Chick Roberts was not so smart, and he was not so discreet, and it wasn't long after he put out the word that he got himself three bullets in the head."

Tremaine paused, sighing heavily. "Here it gets more speculative. My sources are pretty weak and incomplete, but this is the picture I've put together, and it makes a kind of sense.

I think the New Hong Kong people had Chick killed. As soon as they scented their property in the wrong hands and up for sale, they took care of the problem. The first problem. The second problem was finding out where Chick had gotten his stuff. They traced it back to the nephew, and then did him. But . . . they didn't tell the mayor, because they didn't know whether or not the mayor was in on it with the nephew. So you had the mayor putting on the squeeze to solve his nephew's murder. Politics, family loyalty, whatever.

"But New Hong Kong stays on this thing, tracing everything back. They've *got* to find the hole in their security and plug it up, and they have to be certain about it. I think they found it, and it wasn't the mayor. Probably someone up in New Hong Kong who is now a piece of space debris. When they were sure the mayor wasn't a part of it, they told him what had happened, and told him to take the pressure off the case. You *have* been asked to bury the nephew's case, haven't you?"

Carlucci didn't answer, and Tremaine nodded.

"Anything else?" Carlucci asked.

"Isn't that enough?"

"It's all speculation," Carlucci said. "I can't do a goddamn thing with it."

"I won't give you my sources," Tremaine said. "Even if I did, they'd never testify in court, they'd never even give you a statement."

"I'm not asking for your sources," Carlucci said in disgust. He pushed off the bench with his foot, walked over to the trash can, and shoved his empty coffee cup into it. "It does make a kind of sense," he said to Tremaine. "But I'm not going to get any names, am I? The name of the guy who put three bullets in Chick's head. The name of the guy who gutted the mayor's nephew. The names of any of the people who are responsible for this goddamn mess."

"I don't think so," Tremaine said.

"And what the hell is it you want from me?"

"Any information you have about these cases that I don't have."

"There *isn't* anything," Carlucci said. He was lying, but not much. "You know more than anyone. Christ."

"Confirmation that the Chick Roberts case was buried. Confirmation that the mayor has asked you to bury his nephew's case."

"You can't be serious."

"I've got to ask."

Carlucci had to laugh. "Christ, you're something else."

"Is that a 'no comment,' or a denial?" Tremaine asked.

"It's jack shit, is what it is. I told you, not a fucking word is on the record. There is no response to your questions."

"They weren't questions. They were statements. I'm just asking for confirmation."

Carlucci shook his head. "You've been a lot of fucking help," he told Tremaine. Actually, Tremaine *had* been a help, but he wasn't going to admit it. "We're done." He turned and started walking away. "See you."

"Wait. Lieutenant."

Carlucci just shook his head and kept on walking.

One last meeting, this one at night with Hong and LaPlace. Carlucci felt they were getting close, so close to the answers, but he was afraid they wouldn't be able to make it all the way. They sat at the table in the Hong family kitchen; Hong's entire family had gone to the cinema to see *Ghost Lover of Station 13* for the second time.

Carlucci told them everything he'd learned from Tremaine, from Sparks, the odd bits of information he'd gleaned from Monk. And he told them about Mixer.

Hong smiled. "So the spikehead's still alive, stirring up the shit."

"Yeah, except he's not a spikehead anymore. It all got burned away."

"Well, we have something, too," LaPlace said. "Monk may have been wrong about Butler."

"What do you mean?"

"Joseph and I found this guy. You know, a guy who knew a guy. Name's Little Johnny. Wanted to buy his way out of an intent to distribute bust. Kanter had him, called us in to see the guy. Little Johnny seemed to think Butler had killed the nephew. Didn't know why. Little Johnny doesn't know Butler himself. He knows a guy. The guy he knows is Totem the Pole."

"The porno star?" Carlucci asked.

"That's him. King of prong. Little Johnny says Totem the Pole told *him* that Butler had killed Kashen. According to Little Johnny, our man Totem the Pole, in contrast to his on-screen persona as the great humper of women, in real life, well, he likes men, too. Robert Butler, for one. Butler did something for Totem. Apparently Little Johnny did, too, which is why Totem got so confessional with him. Little Johnny tried to get specific about what they did for each other, but I didn't think we needed those kinds of details. The details we needed, though, he wasn't so good with. How did Totem know? Was Butler as confessional as Totem? Little Johnny doesn't know. Little Johnny says Totem heard something the night Butler got killed, that Totem was in the building when it happened, he was downstairs with the woman who lived under Butler. What he was doing with the woman, no one knows. Changing orientation again, maybe. But Totem seemed to think Butler was killed as his reward for killing Kashen. Yeah, to shut his mouth, permanently. We went around and around with Little Johnny, he said this, he said that, cha cha cha. It doesn't all make sense. But some, maybe. We kept Little Johnny in a holding cell, with a promise for release, and tried to track down Totem the Pole."

"You didn't find him, did you?"

LaPlace shook his head.

"We got to his agent," Hong put in. "She said Totem the Pole was shooting a new movie, he was on location."

"Let me guess," Carlucci said. "New Hong Kong."

Hong nodded. "New Hong Kong."

"I don't think we'll be seeing Totem or his Pole in San Francisco any time soon," LaPlace said.

"What about the woman who lived under Butler?"

"She's gone too," Hong said. "We can't find her."

"Shit," Carlucci said, his voice little more than a whisper. He leaned back in his chair and rubbed at his neck. "What do you think, Joseph?"

"Like Pete says, it makes a kind of sense, but we can't do much with it. Butler's dead, Totem's gone and probably wouldn't be much help anyway, and Little Johnny is useless. It just doesn't lead us anywhere."

LaPlace got up from the table, shaking his head and pacing. "This whole thing is going to shit on us," he said. "I mean, I'm not worried that we're in trouble, but everything goes nowhere. We know more, but where does it get us? We're never going to get anything to go to court with, are we? Are we going to get the guy who put holes in the punk's face? We don't know for sure that Butler killed the nephew, but even if he did, he's dead, and are we going to get the guy who put a meat hook through his neck? And the mayor? We can't touch him, and we sure as hell aren't going to be able to get to anyone up in New Hong Kong, are we?" LaPlace shook his head. "Not fucking likely."

Carlucci couldn't disagree with LaPlace. He'd been thinking pretty much the same thing himself. The closer they got, the worse things looked.

"The one thing we *can* get out of this," Hong said, "is knowing what happened, and why. That's worth something. Sometimes it's worth a lot."

Carlucci nodded. "Yes, Joseph, that can be worth a lot. But we don't even have that yet, do we? We're close to knowing what happened, but we sure as hell don't know why." Carlucci shook his head. "What is it? What is worth killing all these people for?"

Carlucci looked back and forth between Hong and LaPlace, but neither man had an answer for him.

TWENTY-SIX

"ETERNAL LIFE," MIXER said. "That's what's getting people dead."

"Eternal life," Paula repeated. It didn't seem real. Maybe it wasn't.

They were sitting around the table in the kitchen of the Saints' place: Paula, Mixer, St. Katherine, and St. Lucy. Early evening, dark outside, two bright overheads lighting the kitchen. On the table in front of Mixer was a stack of eight or nine discs. Chick's discs.

"Not eternal life," St. Lucy said. "Life extension. It's not the same thing."

"Close enough," Mixer said. "People who will want it won't make the distinction. Or won't care. And who *won't* want it?"

"I've heard rumors about New Hong Kong all my adult life," Paula said. "Rumors about this, the New Hong Kong medicos finding the key to life extension. Nothing ever happened, and I stopped paying attention a long time ago. Now you're telling me it's for real?"

"Maybe," St. Lucy said. "Yes, it's for real, though it appears that they don't have all the answers yet. But they're probably very close." She pointed at the discs. "It's laid out here, what they're trying to do, the directions they're working in, how they're going about it. Not a complete picture, but enough."

"What do you mean by not complete?"

"We've got eleven images, eleven 'pages,' you could say. But there are at least twelve. We're missing Part Seven. We can't find it anywhere."

"It's possible Chick never even had it," Mixer put in.

"And there might be more than twelve," St. Lucy said. "But it probably doesn't matter. All the parts most likely would still provide only an incomplete picture. The key thing is, what's on these discs would be enough for some other group with sufficient resources to start up their own research program along the same lines. Atlantis Two, for example. Gottingen Gesellschaft, for another, or any of the other big biotechs. Any of those people would be willing to pay a fortune for what's on these discs."

"Okay," Paula said. "So tell me what's on the discs."

"We brought in someone to make the text translations first," St. Katherine said. "Someone we felt we could trust. But when he'd finished, and he'd given us the translation, we realized what this was worth, and we were no longer sure about him. This is one hell of a temptation."

"So what did you do, kill the translator?"

St. Katherine smiled. "No, of course not. But we do have him . . . in protective custody until we decide what to do next." St. Katherine shrugged. "He understands. It'll all work out."

"And what about the medical expert you were going to bring in?" Paula asked.

"We brought her in next, and she confirmed what we and the translator had guessed at. She's a doctor, the one who kept Minor Danzig alive after the trial. The texts are highly technical and advanced, and she didn't understand some of the details, had to make some guesses of her own, but it's pretty clear what they're after, and how they're going about it."

"Is she in protective custody, too?"

St. Katherine shook her head, smiling again. "No. She's my sister, and I've trusted her with my life more than once. I trust her with this. She also has serious reservations about their research methods, and their projected treatments."

"What kind of reservations?"

"Moral."

Paula was almost afraid to ask. "Why?"

St. Lucy sighed heavily. "They're doing all their primary experimentation on people, that much is clear. Testing and evaluation on human subjects. Teresa, Saint Katherine's sister, feels fairly certain that a lot of the evaluation has to be done through autopsies. Or vivisection. Neither option is a pleasant one."

"Jesus," Paula whispered. "Where are they getting . . . ?" She didn't finish the question, the most obvious answer leaping into her thoughts. "The recruiting vans."

"Probably," Mixer said. "Probably some other source as well, because a lot of the people the vans pull in aren't in such great health, and we're not sure how much use they'd be. Except as a source of raw materials."

"Raw materials?"

"My sister thinks the longevity treatments themselves involve live tissue, blood products, brain tissue."

"So we've got testing done on human subjects, followed by autopsies or vivisection, and treatments developed from materials harvested from other human beings."

St. Lucy nodded.

"And this is what Chick was selling," Paula said. "A blueprint for this fucking shit."

"I doubt he had a clue," Mixer said. "He didn't read Chinese. Probably all he knew was that it was about longer life, and he knew that was worth a fortune."

Paula looked again at the discs. This was what Chick died

for. Fucking great. "Longer life," she said. "How much longer? Forty, fifty years?"

Mixer laughed.

St. Lucy shook her head. "They don't know for sure, of course; they won't until somebody actually does it, but the text in these things," she said, pointing at the discs, "talks about a lot more than that. A hundred and fifty, maybe even two hundred extra years. Bringing the aging process nearly to a complete halt."

"And they want it *now*," Mixer said. "There's not going to be any miracle of reversing the aging process, and who wants to live an extra hundred years as a decrepit old fuck with a body that's falling apart? No, you want to start this as young as possible."

"But you don't think they actually have it yet," Paula said.

"Teresa doesn't think so," St. Katherine said. "Another guess on her part, but it's probably a good guess. Two things, she says. One, that's the impression she gets from the text, the way they talk about promising avenues, dead ends. Two, if they thought they had it—and they'll never be sure, of course, until someone tries it and lives for an extra two hundred years—but if they thought they had the answer, they wouldn't be able to keep it secret. They'll want customers, for one thing. They probably won't care so much then. But for now, they're still experimenting. They can't afford to let this get out. They don't want the competition, and they don't want the bad PR."

"They've got to keep their stream of fresh bodies coming in," Mixer said.

"Jesus Christ," Paula said. She remembered sitting with Tremaine in his car at Hunter's Point, watching the huge crates being unloaded from Jenny Woo's van. Bodies, Tremaine had said. He'd been right.

No one said anything for a long time. Paula kept staring at the discs, as if they had some kind of answer for her. Hell, they had the answers for someone.

"What do we do with it?" she finally asked.

"We were hoping you would have an answer to that," Mixer said.

"Me?"

Mixer nodded. "Chick paid for this with his life." He put his hand on the stack of discs, then pushed it toward her. "They're yours now. You tell us what we should do."

Paula didn't know what to say. St. Katherine put her hand over Mixer's, looking at Paula.

"Minor said you would know what to do. He said you would know what's right."

Paula stared at the discs again. She would know what was right? Maybe they should just destroy the discs, pretend they'd never seen them. As soon as she thought about it, though, she realized it would be pointless. There had to be something else.

"I think we should give them to Carlucci," Paula eventually said. "We should give him the discs, and tell him what we know. He's stuck his neck out trying to find out what happened to Chick. And I trust him."

"Passing the buck?" Mixer said, smiling. "Let Carlucci decide?"

"No. He might not take them. But he probably knows more about this than we do. He might be able to do something, use them to stop this shit somehow." Mixer snorted, and Paula said, "You have a better idea?"

Mixer looked at St. Katherine, then at St. Lucy. They both nodded, and he turned back to Paula. "Okay," he said. "We give them to Carlucci."

Carlucci stood at the head of the alley, in a warm, steadily falling drizzle, and watched the flames of the barrel fires ahead of him. His raincoat kept his clothes dry, but he wore no hat, and his hair and face were wet. He felt certain the last of the answers were waiting for him down this alley. He didn't know if that was going to be good or bad.

He had been home from work for an hour, settling in to watch a movie with Andrea and Christina, when the call from Paula had come. Brief and simple.

"We've got something for you," Paula had said. " You'll want this." Then, before he'd had a chance to reply, "Do you remember where Saint Lucy brought you?"

"Yes."

"We'll be waiting for you."

He'd known, then. Something in Paula's voice. She had the answers. She knew.

So here he was, in a warm and strange, heavy mist that softened the sounds of the Tenderloin night. Carlucci entered the alley, approaching a barrel fire surrounded by several men and women and sizzling from the mist and a rack of fish grilling above the flames. A man held out a brown bottle, said, "Want a beer, paisan? We've got plenty." Carlucci shook his head, said, "No thanks," and continued along the alley.

He passed another barrel fire and slowed, searching the building wall, hoping to recognize the right door. A cloaked figure stepped out of an alcove and stood directly in front of him. St. Lucy. She smiled briefly, touched his arm, then turned back and opened the door for him.

Inside the building, they didn't speak. St. Lucy led the way upstairs to the same small kitchen where he'd first seen Mixer after his trial. This time the kitchen was full: Mixer and Paula Asgard, and a tall, beautiful woman who had to be St. Katherine; and now St. Lucy and himself. On the table was a stack of media discs in cases, maybe ten of them.

"Please, sit down," St. Lucy said.

Carlucci hung his coat on the chair, face and hair still dripping. St. Lucy got a towel for him, while Mixer got up and put coffee and tea and a bottle of Scotch in the middle of the table, white ceramic mugs all around.

"Thanks for coming," Paula said.

"Sure." Carlucci finished drying off, set the towel on the

counter, and sat. He tried to read their expressions, tried to guess whether what he was about to hear was going to be good or bad. But he couldn't tell much from their faces, only that he was in for something serious, and he'd already known that. Then, everyone at the table watching him, it began.

Mixer and Paula, with occasional help from the two Saints, told Carlucci first where the discs had come from . . . and then everything they knew about what was on them—the translations and diagrams, the certainties and the probabilities and the guesses; what New Hong Kong was working on, and how they were doing it. Life extension and autopsies and vivisection and bodies harvested for longevity treatments. Everything.

Carlucci asked a few questions as they talked, but mostly he listened. He grew increasingly tired and depressed as all the final pieces now came together, shifting into place. It was as bad as he'd expected.

"You don't seem all that surprised," Paula said when they were done.

Carlucci managed a slight smile. "I'm not, really." He paused, thinking. "I didn't realize it at the time, but I've had two rather oblique offers of a couple hundred extra years of life if I would forget about all this and bury a couple of murder cases."

"Now you can take them up on it," Mixer said.

Carlucci gave a short laugh. "Yeah, sure. I doubt the offers are still good." He looked directly at Mixer. "I know why the mayor wanted you dead."

"Tell me."

Carlucci did. He told them about Jenny Woo and the rigged body-bags. "You were bootlegging the body-bags with her and Chick," Carlucci said. "The mayor knew you and Chick were friends. He assumed you knew what was going on."

"I didn't," Mixer said.

"I believe you."

Mixer turned to Paula. "You believe me, don't you?"

Paula nodded. "I've never trusted anyone more," she said. She reached out and took his hand of metal and flesh, squeezed it gently.

"There's more," Carlucci said.

"How much more?" Paula asked. "Something about Chick?"

Carlucci nodded. "Yes, about Chick." He told them some of what he had learned from Sparks and Tremaine, about Chick and the nephew and the mayor and New Hong Kong. He even told them a little—leaving out names and details—of what had been going on inside the police force, the orders to bury cases, the pressure from the mayor.

"So now what?" Carlucci asked when he was done.

"We were hoping you might know," Mixer said.

"Me."

"It was Paula's idea to come to you."

"You looked into this mess when no one else would," Paula said. "You've been working on it from the beginning, taking risks. We thought you might be able to do something with the discs. Or you'd know what we could do with them. Something, maybe, to stop all this."

Carlucci didn't say anything for a long time. He felt lost, unsure if he could find a way through this. The last of the answers had been here all right, but that didn't mean he knew what to do with them. He looked around the table, then reached for the Scotch and filled his cup. "Give me an hour alone to think, all right?"

Paula looked at the others and nodded. The four of them got up from the table, and left the room.

Paula and Mixer sat on the fire escape outside Mixer's room, drinking beer and watching the container fires in the alley below them. The rain had become little more than a light, falling mist, warm on Paula's skin. The alley was filled with shadows, figures moving in and out of the firelight, music pounding from a boomer across the way, bells ringing somewhere out on the street. Loud cracks, maybe gunshots, but they were far away, maybe not even in the Tenderloin. Paula could see white and red lights of vehicles moving along the streets at either end of the alley.

"What do you think Carlucci's going to say?" Mixer asked.

Paula shrugged. "I almost don't care anymore."

"Two hundred extra years," Mixer said. "Live into the twenty-third century."

"Christ, who would want to?" Paula drank from her beer and shook her head.

"I would," Mixer replied. "I almost died. Didn't like it. I like being alive, and I'd like the chance to keep on doing it as long as possible." He snorted. "I won't get the chance, though."

"No," Paula agreed. "Neither of us will. If they find the answer up in New Hong Kong, only the rich and the big sharks will get a shot at it. We won't get shit." She shook her head again. "Fuck 'em. Let them have it."

Mixer laughed. "Yeah, well . . . Not everyone's going to take that attitude."

Paula looked at him and smiled. "No, they won't. That'll at least make it a little rougher for those rich fucks."

In the building across the alley, one floor down and just to the left, Paula could see a man and a woman standing next to each other by the open window. Their shoulders were pressed together, and they were talking, smiling. She heard the woman laugh, then saw her pull back and playfully slap the man's shoulder. The man grinned, then put his arms around the woman, and they held each other, the woman digging her face into the man's neck.

"You love her, don't you?" Paula asked.

"Saint Katherine? Yeah, I guess I do."

"It won't be easy," Paula said.

"No," Mixer replied. "But maybe easier than you think.

We've both got gashes scorched in our brains, and they seem to match in a way. It'll work out."

"I hope so."

"What about you and Tremaine?"

Paula shook her head. "Who knows? All this crap, we've never had much of a chance."

"This will all be over soon, one way or another."

"You think?"

Mixer nodded "Yeah, whatever Carlucci decides, there's going to be some kind of explosion. He won't just let it go. Not tomorrow, maybe not for a week or two, but it'll happen." He stared down at the container fires. "And when it does, I've got something in mind for Mayor Terrance Kashen."

Paula looked at him. "What, Mixer?"

Mixer shook his head. "We'll never have to worry about him again. That fuck." He wouldn't say anything more.

Paula looked away from him, back to the couple across the alley. "Chick sure got himself into something this time, didn't he?"

"You still miss him," Mixer said.

"Yeah. Always will. I don't know why. He could be a real asshole, sometimes." She smiled, looking at Mixer. "I guess you know that, don't you?"

Mixer nodded. "Mostly, he just didn't think. He never really meant to be an asshole."

"No." Paula finished off her beer, resisted the temptation to throw it over the side of the fire escape. She set it beside her and pressed her face into the railing bars.

"I've got to start playing again," she said. "I've bailed out on so many gigs lately, Sheela and Bonita are about ready to get a new bass player. Besides, I really miss it. I need it."

Mixer put his hands on her neck, worked at the tightened muscles. "Then do it," he said. He continued to massage her neck and shoulders for several minutes, strong and hard with his left hand, noticeably weaker with the right. The pain felt good, loosened the knots, but she imagined it must be hard on his injured hand and arm. She put her hands over his and stopped them. "Thanks," she said.

"Everything'll be okay," Mixer said.

Paula laughed once and shook her head. "No it won't."

"No," Mixer agreed. "It won't."

Paula pressed her face harder into the bars and stared down at the flames below.

Carlucci sat at the kitchen table and drank bad Scotch, trying to think. The alcohol wasn't going to help him, but he drank anyway, relishing the burning warmth it sent out from his belly. He stared at the stack of discs. Two hundred extra years of life. It wouldn't matter if it was *five* hundred, it would never do Caroline any good. She would still die before she was thirty. The thought of himself and the rest of his family living to be over two hundred years old while Caroline never made it out of her twenties made him ill. He knew it wasn't logical, that they were all going to significantly outlive Caroline anyway, but it still seemed somehow obscene to him.

Carlucci sipped at the Scotch, tongue and lips burning. The building was quiet; he could hear faint sounds of movement above him, but not much else. There was flickering light outside, visible through the kitchen window, but the Tenderloin's night sounds were muted. He felt very much alone.

What to do. Paula and Mixer and the two Saints wanted *his* advice. Because he was a cop? Yeah, he was a cop, and he was supposed to find out who committed crimes, collect evidence, and then arrest those responsible. And if he did his job well enough, a lot of those criminals would be tried and convicted and pay the price this society had decided they would pay. More or less.

But there had been plenty of crimes committed in this business, probably a lot that he didn't even know about yet, and he couldn't make one fucking arrest that would ever stick.

There was no way he could see to make those who were ultimately responsible pay. This time, he could not do his job.

It wasn't his fault, he knew that. It wasn't from lack of effort, or some inadequacy of his. But he still felt ineffectual. There was nothing, it seemed, that he could do.

He got up from the table and walked to the small window. Leaning against the counter, looking down and out through the grimy window, he could just see the alley below, dark figures moving in and out of the light of fires. Why did they have fires? The nights didn't get cold. But there was something comforting about the drum fires, and he almost felt like going downstairs and taking up that guy's offer of a beer. It was a better offer than the ones he'd had from the mayor and the slug. It was an offer he could live with.

Directly across from him, a large, heavy cat sat on the ledge of a lighted, open window, chewing at its claws. A bright light flared overhead, and red embers showered down into the alley, but the cat wasn't in the least distracted. Fat cats, he thought. The mayor, his buddies, everyone up in New Hong Kong.

No, he could not do his job. Which left him with only two options.

Try to bury it all and walk away; let the mayor and Jenny Woo and New Hong Kong all go on, undisturbed, shipping their bodies, doing their research.

Or somehow blow it wide open, and hope nobody else got killed.

Carlucci returned to the table, sat, poured himself some more Scotch, and waited for the others to return.

TWENTY-SEVEN

"GIVE IT TO Tremaine," Carlucci told them. "Give him everything."

Outside the Tenderloin, Carlucci and Paula skirted the DMZ and headed for the Polk Corridor on foot. He'd had too much to drink, and was glad he wasn't alone; he didn't trust his own judgment. The drizzle had stopped, but everything was wet. It was well after midnight, and the sidewalk was almost empty. The street wasn't much busier.

No one had argued with him. No one had offered any other ideas. They had agreed to turn over hard copies of the text and translation and diagrams to Tremaine—Paula had them with her now, tucked up inside her jacket. They would all, Carlucci included, tell Tremaine everything they knew. And Carlucci had taken the discs, promising to destroy them once Tremaine's story was out.

"Do *you* want the discs?" Carlucci now asked Paula. "For Chick's music, his videos? No one but me would know."

Paula shook her head. "No, but thanks. I was thinking of asking you for them, but it's not worth the risk. Like you said, anyone finds out somebody has them . . . whatever music's on the discs, it won't really matter that much if I don't have it."

"I've thought about scattering them around the city," Carlucci said. It was a crazy idea that had come to him. "Drop one on the sidewalk here, toss one onto a roof in the Asian Quarter, leave another in a coffee shop. All around the city. See what the street does with them."

Paula smiled at him. "That's not such a bad idea."

Carlucci shrugged.

"You're not going to do it, though, are you?"

"No."

They continued in silence until they reached the Polk Corridor. There was more traffic, now, more lights and noise, more people. The sidewalks were almost crowded.

"Home," Paula said.

They passed Christiano's, where they'd eaten and talked, where he had told her he would look into Chick's death. It seemed to Carlucci like a long time ago. Things had changed quite a lot since then.

Music banged out of a window across the street, and two women were dancing to it in the street, hopping in and out of traffic, smiling when cars honked at them. A man with a see-through prosthetic arm nodded at Paula, who nodded back. Two heavy women bundled in long coats staggered down the sidewalk, cigarettes in hand, both of them drooling. Other things didn't seem to change at all, Carlucci thought.

A few more blocks, then they cut down a street to Paula's building. Carlucci stopped on the bottom step of the porch.

"You want to come in?" Paula asked.

"No. I should get home. Andrea will be wondering what the hell has happened to me."

"I wish I'd met her."

"Maybe someday."

Paula nodded and sighed. "Who'd have thought?" she said. "When I first tracked you down and asked you to check out Chick's murder. It seemed so simple, then. And it turned into such a mess." She paused. "I'm sorry I got you into this."

"Don't be," Carlucci said. "You couldn't have known. And it was the right thing to do. Sometimes that's what's most important."

"Is that why you think we should give it all to Tremaine?"

Carlucci shook his head. "I have no idea if it's the right thing. I just don't know what else to do."

Paula nodded. It seemed to be enough for her. "I'm never going to find out who killed Chick, am I?"

"No."

"It's over," she said. "But it's not."

"No," Carlucci said. "Things like this are never completely over."

Neither of them said anything for a minute. Paula took out her keys. "How are you getting home?" she asked.

"I'm going to splurge, catch a cab." He paused, then said, "Be careful, Paula. Tremaine does his story, this place'll get hairy when it breaks."

"I know." She shrugged.

"Will you be seeing him soon?"

"I guess."

"Tell him I'll talk to him."

"I will." She gave him a tired smile. "Good night, Frank Carlucci."

"Good night, Paula Asgard."

The mayor's limo, long and dark and silent, was parked in front of Carlucci's house when he arrived. Carlucci paid the cab driver, then waited for the cab to pull away. He watched his house, wondering how long the mayor had been here. He started up the walkway to the porch, thinking about the discs in his coat.

The rear door of the limo opened, startling Carlucci, and the mayor stepped out. Carlucci stopped, halfway along the walk, and waited for the mayor to join him.

The mayor's expression was hard and ugly in the light from

the porch. "If you fuck me, Frank, I'll take you down with me."

Too late, Carlucci thought, *I already have*. "What are you talking about?" he asked.

"I told you to bury my nephew's case," the mayor said.

"No. I asked you if that's what you wanted, and you said no."

"Don't give me that shit, Frank. You understood what I wanted. You knew exactly what I was asking for."

Carlucci nodded, sighing. "I understood."

"I've been hearing things. And I don't like it. And not just about my nephew. The Chick Roberts case wasn't even yours."

"Who's Chick Roberts?"

The mayor's mouth twisted into something that might have been a smile, and he slowly shook his head. "You fuck. I made you an offer, once. Not just your life, but a much longer life."

"I didn't realize at the time what you were offering."

"You do now, don't you?"

Carlucci nodded.

"The offer won't be good much longer," the mayor said. "And you won't like the alternative. Your friend Mixer didn't. Now you bury this shit, and bury it fast, before all hell breaks loose. You understand?"

"I understand."

The mayor glanced toward the lighted windows of Carlucci's house, then looked back at him. "Do you?"

Carlucci nodded. "I understand," he repeated.

The mayor stared at him a while longer, then turned away without another word. Carlucci watched him climb back into the limo, slam the door shut. The engine started, headlights came on; then the limo pulled smoothly away from the curb and drove down the street.

Andrea opened the front door as he came up the steps. "Are you okay, Frank?"

Carlucci nodded. He stepped inside and Andrea closed the door, locking it and throwing the bolts.

"He was parked out there all evening," Andrea said. "It was starting to worry me." Then she wrinkled her nose. "You've been drinking. A lot."

Carlucci nodded again. "Too much." He smiled. "It seemed like a good idea at the time."

"Why, Frank?"

"I'll tell you."

Carlucci took her hand in his and led the way into the kitchen. It was going to be a long, long talk.

Paula stood just inside her apartment, her back against the door, looking around the room. Her gaze stopped on the remaining boxes of Chick's things. She would have to remind Mixer and the Saints that she wanted the music back, all those tapes and discs. All that was left of Chick.

Chick.

She walked into the bedroom, unzipped her jacket, took out the manila envelope filled with the text and diagrams from the discs, and tossed it onto the bed. Then she sat next to it, picked up the phone, and dialed Tremaine's number.

It rang several times, finally was picked up. "Hello?" His voice was husky with sleep.

"Ian. It's Paula."

"What is it? Are you all right?" Voice clearer, now, alert.

"I'm fine," Paula said. "I have something for you."

"What?"

"Everything."

There was another pause, longer. "Should I come over now?" Tremaine asked.

"Yes," Paula replied. "I want you here, Ian."

"I'll be right over."

Paula hung up the phone. She took off her jacket, then got up and sat in her recliner, facing the blank monitor. The disc with "Love at Ground Zero" was still in the player, but she couldn't bring herself to watch it.

"I did what I could, Chick." Her voice was a whisper, she could barely hear herself. "I did what I could."

She leaned back in the chair, closed her eyes, and waited for Tremaine.

BODY BAGS, RECRUITERS, AND MURDER:

New Hong Kong's Search for Eternal Life
by Tremaine

THIS STORY IS not really about "Eternal Life." This story is about life extension. But life extension so great it has the sound and feel of eternal life. Immortality. Life extension of as much as two hundred years.

Imagine living to be two hundred and fifty years old. Good, or bad? More importantly, at what cost?

The answer to this kind of life extension is not here yet, but it probably will be soon. And it will be the medical researchers of New Hong Kong who find it, because they are searching for it now, and they are closing in. They do not care, however, at what cost they find the answer. They do not care what the answer is. And for now, they will do anything to keep what they are doing a secret.

People have been killed in recent weeks, killed to keep this a secret. A guitarist and low-end drug dealer named Chick Roberts has been murdered. William Kashen, the nephew of San Francisco's mayor, has been murdered. Robert Butler, William Kashen's business partner, has been murdered. Rosa Weeks, M.D., and Poppy Chandler: two more murders. Almost certainly there have been others I am not aware of. There might be more to come. There is no way to know how or when this will all end.

But there was a beginning, a time when . . .

EPILOGUE

TWO WEEKS LATER, near midnight, Carlucci stood on the sidewalk outside The Palms, listening to the muted crash of music. Inside, the Black Angels were playing. Inside, was Paula Asgard.

A lot had happened in the last two weeks. Tremaine's story had gone out over the nets, and for the next several days the city was in turmoil. Huge crowds of protesters had surrounded City Hall and kept city officials from leaving for a day and a half, until the police and National Guard had broken through. Someone launched two rockets into New Hong Kong's headquarters in the Financial District, killing over thirty people and injuring hundreds. Small localized riots erupted throughout the city, most followed by large-scale looting and burning of cars and buildings. New Hong Kong suspended flights from Hunter's Point.

The day Tremaine's story broke over the nets, the mayor disappeared. There was a wild scene out at Hunter's Point, crowds at the gates being fought off by security forces. The mayor, in his limousine, forced his way through the crowd and the first gates, wanting to board the last ship to New Hong Kong. But the main security team stopped him—apparently New Hong Kong had hung him out to dry, just as Monk had hinted at, and ordered their security forces to prevent him from boarding. The mayor then left Hunter's Point, and hadn't been seen since. Word on the streets was that the Saints had kidnapped him and put him on trial. Carlucci didn't know if it was true or not, but he hoped it was. He didn't want to ever worry about Kashen again.

The day his story broke, Tremaine disappeared as well. Paula had called Carlucci to tell him. Afraid that New Hong Kong would come after him—enough people had died already—Tremaine had left the city. Paula didn't know where he'd gone, or how long he'd be away. She'd sounded depressed, and Carlucci thought he understood—she'd lost someone else. First Chick; then Mixer, in a way; and now Tremaine.

Carlucci hadn't seen her since that night with the Saints. They had talked several times on the phone, but their conversations were short and awkward, filled more with silences than words. Now, though, he had to see her in person. He hoped it would make a difference. She wasn't expecting him, but he thought it would be a good surprise.

He finally opened the door, the music blasting him, and he stepped into the clouds of music and smoke, flashing colored lights and a loud, jamming crowd. A young guy just inside the door with foiled hair and two metal hands (real or fake?) put one of his hands up, stopping him. He leaned forward, shouted into Carlucci's ear.

"You sure you want in here, old man?"

Carlucci nodded, and the guy shrugged. "Ten bucks. For the band."

Carlucci dug a crumpled wad of money out of his pocket and picked out two fives, handing them to the guy. The guy nodded, slapped Carlucci on the shoulder, and said, "Have a good time, old man."

Old man. Yeah. To the guy, who wasn't much more than a kid, Carlucci *was* old.

He could barely see the band at the other end of the long, narrow room, his view obstructed by the smoke, people at the raised tables, other people walking around or dancing with their hands in the air, and the half dozen blackened wood ceiling supports. Some of the smoke was illegal, he could smell that. There, he caught a glimpse of Paula, pounding at her guitar, wearing a white T-shirt and black jeans, screaming into the microphone. He couldn't make out a single word.

There weren't any vacant seats at the bar, and all the tables were full, so he worked his way to the side wall, found a spot to lean against between a woman in a crash suit and a guy in silver-strips who must have been close to seven feet tall. The smells in the place made him feel good, reminded him of the clubs he'd played in with the Po-Leece Blues Band. A different crowd, different sound, definitely, but something the same—people pressed in together, drinking and smoking, having a good time: there for the music.

A waitress in black T-shirt, cutoffs, and heavy leather boots stopped by, and he ordered a draft. She said something back, the name of the beer, probably, and he shrugged, nodded.

Carlucci had a good view of the band from where he stood, right between two of the wooden posts. Drummer, lead guitar, and Paula on bass and vocals. Loud and fast, a lot louder and faster than he liked, but the energy was fine; he could feel that, he liked that part of it. And the bass pounding through the floor and wall, into his bones.

The waitress came back with his beer, sooner than he had expected; the beer a lot bigger, too, jumbo pint glass. He paid her, and she left. Carlucci looked back at the stage, and saw that Paula had caught sight of him. She was back from the mike, a break in the vocals, and she stared at him, hand banging away at the strings. Then she smiled, nodding once, the smile getting broader, and he knew it was okay. He smiled back at her and put up his hand, feeling kind of stupid. Like an old man.

He saw Paula lean over to say something in the guitarist's ear, and the guitarist nodded. Carlucci drank from his beer and tried to relax, settle into the music. He was still a little nervous.

The Black Angels played one more song, then Paula announced they'd be taking a short break. The quiet was a relief to Carlucci. There was still music playing over the sound system and people talking all around him, but it was quiet to him, the volume turned way down. Paula stepped off the stage and worked her way through the tables and chairs until she stood right in front of him, smiling. Carlucci couldn't help smiling back. She looked terrific—healthy sweat, good color in her face.

"It's good to see you," Paula said. "A hell of a surprise, but a good one."

"I'm glad to see you, too."

She winced. "Phone conversations have been kind of crappy, haven't they?"

Carlucci nodded, shrugged. He held up his beer. "Want some?"

"Love some." She took the glass from him and drank half of what was left. "Man, that's good."

"How are you doing?" he asked.

"Better. Every day better, I guess. Playing again helps. Helps a lot."

"I can see that. You look great."

She smiled. "Yeah, it does that for me."

"How about other things?"

Paula shrugged, the smile fading. "Still lots of different kinds of pain. But it's okay. That's getting better, too. You?"

"All right. I thought for a while I might be forced to retire, but it's all working out." McCuller had taken 'voluntary' retirement—apparently New Hong Kong and Vaughn had been unhappy with the way he'd appeared in Tremaine's story. Vaughn was still Chief, but accommodation had been reached—there were no hypocritical citations, but Carlucci,

Hong, LaPlace, even Santos and Weathers, were all in good shape. Everything was back to what passed for normal.

"Good," Paula said. She took another long drink from the beer. "That other stuff, though. Politicians making a lot of noise about New Hong Kong, but it doesn't look like much is really going to change, is it?"

Carlucci shook his head. "Not really. Closer inspections of shipments to New Hong Kong for a while, a lot of hand-waving about medical ethics, but that's about it. More money will shift around, and the bodies will start shipping again. Alive *and* dead. Like you said, lots of noise, but after a while it'll be pretty much the same again."

"About right," Paula said. "The fucking politicians want to have a crack at eternal life themselves."

"Yes. And the reality is, there isn't a hell of a lot they can do about New Hong Kong, anyway. Unless they want to try to blow them right out of the sky."

Paula smiled. "It's an idea."

"Yeah, ideas everywhere."

"I guess I was hoping Tremaine's story might change things a little more."

"I don't think Tremaine thought much would change," Carlucci said. "He said as much, really, when I talked to him the last time. He said he just wanted the truth to be known. Anything more than that would be one hell of a bonus."

"That sounds about right."

She took one more drink of the beer, then handed it back to him. They didn't talk for a bit, Carlucci trying to gear up to ask her about Kashen.

"Is it true?" he finally asked. "That the Saints put the mayor on trial?"

Paula looked at him for a few moments without saying anything, then nodded. "Yes, it's true."

"What happened?"

"He survived. If you could call it that." She sighed heavily, then went on. "I've seen him. He's a wreck. He's being cared for by an old woman and a young boy who think he's a holy man." Paula shook her head. "He has no idea who he is."

"Was Mixer a part of it?" Carlucci asked.

"Of course. He's one of them, now."

"A Saint."

"Yeah, a Saint." Paula shrugged. "It might be good. For Mixer *and* for the Saints."

Now was the time, Carlucci thought. He'd been holding it back, like holding back a treat, except she had no idea it was coming.

"I've got something for you," he said. "The main reason I came here tonight. I didn't want to wait until tomorrow."

"What?" She didn't seem to know whether to be eager or afraid.

"A message. I thought you'd want it right away."

He reached into his back pocket and took out the small, folded piece of paper, handed it to her. She opened it carefully, then looked at it. A short message. She read it silently, but he knew what it said. He'd had to copy it out himself:

> Paula,
> Settled in, everything's fine. Miss you.
> Wish you were here.
> Love,
> Ian

Carlucci watched her expression change, soften, watched just the hint of a smile appear.

"Love?" he said.

Paula looked up at him, smile widening. "Could be. I may find out someday." She folded the paper and put it in her jeans pocket. "Thanks."

Someone called her name from the stage and Paula turned. The guitarist was waving at her.

"Break's over," Paula said. "You going to stick around for the next set?"

Carlucci shook his head, but smiled. "Not my kind of music. I just wanted to get that to you. I just wanted to see you."

"Thanks again." She stepped forward and gave him a quick hug. "I've gotta go. Stay in touch."

"I'll have to."

"Yeah." Grinning now. "Bye, Frank Carlucci."

"Goodbye, Paula Asgard."

She turned and walked back toward the stage. Carlucci finished the beer, then set the empty glass on the nearest table, which was already half-covered with empty bottles and glasses. He looked back once more at the stage, and Paula, bass strapped on, waved to him. Carlucci waved back, then headed for the door.

At the entrance, the guy with the foiled hair and metal hands grinned. "Too much for you, old man?"

"Yeah," Carlucci said, laughing. "Too much."

He pushed open the door, feeling better than he had in days, and stepped out into the night.